MARY, MY LOVE

Other Works by Cynthia Davis

Fiction

It is I, Joseph	1-58943-004-2
Beloved Leah	1-58288-220-7
Miriam's Healing	978-0-557-00943-5
Rahab's Redemption	1-58288-215-0
Naomi's Joy	978-1-58288-257-4
My Abigail	978-1-58288-269-7

Available from Amazon.com and the author

Non Fiction

From a Grain of Mustard Seed 978-0-557-02763-7

Available from Amazon.com and the author

Bible Studies, available from Cynthia Davis

Walk with Jesus
Enter the Tabernacle
Dancing in the Footsteps of Miriam

Online

www.CynthiaDavisAuthor.com
FootprintsFromTheBible.blogspot.com

To Laura Blessings

MARY, MY LOVE

Cynthia Davis

Thy WORD is a LAMP unto my FEET, and a LIGHT unto my PATH.
–Psalms 119:105

Footprints from the Bible

Davis, Cynthia.
Mary, My Love / Cynthia Davis.

ISBN: 978-0-9844723-0-7

1. Mary--(Virgin)--Fiction. 2. Joseph, carpenter. 3. Bible. N.T..--History of Biblical events--Fiction. 4. Women in the Bible--Fiction. 5. Biographical fiction. 6. Religious fiction. I. Title.

This is a fictional retelling of the story of the early years of the life of Jesus Christ and his parents as found in the New Testament of the Bible. (Matthew, Chapter 1-2 and Luke, Chapter 1-2) Characters and incidents not found in scripture are the product of the author's imagination. Any resemblance to actual persons, living or dead, is entirely coincidental.

Mary, My Love

Dedicated to my grandchildren, who inspired me to tell the story of Mary and Joseph and the Holy Child.

Mary, My Love

Chapter 1

God was a distant premise until the Holy One stole the woman I loved. It was then I learned about faith and love.

My father was a successful carpenter and trader. His tales of travels to Damascus and Tyrė were fascinating to me as a boy. Even though the man remained proud of his descent from King David, I rarely saw him darken the door of the synagogue. He even abandoned his Jewish name, Jacob, for the Greek name Heli. My mother called him Jacob, as did all in Nazareth, but his foreign customers used the Greek name.

"Our son should learn to read Torah," I overheard my mother Sarah begging when I was five.

"If it makes you happy, he may study with the rabbi," my father replied. "It matters not to me."

I was excited to sit at the rabbi's feet in the early mornings learning to read Torah and memorizing the myriad laws. At first I tried to share the lessons with my father.

"We are the chosen people," I told him. "Since Abraham, the True God has promised to be with us. If we are forsaken, it is because we have turned from God to worship idols."

"Your mother must be proud to have you spout such learning," he sneered. "What do you really know of this God? Has God ever done anything for you? When you have experienced the silence of God, in the darkness when you cry out for help, then speak to me about being a chosen people."

"The rabbi says we must turn back to God. Then Messiah will come," I insisted.

With a cuff on the head, he shouted, "Get to work! You waste my time! Spend your time leaning to do man's work. Leave praying to your mother and the women."

His derision made me cringe, but did not stop my desire to learn. Eventually I quit trying to talk to my father about my lessons.

Rebelliously I told myself, "I know God cares. Someday I will find something within the scrolls that will convince my father to believe."

By the time I was of an age to become a Son of the Promise, I had seven siblings. The four girls, Ruth, Deborah, Hannah, and Sarah, were finally followed by three brothers. The twins, Judah and Benoni, and Matthat the baby, clung to mother's skirts as she went about the daily round of tasks. My sisters accompanied her to the well and market. They learned the womanly arts of baking, weaving and cleaning.

When I was almost twelve, my father said, "Soon you will be old enough for me to trust you with simple repairs. It will be several years before your brothers can learn the craft. When I travel, you will be able to help some of the customers here."

Not long afterward, Ezra the rabbi, announced me ready to read Torah, the ceremony that would make me an adult member of the community.

"I will be one of the youngest in Nazareth to become a man by reading and interpreting the scriptures!" I bragged to my father, hoping he would take an interest. "Rabbi Ezra says I have excelled in my studies."

My father's response left me aching from his searing words. "Go ahead! Prattling from a scroll will not make you a man. My son will be considered a man when he can prove his worth by earning a living as a carpenter."

I snapped angrily, "When has my work been left unfinished or rejected by the customer? I have never neglected…"

He grabbed my wrist and threw me out of the shop, bellowing in rage, "Grovel to your mother's God! Do not come back until you learn the respect due a father under the Law you claim to follow."

Humiliated at being thrown into the street, I slunk home to soak my wrist in a cool bucket of water and hide from my siblings' prying eyes. Mother found me when the afternoon shadows lengthened.

"My son, why are you here?" She asked with surprise.

I answered without looking up, trying to conceal the bruise by holding my arm behind my back.

"My mother, Father is not pleased that I plan to participate in the ceremony this Sabbath."

She sighed and looked sadly toward the workshop where a lantern still glowed although no sounds of work emerged.

"My husband has been angry at the God of Abraham, Isaac, and Jacob for a long time. He has never spoken of it to me except to insist that until God proves himself, he will not believe that there is any difference in the Living God of Israel and the worship of the Samaritans and Romans." She laid a gentle hand on my shoulder. After a moment of silence the woman added, "You must decide for yourself whether to stand up tomorrow and take your place as a man of Nazareth."

I took her work rough hand in mine. With a proud lift of my chin I announced my intentions more loudly than necessary, hoping the man would hear. "I will not change my mind now! My father may do as he pleases!"

The evening meal was subdued. Jacob's frowning silence even affected the twin's antics. They usually kept us entertained with attempts to feed the baby. My sisters kept their eyes lowered, focusing on their food. They hurried to help our mother as soon as possible. The meal ended when my father hefted himself to his feet. I stood and faced him.

"My father," my voice cracked and I cleared my throat. "I would be honored if you attended synagogue tomorrow morning."

Even when the man swung around to face me, I refused to flinch. With my head lifted slightly to meet his gaze, I waited.

Without an answer, my father stamped into the street. I swallowed the hard lump of sorrow in my throat. Forcing myself to unclench my hands and breathe naturally, I turned to my mother and siblings.

"Good night," I said, in a tone that was almost normal.

I hurried to my pallet on the roof before the tears in her eyes unmanned me.

"God of my ancestors, help me obey both you and my father. I think you must still care for your chosen people. Send me proof for my father. If you are real, give me a sign," I begged, half ashamed of my need.

Only the night sounds answered me. Far away a wild dog barked and an owl hooted. For a moment I wondered if my father was right. Then I looked up to the stars and remembered how God walked with Abraham and showed him the same stars as a promise.

CHAPTER 2

The Sabbath of my twelfth birthday dawned clear. I said the morning prayers facing Jerusalem as I was taught. The cool water that I splashed on my body left me tingling.

"Here is a new tunic." Tenderly she smoothed the tiniest of wrinkles from my sleeve.

The homespun cloth was soft on my skin. The gift was full of love from my mother.

"Mother used the finest wool to weave the cloth. She would not let me help with the sewing," my sister Ruth informed me.

"This is beautiful, Mother. I am sure no other young man in all Israel has ever had such a fine garment."

"You make me proud, Joseph. You are no longer a child. After today, you will be a man, my son. We must not be late."

She touched my cheek with tears in her eyes then turned abruptly to pick up Matthat from the floor and dust his hands. Proudly I led my mother and sisters to the door of the synagogue. They hurried to find places in the women's section behind the screen.

The rabbi held out a hand in welcome, "Joseph bar Jacob, this is an important day in your life."

He looked down the village street toward the carpenter's shop.

"I do not think my father will be able to come." I told the rabbi, relieved that my voice was calm.

The slight shake of his gray beard was barely perceptible. I knew the man was disappointed on my behalf.

"I see. He is a busy man." My teacher made an excuse for my absent father. "Come then, let us begin."

My heart beat faster as the opening prayers were said. Ezra stood up and looked at me. His beckoning finger brought me nervously to my feet.

"My brothers, today we welcome a new man into our midst."

I took a quick steadying breath and stepped up to stand beside my teacher. When I took the Torah scrolls from the cantor the weight of the papyrus rolls sent a spasm of pain from my bruised wrist up my arm. Ignoring the throbbing, I lifted the Law above my head as I was taught. Then I laid it on the stand. The rabbi held the pointer that directed my eyes to the first line I was to read.

My voice shook slightly, "Hear O Israel, the Lord our God, the Lord is One…"

I forced myself to focus on the words, reading the commandments slowly. Something, maybe a slight stir in the room, made me lift my eyes briefly. Jacob stood in the doorway. Our eyes met. With an effort I brought my attention back to the scroll and completed the reading. When I looked up again, my father was gone. I rolled up the papyrus and handed it back to the cantor.

"Joseph, have you any wisdom to share from the reading?"

I responded to the rote request by the rabbi with a nervous nod. Even though he was not present, my words were for the man who was my father.

"The God of our Fathers orders us to honor our parents. This is the first of the Laws dealing with the relationship between people. The previous four commandments tell us how we shall worship and honor the Lord God, Creator of Heaven and Earth. Therefore, we are to love and obey God first and honor our parents next and do unto all people as the Lord has commanded, seeking good and not evil for one another. Surely then the God of Abraham, Isaac, and Jacob will remember his people."

I did not dare glance at anyone as I took my seat. The final prayers were short. Then congratulations greeted me from all sides.

"Well read, Joseph bar Jacob."

"How proud you make us all."

"What a shame your father missed this Sabbath."

"I hope I do as well," my friend Jonah whispered.

"It is not so hard," I assured him. "Think about the reading and do not look at the congregation."

Even as I shook hands and accepted commendation from the men of Nazareth, my eyes searched for my father. Instead I found Mother. She was waiting outside. The crowd of women encircling her quickly turned to me with exclamations.

"You did well."

"I know your mother is proud."

"He is such a handsome young man."

"Some girl will have her eye on you soon."

Blushing and embarrassed from the giggles of the girls in response to the matchmaker's comment, I turned to my mother.

"He came! Your father was there for the reading," she whispered with delight.

I nodded quickly, "I saw him. Where is he now?"

"Probably working; even though it is the Sabbath."

I knew she was right. It seemed hours later before I was able to get away from all the happy congratulations and praise. In reality, the sun had not reached the high point in the sky. Slowly I walked past my house to the wood shop.

Even a stranger to Nazareth would know that a carpenter worked here. Pieces of timber and cut lumber were propped along the front wall. The smell of sawdust permanently hung in the air. The door was slightly ajar but I did not hear any sounds of sawing or sanding. Rather an odd chipping sound issued from inside.

When I looked in, I saw my father sitting on the workbench closest to the window. His back was to me. Rhythmically one hand rose and fell. He was systematically hacking a plow handle into shavings. The door creaked when I pushed it open. The man spun around defensively. I stood still.

"Thank you, Father."

"You read well. I doubt I did as well."

His praise surprised me and I gasped, "You read Torah and became a Son of the Promise?"

A bark of a laugh was his answer. "At one time I was a naïve as you. That was before…"

The man's voice trailed off and he turned back to the handle. I took a step into the semi-darkness of the shop.

"Tell me," I pleaded.

"I learned all about the Law and the Prophets. That was no help to my mother and sister…"

I held my breath when the sentence trailed off into a growl. When he moved suddenly I jumped in startled reflex. Strong hands held my shoulders and his face came close to mine. I smelled the sour odor of cheap wine on his breath.

"You are a man today. I tell you that God does not protect his people nor answer prayers of man or boy."

The pressure on my shoulders forced me to sit on the vacated workbench. My father stood between the door and me.

"Why do you hate God? Why did you leave Bethlehem?" He mimicked the questions I often asked. After a quick turn around the room my father faced me. "Would you not hate a God whose Law condemned your mother and sister to stoning for that which was not their fault?"

The silence stretched out. I realized a response was expected.

Feeling very nervous, I stated, "I do not understand."

Jacob bar Mattan turned away from me. His hands gripped the sides of the window. In a monotone he began his story.

"I was a year older than you are now. My father was away with my older brothers, your uncles." When I gasped in surprise, the man nodded, "Yes, you have two uncles. I am the youngest son."

I could not think of any response. After a moment he resumed in the same far off tone of voice.

"They had gone to cut wood in the mountains. I was left to complete a table and stools for Hiram the innkeeper in Bethlehem."

Again the man fell silent. I barely breathed, waiting for the story to continue.

"Our shop was next to my home, like this. Sawing and hammering is noisy work." My father's shoulders moved in a huge sigh. Emotion choked his hoarse voice. "While I worked, two bandits entered my house. They raped my mother and my sister. She was only ten. I found them when I entered my house for the evening meal."

My father rested his head against the hand holding the window frame. Then he faced me. Even in the shadows I could see the long buried grief and rage in the man's eyes.

"They were both battered. Their clothing was torn. Barely conscious the women lay like dolls where the men left them. My cry of terror and outrage brought the neighbors running."

"No!" A cry was wrenched from me. Already my mind raced ahead and I was afraid I knew the end of the story.

With decades of stored up bitterness behind the words, Jacob snarled, "Yes! No one would believe that they cried out against their attackers. I was asked again and again if I heard anything. When Mattan, my father, returned, he too asked me if I heard screams."

I suddenly felt older than the man who sank onto the bench beside me. He breathed heavily, almost as if he had finished a race.

"Both my mother and sister swore that they fought and screamed but no one came forward in their defense."

I wanted to say something to comfort the weight of guilt and grief I sensed.

Before I could speak, he quoted coldly, "'If a woman does not cry out against her attacker in the town she will be stoned.'"

With a groan my father buried his face in his hands. I could barely hear him whisper, "I have often thought that I should have lied. At the time I never believed that the rabbi and elders would enforce such a law against women they knew as well as my mother and innocent sister!"

"My father…"

I rested one hand on his bowed shoulder. For once he did not shrug it off. I had no comfort to offer. What would I do in the same situation? The rabbi had instilled in my mind the belief that God demanded, indeed rewarded, obedience to every letter of the Law of Moses. Beside me sat a man whose life had been ruined by blind compliance to those same laws. My own grandmother had died by stoning. The thought was almost more than I could comprehend.

"I could not bear to be near Mattan and my brothers." In a defeated voice my father resumed his recital. "The road led north to Jerusalem. I took it and left behind my identity. My mother had always called me her exalted one, her Eli, so I became Heli."

The man paused and I tried to think of something to say.

A harsh laugh grated on my ears when my father continued, "Working in Herod's Temple did not bring me any relief. The more I saw of the priests, the more I despised them and their religion. Levites were paying off Herod's architects only to have a rival faction pay more for another modification. We spent more time taking apart the previous day's construction than actually building anything. They claim to uphold the laws and to hate Herod and the Romans. All the time they take money to enrich their treasury and obtain prestige."

In an abrupt movement the man stood. He paced to the door and back.

"I headed north when a Greek architect invited me to work at Caesarea. I decided I would not deal with my own people. Demetrius knew I was a Jew. He never asked any questions. I joined him at his pagan feasts to the Greek gods he followed. Too soon I discovered that the priests of Athena and Zeus were as avaricious as the scribes in Jerusalem. Joseph, all priests have only one aim. That is to convince the gullible to exchange their meager earnings for the promise of the favor of some god. The scribes and Pharisees in Jerusalem are no different than the adherents of Artemis of the Greeks or Astarte in Damascus."

I was beginning to understand my father's abhorrence of religion. I opened my mouth to offer some response as the silence grew. My mother's voice calling to Hannah seemed to bring the man back to the present. He faced me. A smile crossed his face, softening the bleakness I had seen during his confession.

"Then I met your mother. She was beautiful. For her I was willing to come here to Nazareth. She understood that I would not attend synagogue." Looking toward the house he shook his head slowly. "I know she has been saddened by my obstinacy. She never asked questions and I never gave her any reasons."

Moved by his confession, I stood and faced my father. Understanding brought compassion.

"Father, thank you for telling me," I said, wishing I could offer more comfort.

The carpenter's hands gripped my arms. For the first time I realized that I was as tall as my father. In a different tone he repeated the words that started the conversation.

"You are a man. You will make your own decisions about God. Just do not expect miracles. Religion is a sham. God has forgotten the Jews."

Before I could reply he released me with a slight push toward the door.

"Go, your mother will be expecting you."

"I will stay if you need help," I offered, even though it broke the Sabbath taboo.

He laughed grimly, "No, my son, I will not be accused of dragging you away from the true faith."

That night I lay on my pallet. I had much to think about.

"God of Abraham, Isaac, and Jacob, I believe you are the One Living God. In the writings of the prophets I have learned of your care for the Children of Israel even when we turn away from you. How then can your Law demand the death of an innocent?"

It was a question I contemplated for years.

Chapter 3

My relationship with my father changed after his revelations. At first he barely spoke. One day he paused to inspect my work. I was completing a table ordered as a wedding gift from the wealthiest merchant in the area to his son, Samson bar Samson. Proudly I watched Jacob examine the workmanship. I knew it was nearly flawless. With a brief nod of approve he completed his inspection.

"That is a fine joint. Samson will be pleased to have this table in his house." My father ran his hand along the smooth seam between two lengths of lumber forming the tabletop. "I have been busy with the large order for the Damascus traders. Joseph, I doubt I could have done better."

"Thank you, Father." I tried to sound humble although I really wanted to jump for joy.

"I am now confident that our customers will have competent work even when I am away. I can take on extra commissions in order to provide appropriate dowries for your sisters."

"Dowries?"

"Joab bar Benjamin has asked me to set a betrothal date for Ruth," he answered.

"For Ruth!" I gasped in surprise.

My father nodded. "It is time. Your sister has been a woman for nearly two years. Deborah, too, will need a husband."

"It does not seem possible. However, Ruth is fifteen so Deborah must be thirteen," I mused. "Ruth is almost too old to be a bride but she has always been shy. Joab will be a kind and undemanding husband for my sister." I agreed as if my father asked for my advice.

Jacob simply shrugged. Still thinking about my sisters, I remembered several times recently when Zachariah bar Ishmael stopped by unexpectedly. My friend had seemed distracted whenever Deborah was near.

"I have seen Zach watching Deb when he came to see me," I remarked.

"Zachariah is four years older than you and the young man was well thought of." Father pondered the match with his lips pursed.

"He helps Rabbi Ezra tutor the younger boys with the difficult Hebrew of the Torah. Ishmael, his father, sent him to study in Jerusalem," I reminded the man.

"It would be an honor if a scholar is interested in your sister." He sighed with a frown, "Perhaps I must look for two dowries. It seems your mother is right. She hinted that I should expect both Ruth and Deborah to wed soon."

"Where have my little sisters gone?" I asked myself. "It was not so long ago when they ran from my teasing. Now, Joab and Zachariah are waiting for father to set a marriage price. I have seen Hannah and Sarah giggling and teasing the boys even though they are only eight and ten."

"You will soon be thinking of a bride for yourself," Jacob interrupted my thoughts. "Likely you will want to set up a shop of your own."

"No, no…I have not even thought of marriage."

"Young Samson is not that much older than you," the man remarked.

"There is no one in Nazareth I desire. I am content to remain in this shop with you. The twins are six. They will soon need to learn simple tasks. You will need me to teach them when you travel."

My father nodded and pointed to my youngest brother happily playing just outside the shop. "Matthat will be a fine builder someday."

I agreed. His pudgy baby hands were surprisingly adept at creating structures from the scraps of lumber he collected outside the shop.

"Son, the empire has need of men who can design in wood and stone," he remarked, not for the first time.

"Why would you say such a thing?" Mother overheard and scolded. "My son would not want to build heathen temples."

The man tossed my brother into the air. The child laughed delightedly.

"Who knows what your God has in store for this child? When he is older perhaps I will have him apprenticed to a master builder. Joseph is adept at creating sturdy, serviceable furnishings and farm implements," he added. "He is my good right hand, although I do not trust him with any elaborate carved work."

I knew he was right. Invariably my hand slipped with the awl at the wrong instant, ruining a perfect design.

Only a few weeks later, Father announced, "Joab bar Benjamin will be betrothed to Ruth."

Two months later my friend Zachariah was betrothed to Deborah. The house became a hive of female activity. It seemed that looms were erected in every corner to make new woolen blankets and homespun material. Hannah and Sarah spent time making small mats. The older girls shared secrets, while creating lovely things for their dowry chests.

"When you are not working for a customer, can you make some simple wood bowls and plates for your sisters?" Mother begged.

I sought refuge in the shop from the immanent nuptials. One afternoon, as I sat on the doorstep polishing a bowl designed to hold fruit, a small girl stopped to watch. I recognized her as the only daughter of Anna and Joachim bar

David. She was their precious jewel. For many years Anna had prayed for a child. Eight years ago her prayers were answered.

"What are you doing?"

The little girl reached out to touch the smooth wood. I stopped rubbing oil into the bowl and held it up. The afternoon sun lit the rich tones in the wood so that it shone.

"I am making a bowl for Deborah's dowry."

"It is lovely and soft as kitten's fur." Her small face became almost dreamy as her fingers explored the smooth surface. Dimples appeared when she smiled at me. "Will you make me a bowl like that for my dowry chest?"

"Aren't you too young for such things?" I asked in my best big brotherly tone.

Brown eyes sparkled and she tossed her hair in imitation of an older flirt. "A girl is never too young to plan for her wedding."

I had to chuckle. In response she placed small fists on her hips and stared at me with a severe frown. I choked trying to hold in the gales of laughter that threatened.

Suddenly she relaxed and began to giggle. "I do not want it right away, silly!"

My whoops of merriment brought my siblings to the door. I saw them looking from little Mary to me. Matthat trotted over to his friend.

"Do not mind my brother," he advised, pulling her hand. "Come inside, Mother just made some sweetmeats."

I was left alone again. Memory of the little girl brought a smile to my face many times during the next week. Then the weddings were upon us.

A whirlwind of baking, chopping, and harassed activity preceded the week-long celebration. My father brought huge jars of wine from Sepphoris for the feast. Both Ruth and Deborah were lovely in their elaborately embroidered gowns.

"Here is my gift to you," Father tied a heavy dowry necklace around the neck of each woman.

Ruth sobbed her thanks and kissed his cheek before allowing her bridesmaids to cover her face with the veil.

"My father, you are so kind!" Deborah whispered, with a kiss for her father.

"My sisters are beautiful," I announced proudly while I watched the bridesmaids lead them to their litters.

The groom and his attendants met the procession in front of the synagogue. Zachariah bar Ishmael lifted Deborah from her seat. Ruth's attendants stopped beside Joab bar Benjamin. The man bowed in homage before lifting my older sister out.

Ezra smiled as he pronounced the simple words that ended the betrothal and completed the marriage. With great clashing of cymbals and blowing of pipes the procession marched back to our courtyard. Shouted best wishes came from our neighbors as they joined the crowd.

"Happiness to you all!"

"Blessings on your marriage!"

The celebration continued for a week. Every dawn Mother sank down on her pallet only to rise at noon to make preparations for the evening.

"I am glad we made plenty of bread," she said surveying the food left on the last day. "It will stretch the meat and vegetables."

"Can't we have just one of the sweet cakes?" My younger siblings begged.

"Later," Mother promised.

"Bring more wine from the shop," Father told me. "We must not run out."

At sundown, the feasting and dancing started again. The women formed a circle and led Ruth and Deborah in the steps. Then the men encircled the women as the pounding instruments sounded the rhythm. Left and then right the company revolved in the ageless dance of love and fertility.

"In the same way Abraham and Sarah celebrated their wedding," I thought to myself, feeling a bit lonely. "Now my sisters have a new life with her husband in her new home with his family."

"What a wonderful celebration," Mother smiled. She looked contented as she leaned against her husband. "Their lives will be blessed by God."

"Our daughters have been well honored by all Nazareth," the man agreed.

In an unusual gesture of fondness, my father touched his lips to Mother's forehead. The couple turned away and entered the house. Watching them go, I thought of my parent's love and how Sarah had transformed Jacob from a wandering carpenter to husband and father. For the first time, I felt guilty about not wanting a wife.

"It is the duty of every young man to find a good Jewish bride and raise a family so God will bless the union and the nation." I remembered the rabbi's instruction.

Suddenly discontented, I began to clean the courtyard. The twins joined me but they found it more fun to throw the food at each other than actually pick up the mess. My mind was occupied with thoughts of choosing a wife and raising a family. I did not even scold the boys for their antics. Late in the night, I sat in my blankets on the roof. My thoughts turned to my sisters. I hoped they were happy.

"God of my fathers," my prayer winged heavenward. "Bless my sisters. Make them joyful wives and fruitful vines to your glory. Is there a mate for me?"

For a while I lay thinking about the young girls at the feast and in Nazareth. I could not imagine any of them as my wife. Finally, I rolled into my blankets and fell asleep still wondering if I would ever be a husband.

CHAPTER 4

The years slid by. I was busy and content. Mother and my sisters often proposed some young woman as wife. Each time I found some reason to refuse.

"Elizabeth is too young."

"I could not live with Delah's laugh."

"Tamar is partial to David bar Joash."

The one girl in all Nazareth whose company I enjoyed was little Mary. I did not forget her request to make a smooth bowl for her dowry trunk. In my spare time, I worked on an entire set of bowls and platters of the finest oak. Often the child visited my shop. She seemed to like sitting quietly on a stool in the corner, just watching me work. It was a novel experience to have a female in the workshop. My mother and sisters rarely entered. Mary did not seem to mind the sawdust and I enjoyed her conversation.

"Does your mother miss your help?" I asked occasionally.

"I have finished my chores," she invariable replied with an emphatic nod.

Sometimes the girl brought a spindle and wool or a piece of embroidery to work on as we visited. One spring morning she held a small wood box when she arrived.

"Yesterday I found a lizard. I do not think they are evil, do you?" She asked seriously.

Pausing in my sawing, I shrugged, "God made lizards just like he made dogs."

She smiled in relief and set the box carefully on the workbench.

"Come here," she whispered.

I bent over as she carefully lifted the lid. A small lizard sat quietly in the bottom of the container. Mary looked up eagerly.

"Isn't he lovely? Have you ever seen such glistening skin?"

"He is quite handsome," I agreed.

"Can you keep him here?"

"You could turn him loose," I suggested.

Gently, the girl's finger touched the creature. He moved slowly, dragging one leg.

"He is hurt," she pointed out. "If I let him go now, he will be eaten by a cat or bird."

I could not resist her appeal or the tears in the ten-year old girl's brown eyes. Helplessly, I nodded. Her sudden exuberant squeeze almost knocked me off balance.

"Thank you!"

She replaced the lid almost reverently.

"What will you feed him?" I teased. "Lizards eat bugs."

"He eats tiny pieces of meat. I have already fed him today."

So my shop acquired a mascot. Even after his leg healed, the creature refused to leave although the box was discarded. I never ceased to be amazed by the daily appearance of the lizard. He emerged from some dark corner whenever Mary appeared. I left the animal alone. His presence gave the child a reason to visit and I was glad. Other wounded animals were brought to the shop from time to time.

"You have a gift with animals," I told the girl. "They do not fear you and let you touch and tend them."

She shrugged, "All creatures need help sometimes."

Mother noticed Mary's visits, too.

"Are you fond of Anna and Joachim's daughter?" She asked on afternoon as I watched the girl walk up the street toward her home.

"She is a sweet child."

"Is that how you see her?" Mother asked sharply.

"How else?" I stammered feeling like a naughty child under her piercing look.

"Mary is almost a woman."

"She is only a little girl," I insisted.

Peering after the subject of our conversation, I wondered if I was wrong.

"Soon people will be questioning her presence in your shop. I have already heard a few whispers at the well."

I felt my brows draw together angrily. "They have no right to suggest anything! Mary keeps me company with her stories."

My mother touched the hand that I was surprised to see was clenched in a fist.

"I think it is more than that," she suggested gently.

I shook my head. When the woman left, I stood for a long time thinking about what she said.

"She keeps me company," I repeated to convince myself.

When Mary did not visit the next day, I found myself unable to concentrate on my work. I sat on the bench and was surprised when the lizard crawled from his corner to lick the tips of my fingers where they dangled between my knees. Softly I addressed the creature.

"Are you hungry?" I asked softly. "Or do you miss Mary, too?"

When I moved, the animal vanished into the shadows but he came out the next day to accept a small piece of raw meat from me.

"Is Mother right?" I asked the creature. "Mary has been coming here for, can it be four years? She must be nearly thirteen, since she is about the same age as the twins. That is old enough to marry…"

The realization made me stare blindly out the door. Suddenly I could not stand the thought of Mary being wed. Restlessness chased me from the shop. Despite the several half-finished projects waiting, I strode out into the cool fall afternoon. With no destination in mind, I found myself walking up the dusty street past the synagogue.

"Joseph, what a pleasant surprise," the rabbi called. "Come, share some fresh bread. Reba has just taken it from the oven."

I mumbled some excuse and kept walking. A little further along the street, I realized I was nearly to the neat home of Joachim. I stumbled to a stop just as Anna stepped through the door to shake a rug.

"Joseph, what a pleasant surprise," she called cheerfully. Did Joachim ask you to look at the table?"

"I…that is…um…."

My tongue seemed to have deserted me and taken coherent thought with it. I had no idea why I stood in the street outside the very house I should stay away from if I wanted to silence the gossips. Anna took pity on my confusion.

"Do come inside and see if the wood can be repaired." She led the way into the house. "See, the edge of the table top has cracked."

A soft voice was singing somewhere nearby. With an effort, I focused on the piece of furniture. The wood had separated at a joint. It would be simple to repair.

"I can easily fix this. Shall I get my tools now?"

"There is no rush, Joseph," she smiled.

The rustle of clothing signaled Mary's appearance.

"Mother, who is here? Joseph, what a pleasant surprise!"

It was the third time someone greeted me with the same words. For some reason my heart began pounding frantically at my little friend's salutation. I swung around so suddenly that my elbow bumped into a vase of flowers. Only Mary's swift response saved the pottery from smashing to the floor. In her graceful movement, I saw that the child was truly a woman. My mother was right.

"Mary…Anna…," I stammered. "I must go. Tell Joachim I will come tomorrow to repair the table."

"Only if you have the time," Anna insisted. "There is no hurry."

"Yes…of course."

Somehow I was looking at Mary not Anna. Her smile no longer held the teasing of a girl. Rather her lips offered the promise of a woman. The room suddenly felt too small. How I got back to the street, I never remembered. I nearly ran past the last few homes until I was on the hillside outside Nazareth. The truth pounded in my blood.

"Mary, my companion and friend, is not a child. She has blossomed into a winsome young woman under my nose," I panted. "Men will be flocking to ask Joachim for her hand in marriage."

I felt a terrible ache when I voiced my thoughts. For a long time I paced the hills. The sun was setting in the west when the truth struck me.

"I love Mary," I stated. "I want to hold her in my arms and make her my wife."

Stunned, I sank down under a tree. Desire and longing swept over me. I looked up and made a promise to the darkening sky.

"God, I will love her with my very life," I vowed to the darkening sky. "I cannot bear to see Mary wed to another. Let Joachim look favorably upon my proposal."

It was dark when I made my way home. My mother's raised eyebrows were the only indication of her concern.

"I had to think," I told her.

A gentle hand plucked a branch from my hair and dusted some pine needles from my robe. She pointed to a simple meal of flat bread, vegetables, and beans.

"Eat your dinner."

Lost in my thoughts of how best to approach Joachim, I ate in silence. I wondered if the man would hold my age against me. After all, I was twelve years older than his sweet daughter. Late into the night I tried to prepare for any argument.

"The shop is well established. Mary will not go hungry," I reassured myself. "I will build her a lovely home. Only the best will do for the daughter of Joachim."

It turned out that I barely needed to convince the man. At first light, I donned my best robe and trimmed my beard. Oiling my hair was not something I normally did, but on this day I carefully coiled the ringlets over my ears and smoothed my hair before adding a turban. Formally dressed, I presented myself at the synagogue for morning prayers. Joachim was present, as I expected. After the brief service that seemed to my hopeful heart to take forever, I approached Mary's father. The man paused in his conversation with Ezra when I stopped beside the pair.

"Joseph, I hear you will be repairing our table. That is kind of you. I know you are a busy man."

It was not how I hoped to begin the discussion but I nodded, "Yes, I plan to come later today to repair it."

The man half turned back to the rabbi. I did not move.

"Was there something else?" Joachim's raised eyebrow and half smile barely encouraged me to continue.

Suddenly, I was very nervous. Blood rushed to my face. The interview was not going as I hoped.

Taking a deep breath, I blurted, "Joachim bar David, I would speak to you of your daughter, Mary."

Several of the men talking with each other paused to listen.

"Go ahead," the man said slowly.

"I would like to marry her."

I felt my face turn fiery red. I was sure I sounded like a youth of fifteen rather than a man of twenty-five.

The rabbi smiled, "You will want to talk privately."

He stepped away to engage Joash bar Adam in conversation.

In an agony of discomfort and confusion, I stared at the mosaic floor. Joachim cleared his throat. I looked up.

"The rabbi is right, we need to talk." The older man motioned me to be seated on a nearby bench.

Nervously, I ran my hands over the edges. I recognized my father's workmanship. Never before had I noticed that the wooden seats, lining the synagogue walls, were made by Jacob.

"So you think you want to marry my daughter. Why?"

The feel of the wood under my fingers soothed the turmoil in my mind. Confidently I lifted my head.

"I cannot bear to see her married to anyone else."

"Are you so fond of my Mary, then?"

The father's love was plain. Steadily I met his concerned look.

"Yes, Joachim, Mary is precious to me."

I saw resignation slowly appear in the gray eyes staring at me. The silence stretched out until I thought my heart would stop.

Finally he nodded, "Then it is good. You are a fine man, Joseph bar Jacob. My daughter is fortunate that you desire to wed her."

"We will live here in Nazareth," I assured him. "I will not take her away. Our doors will always be open."

Another nod, more convincing this time moved the graying beard.

"Come, my friends," he called. "Bear witness to my joyful news."

As the men crowded around, Joachim stood. I followed suit. The man grasped my right hand with his.

"Joseph bar Jacob will be betrothed to my daughter Mary in a month's time."

Congratulations and a few jokes were tossed my way, but I barely heard them.

"When you come to repair the table, we will discuss the details." My future father-in-law nodded to me before hurrying away.

After enduring a few more minutes of advice and compliments, I managed to escape. My mother was not surprised by the news. Her lined face glowed.

"My son, Mary will make you a wonderful wife. It will be lovely to have a young woman nearby again. Your sisters are busy with their families and do not have time to visit often."

"I never realized…" I stammered. "You must be lonely now that my brothers travel with Father."

"They are young men now," she replied. "Sometimes it is hard to remember that they are thirteen and fifteen. I miss their boyish antics, but I know they are a great help to Jacob."

"I have never wanted to travel," I murmured. "They enjoy going to Sepphoris and further north into the Gentile towns and to Damascus."

Not for the first time, I wondered if my father was disappointed in me. Mother patted my arm. She seemed to read my mind.

"Your father is proud of what you have done with the shop here. Your brothers are wanderers and seekers like my Jacob. They enjoy the thrill of distant sights. I am blessed by your obedience to the laws of our people."

Overwhelmed with emotion, I hugged the woman who bore me. Gently my mother shoved me toward the door.

"Go, Joseph, my son, fulfill the mandates so that you may wed your Mary."

Somewhat nervously I paced the distance between my shop and the home of Joachim. In my hand I carried the few tools I would need to repair the table. As I drew nearer, my heart began to pound. It seemed to travel to my throat and lodge there. I swallowed several times, but my voice was still a rough croak when I responded to Anna's greeting.

"Joseph, welcome to our home. Come and sit with Joachim."

"Thank you," I cleared my throat and tried again. "You are very kind, Anna."

Joachim rose at my entrance. He held out the ceremonial washing bowl. I dipped my fingers into the water and dried them on the towel he held out.

"Welcome to my humble home, Joseph bar Jacob," he greeted me with a formal salaam. "We are honored by your presence."

In the prescribed ritual I returned his bow. "I am privileged to be the guest of Joachim bar David."

"Come, let us break bread."

The man motioned me to a low couch. Anna brought out a steaming platter of bread. My host took a loaf and broke it in half. With an inclination of my head I accepted the bread of hospitality.

Then we shared a cup of wine. The importance of the meeting was brought home to me when I took a sip of the liquid. This was not the common thinned wine that every family drank. The rich flavor flowed down my throat.

"You are most generous in your hospitality." I bowed my thanks to Mary's father.

"The house of Joachim is privileged to have the son of Jacob bar Mattan here."

After a few more pleasantries, Joachim brought up the topic of my visit.

"Joseph, son of Jacob of Bethlehem, my daughter Mary will become your betrothed by the giving of dowry gifts in the presence of the congregation at the next full moon during the feast of Purim. My daughter has beauty like Esther of old," he added proudly. "It is a most propitious time. You will be wed before Passover next Nisan."

I was reminded that Joachim was very conscious of his Davidic descent. Unlike my father, this man was proud of his lineage and claim, however distant, to the throne of David. For as long as I had known him Joachim's life centered on keeping the feasts and laws of Israel. It was not a surprise that he would see Mary's betrothal at Purim as a holy act.

"So be it. For my bride I will prepare gifts fit for her beauty. She will have such evidence of my craft and care that all will know her worth. Mary will have a home to call her own built beside my father's house."

My thoughts raced back over the years to when a small girl requested a smooth bowl for her dowry chest. Each season I had added a bowl to the collection, never dreaming that I would be the groom. His approving smile reassured me that my future father-in-law was pleased.

"Well spoken. To her groom my daughter will bring a dowry symbolic of her accomplishments and grace. I will speak to Ezra. The documents will be drawn up for witnessing at Purim."

Joachim poured another cup of wine. We drank to the agreement. With the business completed we could both relax.

"My Mary will indeed be blessed with you for a husband. She will not know hunger and her furniture will be stout."

His words reminded me of my other errand.

"I will repair the table now if you wish, Joachim."

Nodding and almost jovial, the man stood beside me as I pegged and repaired the crack. My iron bit dug quickly into the wood. Joachim bent forward to watch.

"I have never seen a man drill so quickly," he remarked.

The neat holes complete, I showed my future father-in-law the tool.

"The bit is of iron from Greece and well worth the price. It seemed an expensive extravagance when I purchased the drill from a trader. Many times I have been most grateful for the iron bit. It cuts down the time required to make a hole with the old awl and file method. I acquired an iron saw blade also. That too has been a great help."

"I can see that this is an amazing instrument."

His nod was appreciative as he handed back the drill. Swiftly, pegs were fit to the holes. I spread a thin layer of the gray glue between the two pieces of table before clamping them together with wood slats and leather straps. The leather pulled the table pieces into place. I wiped off the drops of excess glue that squeezed through the crack.

"When the seam dries, I will sand and smooth it," I explained.

The entrance of Anna, followed closely by Mary, interrupted our conversation. I felt my face flush when the women smiled at me. Surreptitiously I wiped my hands on the work apron I had donned to fix the table. Anna's questioning look was met by a smiling nod from her husband.

"It is good," the woman smiled happily. She took my hand and laid Mary's soft palm in it.

Almost of its own accord, my fingers curled around the small hand. My embarrassment fled when I felt her return the pressure. Amazed, I looked down at my promised bride. She barely came to the middle of my chest.

"Mary, I…"

My words were lost when the girl smiled. In her bright eyes shone a trust that made my heart swell with pride even as I felt unworthy of such devotion.

"It is good," Anna announced again with a broad smile and several quick nods.

Her words broke the spell lingering between Mary and me.

My betrothed looked at her parents. "Now may I visit Joseph at his shop?"

It was partly a question and partly a statement of intent.

Joachim cleared his throat. "Well…"

His wife stopped the man before he could refuse.

"What can it hurt once the betrothal is announced? After the promises are witnessed Mary should be able to see Joseph sometimes. Besides, Sarah is nearby."

Somewhat grudgingly, I thought, her father nodded his agreement.

"Very well, after the betrothal is made public at Purim."

"Thank you, Father!"

Joyfully the girl hugged first father than mother before bestowing a radiant smile on me. Again I was struck speechless by her beauty and vitality. It was a miracle that someone so young and lovely was to be my bride.

"You should tell your family," Anna suggested.

She nudged me toward the door when I stood rooted to the floor drinking in Mary's beauty.

Joachim grinned. "This Sabbath is the full moon of Purim. It is only three days away. I will speak to the rabbi."

His words followed me down the street. In a happy daze I greeted my friends and neighbors.

"And the betrothal is this Sabbath! There is so much to do." Sarah was delighted and immediately ordered, "Bring me your best tunic and robe and I will clean them. A new turban would be a good thing. Oh, and I must tell your sisters. You send word to your father. Jacob will want to be present."

"It is fortunate that he and my brothers are so near and not in Damascus or Ephesus. I will find a boy willing to run to Sepphoris with a message for Jacob bar Mattan, the carpenter," I grinned obediently as my mother dispensed orders.

The men hurried home. My father greeted me with a hearty slap on my back.

"So you have decided to take a bride. It is a good time. Your shop is prospering and I hear good reports of your work.

The best thing I ever did was let you take over the business here in Nazareth."

I was saved from responding by congratulations from the twins and my youngest brother.

Judah made us laugh when he mused, "Now I can look for a bride. Eunice in Damascus, perhaps or Chloe from Magdala, maybe Sarah from Cana."

"If you have so many to choose from, I do not think you are ready to settle down," Mother cautioned with a smile.

We shared a happy meal the evening before Sabbath. Everyone was relaxed and at ease except me. Whenever I thought of the morning ceremony, my hands began to tremble.

"Look, he is shaking like a girl. Is my big brother afraid to give up his single life?" Benoni teased.

My frown did not stop everyone from joining in the laugh. Seeking serenity I strolled outside.

Looking up at the silent, distant stars, I begged, "Make me a good husband. God of Abraham, Isaac, and Jacob, is this how the patriarch's felt when they met Sarah and Rebecca and Rachel and Leah? Mary is a special girl and I am only a humble carpenter. Keep me from being a fool."

It was late when my vigil ended. A measure of calm had returned. I had to trust that everything would be fine.

"I will be with you," a voice deep within seemed to whisper. "Your love for Mary will be enough."

I clung to that promise as I drifted to sleep.

Chapter 5

The ceremony at the synagogue the next day was simple.

"Here is the agreement for betrothal between Mary, daughter of Joachim bar David and Joseph bar Jacob, the carpenter," announced Rabbi Ezra, holding up a scroll.

The document listed the modest dowry my bride brought and the items I promised to provide for her comfort. Mary stood at my side blushing, while friends and neighbors expressed best wishes and the hope that the year of betrothal would pass swiftly and comfortably. Eventually everyone began to drift down the street to their own Sabbath meals.

"In all but the marriage bed, you are husband and wife. If anything should happen to you, Mary will be considered a widow. You are responsible for her safety and happiness just as you will be in a year when you share a roof," the rabbi reminded us.

I nodded and drew the slim figure close to my side. "It will be an honor to provide for Mary."

As token of my devotion I pressed a tender kiss on top of my betrothed's head before she walked home between Anna and Joachim. My father put a hand on my shoulder as I watched the family leave.

"You have much to do. There has to be an addition to the house and whitewashing of the entire place as well as building furniture."

I turned to the older man at my side. "I would be honored if you would help me, Father."

"Feeling a bit overwhelmed by all you need to do?"

Jacob's hearty slap on my back and laughing question signified his assent. I joined the laughter as we walked home. It would be good to work beside my father again. I could get reacquainted with my brothers, too. The man would have started work immediately had not Sarah reminded him sharply.

"Father, it is the Sabbath. Work can start tomorrow."

Over the next few days I was glad for their help. The framing for the new rooms went up quickly with five pairs of hands. By the next Sabbath all that remained was a coat of whitewash.

Mary found time during the week to visit the shop. I was working on a chest for Jonathan the miller. Her arrival made me drop my work to hastily dust off a bench. Fumbling, I found a clean cloth to cover the seat. She stopped me with a touch of her small hand on mine.

"Joseph, you never used to worry about making me a clean place to sit. I am the same person I was a month ago."

"You are my promised bride and very special to me."

Judah's chuckle choked in his throat when Father frowned at the young man. At Jacob's signal, my brothers left me alone with Mary. Suddenly I was tongue-tied. The girl motioned toward the nearly completed rooms.

"I saw your work. I did not expect you to have so much done."

"My brothers helped."

Mary stood up to cross the room. Light spilling through the window caught in her dark hair where it was not covered by the newly donned veil. Now that she was betrothed custom dictated that she had to wear the head covering. I was glad she did not fasten it tightly as many young women and matrons did.

"Is this ours?"

Her question called me back from contemplation of the dancing light in her hair. The girl was stroking a tabletop leaning against the wall. With a couple of steps, I stood beside my bride.

"Yes, I have started that for our table."

Bravely, I laid my rough hand over hers where it rested on the wood. She did not pull away and I was thrilled. Her other hand traced the whorls in the wood.

"It has a lovely grain."

"I chose this piece especially for that design."

Mary seemed oblivious to my pleasure at her presence. I swallowed convulsively when the soft hand under mine turned over and small fingers twined with mine. When she looked up her dark eyes were serious.

"Joseph, I am a lucky girl. I will try to make you a good wife," she promised.

"I know you will."

The hoarseness in my voice came from the lump of emotion that threatened to choke me. Suddenly not trusting myself, I stepped back from the loving look in Mary's eyes. My hands shook with longing. The young woman tilted her head as if confused. Something in my demeanor reassured her and a tender smile appeared.

"You will make a good husband. God brought us together."

Before I could move, my betrothed bridged the distance between us. Stretching up she placed a soft kiss on my cheek and hurried out.

"I will come back tomorrow," she called over her shoulder.

Jacob found me energetically sanding the tabletop.

"A year is a long time," he noted.

I pretended to be engrossed in creating a satin smooth finish. A friendly hand rested on my shoulder.

"Mary is a jewel worth waiting for. Like me you have waited for the one woman who trapped your heart. A pleasant torment it is, too."

I heard the amusement in my father's tone and turned abruptly to face him.

"A year is too long," I said, my voice ragged.

"Keep busy," he counseled. "Time will pass more quickly."

Indeed my nervous energy was almost reckless. I worked feverishly in order to spend the wonderfully tormenting afternoons sitting with Mary in the sun on the doorstep. After a short time our daily rendezvous was an accepted part of life in Nazareth. Women on their way to and from the market called greetings.

"Good afternoon, Mary and Joseph."

"Today is lovely after last night's rain."

"How is your mother?"

I sometimes wished we could sit in the courtyard away from the prying eyes and knowing smiles. However their presence helped ease the tension I felt when I found myself alone with my bride-to-be. I longed to clasp the girl in my arms and shower her small face with kisses, but I was afraid to frighten the young woman. Ever so trustingly she held my hand as we talked of hopes and dreams.

"I have finished the blanket for our bed," she told me one afternoon.

The scent of the herbs she used to wash her hair was distracting. I longed to bury my face in it where her head rested on my shoulder. When I did not comment, she stirred.

"Is the table finished?"

"Um," swallowing, I cleared my throat, "Yes. I just have to give the wood a final oiling and polishing."

"What will you make next?"

"There are some jobs that must be completed for customers. Then I will begin a chest for you to keep blankets in."

Mary smiled up at me. "That will be wonderful. Do not make it too large. Blankets take a long time to weave and I will be too busy as your wife to do much weaving."

"Really?" I teased with a raised eyebrow.

Her glowing face was a pleasure to watch. She began to list duties on her fingers.

"There is cooking, cleaning, getting water, and mending your clothes."

The last was added mischievously as one finger played with a tear in my sleeve. Standing and looking down at me, the girl blushed shyly before bending close.

"Someday I will have our children to tend," she whispered and darted away.

Passover approached, reminding me that in a year I would be a groom. It came unusually early in the season. Snow still clung to the heights and the nights were chill. The rabbi commented on my work after prayers one morning.

"It has been only a month since your betrothal. I see you and your brothers have been hard at work. Mary is a fortunate girl. Not all grooms build a separate home for their bride."

I knew he was right. Often the couple simply moved in with the groom's family.

"Mary deserves a home of her own," I replied.

The next day Mary paused at the shop on her way to the well.

"Joseph, I must help Mother prepare for Passover. I will not be able to visit until after the Feast. My parents want me with them this year."

"It is the last you will spend in their home," I agreed. "I will miss your daily visits."

However, I was busy with my own preparations. Passover meant I spent more time at the synagogue. It was the one time of the year that Jacob attended the services. During the daily prayers, the rabbi quoted myriad prophets to prove that the time was ripe for God's Servant to redeem Israel again. Afterward the men stood and mused about Messiah. Again and again, as it had been since before I was born, the arrival of a Deliverer was pondered.

"Surely God will not tarry much longer."

"Why doesn't God send us a Deliverer like Moses?"

"I wonder if we would recognize Messiah," I commented to Father as we walked home.

He shrugged, "Even the priests in the Temple cannot agree on the interpretations of the prophecies. They call for Messiah whenever Caesar orders some new tax or restriction on our lives through his puppet Herod."

Like all families in Israel, we remembered the great saga of Moses and Pharaoh on the night of Passover. Mother prepared the special foods and brought out the platters used only for the Feast.

"The bitter herbs, unleavened bread and roasted lamb remind us of God's deliverance centuries earlier. Do not forget the place for Elijah," she reminded us when we set up the table for the meal. "We want to be ready. The prophets say Elijah will come to prepare the way for Messiah."

The family meal was enlivened by stories my brothers shared of their travels with Father.

"Don't you wish you could visit Damascus?" Judah asked.

"It must be interesting to see all those places," I shrugged, "but I have found something more valuable here."

Anxiously I awaited Mary's visit when the Passover ended. She did not even wait until the afternoon. I had barely started measuring a new piece of wood when I sensed her presence. Delighted I took a step toward her.

"Mary!"

Something in her face and stance slowed my steps. Was it the early morning light in the shop or did the lovely face seem more radiant than usual? My bride stood just inside the entrance with her hands folded in front of her. As usual the veil on her hair was loose and the glossy waves caught the light. When the girl did not speak, I took a hesitant step forward. Then I saw the hint of tears brimming in her eyes.

"Mary? Are you ill?"

I reached for her hand, intending to lead the woman to the seat. Her small hand turned to hold mine. I found myself being led to the bench. Then she knelt in front of me. I was appalled and reached for the slender shoulders.

"Mary, what are you doing? Why do you kneel at my feet? You should be sitting here."

Again her soft hands captured mine. Surprisingly tightly the woman held my palms between hers. She looked up at me.

"Joseph, I have something miraculous to tell you." Her voice sounded different than usual although I could not name what was changed.

"My love, sit beside me."

Again I tried to urge Mary onto the seat. The girl insisted on remaining on the floor.

"Listen to me," she said urgently.

My efforts to lift my betrothed up from the floor ended. I sensed that the message was not something I wanted to hear. My heart began thudding slowly and painfully.

"Tell me what is so important."

My beloved drew one of my hands to her cheek and rested her head against my rough palm. "Joseph, I know that what I have to say will seem…" She searched for the word, "…unbelievable."

Of its own accord, my free hand lifted a wavy strand of hair. Absently I wound the silky length around my fingers. The movement stilled at her pronouncement.

"I have seen an angel."

"What?"

I bent forward to look in the dark eyes. Fearlessly the woman returned my gaze.

"It is true."

I felt my brows draw together. Trying to be reasonable, I forced myself to speak calmly. “Angels do not visit Nazareth. Even prophets have ceased from Israel. Why do you think you saw an angel?”

“His name was Gabriel. I was alone, mixing the dough for the Passover bread.”

As she looked past me, I saw the tension leave the graceful young body. An almost dreamy look transformed the face I stared at. My mind sought a rational explanation. Why would my bride believe an angel spoke to her? Was it possible?

“Suddenly there was light all around. It was like midday, except I was in the house. From the light I heard a voice, ‘Hail, Mary, you are blessed above all women.’ I was terrified.”

A tremulous smile accompanied her admission. Tenderly I stroked the tendrils of hair from her forehead.

After a moment Mary continued, “The bread dough fell from my hands and I covered my face. But the voice was soothing…”

Her sigh of remembrance caused me to clench my fingers around the strand of hair I still held. Who was this stranger in Joachim’s house? At Mary’s gasp of pain, I released my grip. Contrite, I smoothed the hair into place.

“I am sorry.”

The young woman smiled tenderly, “It is hard to believe.”

“What did this ‘angel’ do?”

I was more than half convinced that this was no messenger from God but a human intent on harm. My mind tried to decide who in Nazareth would do such a thing.

As though reading my thoughts, Mary stated, “This was no man. No hand touched me. The angel’s words were a message from the One God.”

My hands were captured between the soft palms of my betrothed.

“Tell me,” I gasped in a whisper.

Soft eyes held mine as my beloved recited, "'Do not be afraid, Mary. You have found favor with God.'" After a brief pause she plunged on. "'Behold, you will conceive and bear a son. You will call his name Jeshua.'"

I started to speak but the woman kneeling in front of me shook her head. Her brown eyes had softened.

"This is not a prophecy of some future son of ours, Joseph. That is what I thought at first."

Again I felt my heart thudding in my chest. Fear gripped me. I shook my head, not wanting to hear any more. Mary's gentle hands still held mine. The woman tightened her grip on my now shaking hands.

"Then the angel told me. 'He will be great and will be called the Son of the Most High. The Lord God will give to him the throne of his father David. He will reign over the house of Jacob forever and of his kingdom there will be no end.'"

"Messiah? It cannot be. You misunderstood."

Head shaking in denial I found myself on my feet. Mary still knelt by the bench. Facing my promised bride, I hoped she would nod and agree. In a graceful movement, this woman who seemed a stranger rose and turned to me.

"Joseph, I questioned the angel."

A tear slipped out to lie gleaming on one cheek when I said nothing.

"This is not something I expected. God chose me, chose us, for this honor."

"Honor? How can you claim this is an honor?" I demanded angrily and was immediately ashamed.

Mary drew herself straight and lifted her chin. "The child I carry is of God. No man touched me."

The pride in her words stopped my pacing.

"How?"

I had to know even though my heart was breaking. Hands crossed at her breast, Mary gazed beyond me out the window.

The light suddenly seemed brighter and was reflected in the lovely face.

"The Spirit of God…I have never felt so alive! A rush like warm water washed over me invigorating and comforting. There was such peace that I slid to the floor unable to move. Still I was bathed in such warmth…"

Mary's eyes returned to me. The woman took a step toward me and held out a hand.

"It was a loving caress, like when you have held me in your arms. Yet it filled my whole soul. I knew it was God.

"No! Do not blaspheme," I shouted, turning my back on the rapturous figure. "Better to have betrayed our vows with a man than to blaspheme."

I flinched from the gentle hand on my arm.

"Joseph, I do not lie."

"No! Leave me."

Hoarsely I denied her claim, shaking off her hand and stumbling away from the girl. Head bowed I stood in the middle of the shop. I heard the woman moving away.

"You have seen no angel. I saw and doubted still. God will reveal the truth," she said softly.

"No!"

I was not sure if she heard my last anguished gasp. When I turned the room was empty. Only the spot where she knelt was evidence of the girl's presence. Reeling and devastated, I smashed a fist against the tabletop. The perfection of the smooth finish mocked me with a reminder of my love and her betrayal.

Chapter 6

Unable to work, I threw on my outer garment and stormed from the building, nearly trampling Benoni. He backed away from my rage without even a question. Blindly I headed for the hills beyond Nazareth. If anyone greeted me, I did not hear. Mary's words repeated their terrible litany in my head.

"Bear a son…God chose...no man…I do not lie."

Faster and faster I walked, until I was running up the mountainside. The same grove of trees that saw my decision to wed Mary received me. Like a mad man I smashed my hands against one trunk and then another until my rage was spent. In despair I fell to my knees.

"God, why do you mock me? I believed you gave me Mary's love. Now she admits that she carries a child which is not mine!" Renewed anger set me to pacing. Suspicion fueled the fire. "Joachim was eager to accept my offer. Did he know that his daughter was no virgin, even then? Was I the dupe all along?"

I heard the animal growl that came from my throat. If the man had been near I would have choked an answer from him. My head began to pound from my emotions and unanswerable questions. Sinking down with my back against a tree, I buried my face in my hands.

"God, the girl blasphemed to cover her lie. How can you not strike her down?"

A memory of her radiant face gave me pause. The innocence and beauty of her announcement came back to me. I dared not believe it true.

"God, is Mary a victim of some hoax? God, did you steal my bride?"

Throughout the day I alternately paced and sat, prayed and cursed, raged and wept. The evening shadows started to darken the grove when a horrifying thought occurred to me. I crashed to my knees, gripping a sapling for support.

"I do not accept Mary and her child, she will be stoned!"

The pain that grabbed me by the heart radiated throughout my body until I could almost feel stones striking me. I slid to the ground in agony. My father's recital of what happened to his mother flashed into my mind. Groaning, I covered my head. With my eyes closed I saw the rarely used pit outside of Nazareth. Only once had I seen anyone stoned there. A man convicted of blasphemy had been dragged to the place. Every man in town had taken turns throwing rocks until the body was an unrecognizable bloody pulp.

"No!"

I sprang up, eyes wide with the remembered horror. I could not condemn any woman to such a death. Sanity slipped me a lifeline.

"There is another option," I whispered. "I can send her away until the child is born. No one need know."

I tried to ignore the insistent voice that hissed 'you would always remember'. The shadows grew as I resumed my pacing. My pride shied away from naming the child as mine. True, the gossip could be stared down. Many men sampled the marriage bed during the betrothal. No one would condemn me. I would be the only one to know the infant was not of my seed.

"God…"

Worn out from the day's passion, I sank to my knees. The Name of the Most High was all I could say. Over and over I repeated the word.

Eventually, I resolved to divorce Mary and send her away to preserve her life. Exhausted, I leaned against a tree trunk and closed my eyes. I must have dozed. The dream, when it came, held me tightly even after I awakened. As Mary said, the angel was a figure of light without real form. Even in my sleep, I felt my heartbeat quickening.

"Joseph, do not be afraid. You may take Mary as your wife. The child is conceived by the Spirit of God. She will bear a son. You will name him Jeshua. For just as his name means 'God saves', so this child will save all people."

Then the messenger from God was gone. The peace that enveloped me left me comforted. Gradually, I opened my eyes to stare at the surrounding trees. The grove was in darkness but my soul was in light. Moonlight filtered through the sparse early spring leaves to illuminate the trunks and the ground. Slowly I sat up, reassured and unafraid. God had stolen my beloved but I would not lose her.

For a long time, I sat with my back against the rough bark of the cedar tree. Absently I gathered a fistful of the soft dirt to let it trickle through my fingers only to gather it up again.

The words of Isaiah came to me, 'A young woman shall be with child, and you shall call his name Emmanuel.'

"Emmanuel." I said the name aloud. "God is with us."

The meaning had never seemed so real and possible. Suddenly, God was not a distant figure from the past who only spoke to Abraham and Moses. The One whose true Name was too holy to be spoken had come to a fourteen year-old girl in Nazareth.

"Mary is pregnant by the will of God," I whispered in awe.

My words were absorbed by the night breeze and my heart thudded at the audacity of such a thought. The memory of my dream reassured me. The touch of the soil in my fist convinced me that I was awake. I watched the moon set. The pre-dawn darkness on the hillside was not frightening. Angels still seemed to hover nearby. A red glow in the eastern sky foretold the dawn.

"I must go to Mary."

Confident in my decision, I strode down the path. Without pause, my feet carried me to the house of Joachim and Anna. It appeared that no one was awake. For a moment I hesitated before knocking. A rooster crowed to welcome the new day and a dog barked in reply. My pounding brought Joachim to the door. His hastily donned garment and uncombed hair told me that I had awakened the man.

"Joachim, I want to wed Mary!"

My statement caused the man to pause in rubbing the sleep from bleary eyes.

Somewhat irritably my future father-in-law frowned, "My son that is settled. You and Mary are betrothed."

I took his arm when the man began to close the door. "Joachim, I want to wed her now!"

He raised an eyebrow in response. His gaze traveled over my bedraggled appearance. Glancing down, I belatedly remembered that I was covered with dirt. Pine needles clung to my beard. I plucked a cluster of leaves from my sleeve and shook out the hem of my cloak. Still Joachim stared at me.

"Or as soon as it can be arranged," I temporized when he did not answer.

A hint of anger crept into the older man's reply. "Joseph, do you dare imply that there is a reason for such haste?"

I realized Mary had not shared her news with her father. The interview was not going to be easy.

"I…that is…" I stammered for a moment until I heard again, 'Do not be afraid'. Lifting my chin and looking Mary's father in the eyes I nodded. "Yes, Joachim."

Then I waited for his rage to subside. With a howl of anguish, the man struck my cheek. Angrily he sputtered imprecations about my age and family. He finally came to the end of his tirade.

"A man of your age should be ashamed of taking advantage of my Mary's innocence," he panted.

The man's hands fell limply to his side. Looking beaten, Joachim pulled me into the house. I winced at the sorrow in the tone when he called his family.

"Anna, bring Mary."

There was a rustle of material and the two women entered. Mary's unbound hair still seemed to retain light from the day before. Her eyes sought mine. In answer to her unspoken question, I crossed the room to take her small hand. It was cold and shaking. I drew her close against my side.

Joachim frowned but I felt the tension leave my bride. Only then did I understand that the confidence of the day before was partly a façade. I bent my head to place a kiss on top of the girl's head. Anna broke the silence. Looking from her grimacing husband to my protective stance the woman relaxed.

"You have decided," she said softly.

I nodded calmly.

"Wife, what do you know of this?" Joachim asked in a hoarse voice.

The woman patted her husband's clenched fist. "More than you, my husband. All is well, though. See how Joseph is taking care of our Mary?"

"So he should, if what he says is true."

The man looked at his daughter. His mouth tried to form the words.

Finally he gasped, "Mary is there a need for haste?"

The girl repeated her mother's words. "Father, all will be well. It is not something I planned."

In renewed rage the man glared at me. "No, you are innocent."

Mary left the circle of my arms to face her angry father.

"My father, hear me. Joseph did not plan for this either."

"He should know better," Joachim growled.

Anna intervened when the girl would have spoken again. The woman took charge.

"I will talk to your father. Now there is much to be done. Joseph tell your family the ceremony will be tomorrow. If your mother can help, it would be appreciated. Joachim, go to the rabbi."

When we did not move, she gave us each a none too gentle push toward the door.

"Go!" She ordered. "Mary and I have much to do."

I found myself outside in the street beside the now bemused Joachim.

"Anna knew. Mary told her mother," he mumbled.

The man sounded hurt. He narrowed his eyes in my direction. I was a convenient scapegoat for his anger.

"If you ever do anything to harm my daughter I will find you. Crucifixion will not be punishment enough."

I shuddered at the mention of the cruel Roman punishment reserved for rebels and murderers. In Nazareth we heard stories of crosses along the roads leading into Jerusalem and Damascus.

"My friend, Mary is more to me than life itself."

I offered my hand in reconciliation.

"But not worth your restraint," the man growled.

My proffered hand dropped and I felt myself stiffen in outrage.

"Joachim, I will see you at the synagogue."

I knew that if I spoke again it would be in rage. Mary had not told her father of the angel's visit. It was not my place to do so. I swallowed my pride and hurried to inform my mother of the change of plans.

Chapter 7

Mother did not ask any questions before rushing off to help Anna prepare a feast. I fled to the shop seeking silence and solace. Joachim's anger had shaken my assurance and the memory of my dream. I did not doubt the rightness of my decision. What I sought was reassurance that it was what God wanted.

"God, you ask a lot of me. I thought the neighbors would be hard to face, not Joachim."

Jacob interrupted my prayer. "Doesn't the father have a right to be aggrieved? I would have whipped your sister's husbands for a similar reason."

Startled, I spun around. Anger that I thought suppressed burst out. My fists clenched and I took a step toward the man.

"You do not understand the situation. How dare you judge me? I have decided to do what is necessary for Mary and the baby."

With raised eyebrows my father studied me. Then he quietly asked, "Then the child is not yours?"

I felt my head jerk up as though struck. His nod of understanding and unvoiced condemnation was too much.

I grabbed my father's arm and announced, "No! The child is mine."

Skeptically the man studied me. Eventually he gripped my arm in return.

"My son, I accept your claim. The child will be welcomed into this household."

Joachim and Anna, Jacob and Sarah as well as my siblings attended the ceremony before the rabbi. We walked together to the synagogue. I met Ezra's sad eyes without flinching. The simple words that asked the Holy One's blessing on our union and the prayer for many sons were swiftly concluded. The old man laid Mary's hand in mine.

"Go in peace, my son and my daughter. May God protect and bless you both."

When we did not move, the man grinned. "You may kiss your bride."

Gently, almost reverently I touched my lips to Mary's. Memory of the child she carried swept over me and I drew back. It did not seem appropriate to kiss the girl chosen to bear the Messiah.

"Come, Anna has prepared a feast," Joachim interrupted in a voice filled with false heartiness.

As we walked the short distance to Mary's home, Joachim shouted the news to curious friends.

"Come and celebrate with us. Mary is now a wife. Joseph bar Jacob has made her his wife."

The words carried a double meaning for my ears only. Glad of the excuse to celebrate, many neighbors flocked after us. Joachim ushered me to a low seat. Mary sat beside me, the bridal headdress covering her lustrous waves of dark hair except for a few curls on her forehead and cheek. The girl held my hand. I squeezed her quivering fingers and was rewarded by a small smile. Then we were overwhelmed by the good wishes of friends.

"Congratulations, Joseph."

"Blessing on your home, Joseph and to you Mary."

"Shalom, my children."

"May God grant you many sons."

The glances of the women strayed knowingly to Mary's slim figure. In the masculine heartiness I sensed sympathetic understanding. Some of them had not kept the betrothal year either.

My mother and Anna seemed to be everywhere. They carried out an endless supply of food and drink. I watched the guests consume cup after cup of thin wine. Eventually, everyone drifted to their homes. The day was spent and the moon perched on the horizon.

"Not a moment too soon," sighed Anna dropping onto a vacated pile of pillows. "We have only one more jug of wine."

"Mother, it was lovely." Mary embraced her mother.

Then my bride kissed her father. He clung to her for a long minute before laying her hand in mine.

"Deal with her gently," he said.

I remembered his threat of wrath if I failed his daughter. Almost reverently I led Mary to my home. Picking up the slight form, I stepped into the house. The Roman custom seemed somehow necessary. I had to prove that the woman was my bride.

Jacob stood beside my mother.

"Welcome to our home," he said with a forced a smile for Mary.

Sarah looked very tired but smiled tenderly at us. "My son, we will go to Deborah's home this night. You will have privacy with your bride."

With a kiss on my cheek and then on Mary's, Sarah led the way from the house. My father's grip of my shoulder was reassuring. Then we were alone for the first time since the interview only days earlier in the wood shop.

Mary did not move, even when I held out my hand to her.

"Joseph, why?" She asked timidly.

"What do you mean?"

I stepped toward my bride. One outstretched hand stopped my advance.

"Did you marry me from pity or because you believe?"

"God sent an angel to me, too. I had a dream…" Briefly I paused then added, "I know you did not lie."

"Joseph!"

Joy suffused her young face. In a moment I held my wife in my arms. She buried her face in my chest. I felt tears soaking my tunic.

"I am so glad," she sobbed. "Pity would have been awful."

"Mary, my love," I whispered.

It was all I could say. It was enough. I smoothed the dark hair and kissed the top of her head. How long we stood in the center of the room, I do not know. Eventually she stopped sobbing. Still I held the woman.

"God chose you because you are a faithful and honest man," she stated. With a tilt of her head, my bride looked up at me. "I could have not asked for a kinder groom. Few men are willing to take a child not their own. I know very well how hard it must have been to accept my story."

"I did rage at God," I admitted with a rueful smile and lowered head.

"You would not have been human if you had not." Her hand gently touched my cheek. When I did not reply she added, "It is a hard story to accept."

Mary led the way to the bed lovingly prepared by my mother. Taking a seat, she pulled me down beside her. In the flickering lamplight, I saw a gentle smile. Gracefully my bride removed her veil and loosened her hair. My heart jumped into my throat choking off any utterance as the glossy waves cascaded over her shoulders. Shifting slightly she removed the gown that covered her tunic. I sat frozen when the girl removed my turban and outer garment. Swallowing desperately, I caught her hands.

"My wife, you carry Messiah. I will not take you as wife until he is born."

"Joseph?" She tried to argue.

Holding her hands captive I tried to explain. "No, Mary. The angel told me to…not to…I shall not…"

"I am sorry," the woman stated.

She freed her hands to slip them around my waist. The head that rested against my chest was both comforting and disturbing. Although I ached to caress my wife, I was almost in awe of her.

"There should be no doubt that your son is Messiah."

My voice sounded stern and Mary drew back to ask, "Do you still love me?"

"More than life itself," I responded truthfully.

"Then will you hold me in your arms?"

Her innocent question made my heart pound.

"Yes, my love."

I drew her close. So we slept. Rather Mary slept. I lay beside the woman marveling. Why had I doubted her? What did it matter if she bore Messiah? Mary was my wife as I had dreamed and desired. The reality was so different than I expected.

"God help me to be the husband Mary deserves. I will protect her and the child she will bear," I vowed silently.

Chapter 8

The first few days were the worst. An unusual number of customers made a trip to the doorway of the carpenter shop.

"Joseph, my plow needs tightened."

"Can you fix this cracked chair?"

"Is my stool done yet?"

All the questions were expressed casually while eyes roamed past me trying to catch a glimpse of my bride. I had to grit my teeth against an aggravated response to their overt curiosity. The women were no better. I knew they eyed my wife with calculating eyes when she accompanied my mother to the well.

Eventually the gossip began to die down. It was replaced by rumors from Jerusalem of Herod's latest folly. Merchants from the capital whispered that the King was plundering the tombs of David for the gold inside. At the synagogue there were arguments after the Sabbath service.

"We would be better off without a mad man on the throne."

"Would a Roman governor be any better?"

"We already pay taxes to Herod and the Temple. We do not need more taxes from the Empire."

"The King is not even a Jew. How can he know what we need?"

"He is old and sick. Who knows if his sons will be any better?"

"Surely now is the time for God to send Messiah."

"With one of David's line on the throne, we could drive the heathen from Israel."

"Messiah will purify the nation as in the days of Isaiah."

I kept my mouth closed and thought of the unborn child. It would be hard to keep the child safe from feuding factions.

Before the next Sabbath Mary came to my shop.

I grinned and dusted off the bench for her. "I am happy to see you here again. This is how I remember it. Besides it gave me a chance to stop work."

For several moments my wife looked at me with such love in her eyes that I felt humbled. Then she looked down and twisted the ends of her veil.

"My husband, I would like to travel to see my cousin, Elizabeth." I must have looked as startled as I felt because she hurriedly explained, "The angel that came to me told me that Elizabeth is with child."

"Your cousin, the wife of Zechariah the priest is pregnant? How can that be? She is an old woman past the age of child bearing."

"Yes, Elizabeth is Zechariah's wife. Just listen to what the angel told me."

My wife squeezed my fingers. With eyes almost closed and a slight smile on her lips, the young woman quoted the angel, "'This is the third month with her who was called barren.' My cousin, old as she is, is also going to have a child."

My eyes must have shown doubt because my wife stood up and lifted her chin.

"God gave a baby to Abraham and Sarah when she was ninety-nine. Rebecca bore Isaac at an advanced age, too."

"Those were long ago," I argued feebly.

"Joseph, I want to visit Elizabeth to see if it is true."

My mouth opened to argue but I shut it. Looking at the young woman, still almost a girl, I understood that she needed the assurance only her cousin could give.

"Is it safe for the baby?"

As soon as the question left my lips, I knew it was foolish.

Mary smiled, "My husband, God has his hand on me and on this child. Do not be afraid."

"My love, I can see that this is important to you. I will arrange for you to go with the next caravan south."

Like a happy child, my wife hugged my neck and kissed my cheek before dancing from the shop.

"You are so good to me, Joseph bar Jacob!"

In the silence after she left, I stared at the door. I had to swallow the lump of loneliness already building in my throat.

"God, why do you continue to test me?" I grumbled.

In the morning I sought a caravan in the market. Mary was fortunate because I found one immediately.

Jeremiah bar Hosea stated, "I am traveling to Jerusalem with a load of olive oil. Of course Mary may come. Indeed, my wife Rebecca accompanies me on this trip."

I ignored his unspoken curiosity and responded, "Thank you, my friend."

Mary was already happily chatting with the older woman while the trader's young sons chased a puppy around and between the donkey's legs. An irritated kick by one of the animals reminded the boys to move to a safer distance. Mary gave me a quick kiss when Jeremiah started up the road.

"Do not worry, Joseph, I will be back before you can miss me."

I could have told her she was wrong but her light footsteps carried her after Rebecca. Already lonely, I watched until the small caravan was out of sight down the road.

Joachim came to see me the day after his daughter left. I looked up at the sound of a heavy footstep.

Angrily he blurted, “Why have you sent her away?”

I rose from the bench where I was absently sanding a piece of lumber. Even across the room I felt the man’s rage.

“My father…”

“Why did you send her away?” he repeated. “You married my child. Now she is exiled. It would have caused less talk if we had sent her away secretly before the wedding.”

“Joachim, I have not cast off your daughter.”

I had to raise my voice because the man continued to pace around the shop accusing me of abandoning his daughter. At last I stepped in front of my father-in-law. He glared at me. I half expected the man to strike me. Instead he crumpled onto the just completed chair nearby.

“Joseph, do you seek to shame my child?”

It was the cry of a broken-hearted father.

I crouched beside the man.

“Joachim, I have not sent Mary away. She begged to go to see her cousin Elizabeth. There is word that your niece is pregnant.”

My visitor sat back in stunned surprise. “Who brought such news? The woman is older than I. Her mother was wed to my oldest half-brother, son of my father’s earlier marriage.”

“The same messenger who told Mary that she will bear Messiah.”

I waited for disbelief or scorn. Instead the man sighed. He raked a shaking hand through gray hair. Haggard eyes lifted to meet mine.

“Is there no end of the surprises this angel messenger left? Why does God require this of me? My only child, my sweet girl, is the object of scorn and gossip. I have to stand by and say nothing. How can God ask this of me?”

“I ask myself the same thing.”

My confession seemed to surprise Mary’s father for he raised his eyebrows.

"The gossips look at me too. I hear the whispers…"

My voice trailed off as I remembered the innuendoes overheard as I walked from the synagogue only that morning.

"There is Joseph, hurried the betrothal along, didn't he?"

"What can Mary see in such a man?"

"No wonder she has gone away already."

"Maybe he sent her off."

"What if the child is not his and he found out?"

"Do you really think so?"

"I would not be surprised."

Shaking my head to erase the titters, I again addressed my visitor. My hand gripped Joachim's.

"We know the truth. That will have to be enough. Surely God does not ask more of us than we can bear."

"I hope you are right, Joseph. I am proud to call you son."

Calm now, Joachim rose. I saw tears in his eyes. My own eyes were damp at the thought of the dreams that would not be fulfilled for my friend.

"Mary will return in a short time. All will be well."

It was longer than I expected before my wife again graced the streets of Nazareth. Jeremiah bar Hosea and his family returned. Mary was not with them. I met the group near the market.

Before I could speak, Jeremiah called out, "Joseph, just the man I was going to find. Mary did not return with us. She bid me beg you to let her stay until time for Elizabeth, wife of the priest, to be delivered."

Numbly I nodded. I felt the held breath of the listening neighbors.

"It is quite the talk of Bethel," continued Jeremiah. "The woman is long past the age of childbearing and Zechariah is even older. It seems the man was struck dumb when he heard the news."

A guffaw from the merchant brought a smile to my lips and giggles from the crowd.

"I am sure Mary will be of great help to her cousin." I said calmly although my heart ached for my wife.

Rebecca noticed my sadness.

She leaned close as if to confide a secret, although she barely lowered her voice. "It is true, you know. I saw Elizabeth myself. There is no doubt that she is pregnant. She is full of such joy and talks of nothing else. I even heard her claim that it was an angel that told old Zechariah he was going to be a father."

Her announcement sent off a ripple of giggles.

"Whether that is true or not, it is obvious that Mary will be needed by her cousin," she added.

"Then I am glad she stayed."

Out of the corner of my eye I saw Joachim sigh in relief. Now the gossips would be diverted with discussions of the amazing pregnancy of Elizabeth.

The evenings were lonely without Mary. My mother brought me meals after noticing that I did not take the time to do more than munch a slab of bread and piece of cheese once a day. More often than not I simply picked at the food wondering when my wife would return. Her arrival after three months took me by surprise.

"Joseph."

I swung around from fitting a board in place to see my beloved standing in the shop doorway.

"Mary!"

My surprise must have been all she hoped for. Giggling gaily, the girl met me in the center of the room. Joyfully I caught her up and spun around. Dark waves of hair tumbled free and cascaded over my face.

"You are back!" My delighted statement was unnecessary as I held the woman tightly in my arms.

"Of course, my husband." I heard a soft giggle against my chest. Mary drew back slightly to look up at me. "Have you missed me?"

"More than you can imagine!" I pressed a kiss on her forehead.

"I missed you, Joseph," she admitted, "but Elizabeth needed me. She was overwhelmed by being pregnant at her age."

"Tell me. Rebecca and Jeremiah did not know any details. All they could say was that Elizabeth is with child."

I carried my bride to the bench and gathered her onto my lap. The woman snuggled into my arms.

"It is true. My cousin who endured the pity of so many because of her barrenness is now the talk of the hill country around Jerusalem. Zechariah is beside himself."

A smile crossed the young face.

I chuckled, "I can well imagine that."

Her next words caught me by surprise. I paused in my task of wrapping the dark hair around my fingers.

"Zechariah had his own angel visitation."

"Really?"

"It is true. He was serving at the temple."

Her vigorous nod uncoiled the strands from my hand. The girl moved slightly to make herself more comfortable.

"Zechariah is of the house of Levi. You know how King David set the priests in ranks for service in the temple. Now there are so many that each priest has only one day a year to serve. Zechariah has always taken the honor most seriously. This year it was his turn to burn incense at Yom Kippur. That is something that a priest can only hope to happen once in his lifetime."

Mary's eyes took on a faraway look. She was quiet for a minute. I thought about the privilege the old man had looked forward to all his life. To serve on such an important feast and to burn the incense before the Holy of Holies must have filled the priest with awe.

“Elizabeth told me what happened because Zechariah is unable to speak,” Mary smiled.

“How?” I asked, and then clarified when the woman looked confused. “How did he tell her?”

One hand reached up to caress my cheek. She teased me with a smile. “Joseph, my husband, when we have been married as long as my cousins have, there will be no need for words either.”

I shook my head and cocked my head waiting for her explanation.

Mary continued, “Zechariah long ago taught Elizabeth to read and write. When he returned from serving in Jerusalem he could not talk. Of course my cousin was frantic. Then the man took a scroll and wrote out his experience.”

Again Mary paused to remember and repeat what she was told. I waited patiently; glad to have my wife home safely.

“When he laid the incense on the altar, an angel appeared to him in the cloud. The news was unbelievable to the old man. ‘You and your wife will have a son. You will call his name John.’ I am sure my cousin was astonished. He is such a precise, level-headed, law abiding, sensible, old man. The idea that he was in the presence of an angel must have shocked him deeply. Such things do not happen to dignified Jews in this century.”

A smile danced across my wife’s face.

I shared her chuckle, with an aside. “Some would say that, but it seems to be happening regularly to unsuspecting and unprepared men.”

A giggle trilled out and my wife nestled closer to me. I did not want to disturb the contented feeling that flowed through me now that Mary was home. Silently I held the woman.

“The angel proceeded to prophesy to Zechariah about his son. He was told, ‘You will have joy and gladness, and many will rejoice at his birth, for he will be great in the sight of the Lord. He must never drink wine or strong drink; even before his birth he will be filled with the Holy Spirit. He will turn many of the people of Israel to the Lord their God. With the spirit and power of Elijah he will go before him, to turn the hearts of parents to their children, and the disobedient to the wisdom of the righteous, to make ready a people prepared for the Lord.'"

Suddenly serious, the woman looked up at me. She repeated, "A people ready to greet Messiah."

Mary pressed one hand to her just rounding belly. I covered it with mine. A huge lump formed in my throat. I swallowed hard. There had remained a tiny thread of doubt in my heart.

"God forgive me. Our God had given proof of his plans," I whispered.

Mary nodded against my shoulder. "Zechariah could not get past his disbelief. He argued with the angel, claiming that both he and Elizabeth were too old. 'I am Gabriel and stand in the presence of God', the figure said. 'You will be unable to speak until all these things come to pass.' Then my cousin was alone. When he finally stumbled back to the people, everyone realized that something unusual had happened. He tried to explain with signs until one of the other priests stepped forward. 'Our brother has seen a vision. God will open his lips at the opportune time.' Then they hustled him out of sight. Of course the High Priest Annas demanded to see Zechariah."

I groaned slightly remembering what my father said about this man who courted favor with both Herod and Rome in order to stay in power.

The woman in my arms shook her head sadly. "When the man wrote out what happened, he was scornfully told, 'God no longer deals with the barren. You have been misled by your carnal desires. Return to your wife and do not mock our intellect with these tales. God has struck you dumb for presumption.'"

"Poor Zechariah," I muttered, seething at the blind cruelty of the High Priest.

"Yes," Mary agreed, "the poor man shut himself up for a week after he came home. Elizabeth told me she heard him moaning and knew he was praying. He refused all food until she finally marched into his seclusion and demanded an answer. Then he wrote down the vision."

"What did Elizabeth think of such a story?" I wondered aloud, remembering my own experience with reports of angel visits.

"My cousin said she scolded her husband. 'How can you doubt such a messenger? The High Priest speaks from jealousy because he has never seen an angel.'"

"Why are women so much more willing to believe the messengers from God? We men struggle for a rational explanation."

Mary smiled and kissed my cheek. "You believe now."

"Yes, but it was not easy."

I captured another strand of her dark locks and tugged gently so that our lips met briefly.

"How did Zechariah come to accept the news?"

"Elizabeth finally coaxed him to eat and they lay together. A month later when my cousin missed her monthly flow the man strutted around with such a grin she was glad he could not speak. Zechariah went to the well and market for his wife. She refused to go out."

"Why? I would think she would want to share her news." I frowned, confused by the older woman's actions.

"I wondered that, too. Elizabeth said, 'They would have stolen away my secret joy.' When she finally did venture to the market after five months, the comments were full of amazement."

"I am sure they were."

I could well imagine the stir that Elizabeth's pregnancy and Zechariah's muteness caused in the small town.

Mary smiled, "When I arrived, Elizabeth was so glad to see me. I think the whispers and speculation were tiring her out."

My mind turned to the gossip around the well in Nazareth. I drew my wife closer wishing to protect her from the inevitable comments that would start again now that she was back. Mary understood my silence.

"Joseph, we cannot stop the mouths of the neighbors. You and I know the truth. That will be enough."

"My love, I wish I could spare you. If they knew that you carry Messiah..."

The vehemence in my tone made the girl open her eyes wide with surprise.

"God will make the truth known," she assured me, "just like God did for Elizabeth, when I arrived."

"Tell me."

Mary snuggled close and continued her story. Her face glowed with serenity.

"Elizabeth started across the room to greet me. Then she stopped suddenly and put a hand on her belly. She said, 'Blessed are you. Who am I that the mother of the Savior comes to me?' It was a final piece of proof that this baby is of God."

A sigh of contentment slipped out as my wife smoothed her gown over the tiny rounding of her figure.

"My cousin told me, 'When I heard your voice my baby leaped with joy.' God confirmed my child through Elizabeth's baby."

I laid my rough hand over the girl's small fingers. "Yes, and your presence affirmed her child also."

"You do understand! Our joy was so great that we sang together, praising God for raising up salvation for the people." Mary began to sing softly. She slipped from my lap to pirouette around the shop as she repeated the joyous chant, "His mercy is for those who fear him from generation to generation. He has shown strength with his arm; he has scattered the proud in the thoughts of their hearts. He has brought down the powerful from their thrones, and lifted up the lowly; he has filled the hungry with good things, and sent the rich away empty. He has helped his servant Israel, in remembrance of his mercy, according to the promise he made to our ancestors, to Abraham and to his descendants forever."

I marveled at the radiance of my wife and smiled, "Surely just so did Sarah and Rebecca proclaim their joy when they conceived. This child is the fulfillment of their longings and the longings of all Israel."

"Yes, my husband, our son is the One promised from the beginning."

Flushed with joy, Mary sank back on the bench beside me. I drew her close briefly. After a moment she stood up.

"I must prepare the meal. Tomas the trader will eat with us tonight. He was kind enough to let me accompany him on his way north."

"I will join you soon," I promised to her retreating back.

I repeated part of Mary's words as I put away my tools, "'He has scattered the proud in the thoughts of their hearts. He has brought down the powerful from their thrones.' God of Abraham, Isaac, and Jacob keep this child safe from the proud and powerful."

Not for the first time I felt a twinge of fear. I could not worry long, however. My nose promised me a delicious, if simple feast prepared by Mary. I greeted Tomas as he strode up the street with my father. They regularly traveled together and Jacob was eager for news. I waved the men ahead of me into my home. Water stood ready for washing. Mary stood in the background like a proper Jewish wife, until I invited her to join us at the table.

"My bride has been gone three months visiting her cousin," I explained to our visitor. "It seems fitting that she be at my side now."

"You'll get no argument from me," chuckled the Greek. "Our women always eat with us."

I realized that I really did not know much about this man despite his relationship with my father.

"Have you a family?"

My inquiry loosened the man's tongue. He had a lovely wife, Priscilla, two daughters, beautiful beyond compare and a stalwart son, almost old enough to learn his father's trade.

When the conversation turned to news outside Nazareth we learned that the king had authorized Roman style gymnastic events.

"It is rumored that Herod will invite Romans and perhaps even the governor of Syria to be honored guests at the games. It is his way of gaining greater favor with those who hold the real power. The king grows even more insane," Tomas whispered. "In his paranoia another of his sons has been executed."

"What is the charge?"

The man shook his head at my question. Glancing around nervously the trader whispered, "There does not need to be a reason. Herod believes the slightest breath of suspicion and reacts."

"Then only Antipas and Philip remain alive?" My father asked in amazement. "Herod had fathered twelve sons and three daughters by his ten wives, and only two survive?"

Our visitor glanced backward as if walls had ears. He lowered his voice further, "Yes, it is said that it is better to be Herod's pig than his son."

Jacob burst out laughing and slapped his thigh. "So he still does not eat pork. What a good, religious Jew!"

"Beware," cautioned Tomas.

I changed the subject when the man continued to look nervously around.

"No one here will betray you. What is the other news of the Empire?"

Glad of the excuse, the trader told of events as far away as Alexandria and Tarsus.

Later, I lay beside Mary. Her hand slipped into mine.

"Joseph, Herod must never learn that our baby is Messiah."

I felt a chill grip me and nodded in the dark. "No, my love. There is no way the King of Judea will hear of a birth in such a place as Nazareth."

Comforted, my wife slept close to my side. For a long time I lay awake staring into the night. Placing one hand ever so gently on Mary's almost flat belly, I swore an oath.

"Herod will never harm this child."

When I slept I dreamed of a child who played in the streets of Nazareth and called me 'Abba'. The rays of the morning sun awakened me. Mary was gone from my side. For a moment, I felt panic until I heard humming and the clink of pottery. Rolling over, I saw my wife. She was bending over the fire stirring something in a pot. Now that the lid was off, a savory smell filled the room.

"What are you making?"

At my question the woman turned and smiled. A graceful gesture indicated the plate of fruit and cheese covered flat bread beside my pillow.

"Finally awake, lazy boy? I have already been to the well and made your breakfast. This stew is for your dinner."

"What time is it?" I asked in surprise.

"Time for you to be in your shop, my husband."

A twinkle in my wife's dancing eyes belied the frown and the hands on hips as she tried to look severe. Feeling like a young man, I stood up. Before the woman could move I caught her around the waist. She laughed when I whirled around so the small feet left the floor.

"So, Wife, you think to command me to work?"

My chuckle was answered with a girlish giggle. Suddenly bold, I kissed her laughing lips. For a second the world stopped and then began to spin faster. Mary responded eagerly and I forgot everything except my love for the woman in my arms. I was the first to draw back.

"Mary, I..." Half-ashamed, I did not want to apologize for the feelings I could not deny.

My wife drew my head down again. “Joseph, have no fear. God made man and woman for each other.”

Our second kiss was less tempestuous but I still felt off balance when I lifted my head. Regretfully I stepped back from my bride. Throwing on my work robe, I belted it tightly and strode to the door.

“I must go,” I insisted.

There was much to do because Tomas brought many pieces of lumber. Some was for projects already commissioned. One fine piece I set aside.

“This will make a bed for the baby,” I told myself.

Tomas left with my father in the morning. They planned to travel together to Sidon. Jacob took a matched set of bowls to a Greek customer in the cosmopolitan city. I sent along a curiously designed folding table for the same man. It was good to have Mary in my home and work to complete in my shop.

CHAPTER 9

Mary's return and the news of Elizabeth's son kept the tongues of Nazareth wagging for a week. A rumor from Jerusalem soon caused new concern. All the men of the city gathered at the synagogue when Abel bar Ezra, son of the rabbi, returned from the capital.

"They say that Caesar plans to conduct a census of all the people," he announced after the prayers.

Immediately an uproar broke out.

"That is just an excuse to extort more taxes!"

"How dare anyone order such a thing? We have our own king!" Young Samson shouted.

I felt sorry for the boy when my father turned on him scornfully. "Herod will do anything it takes to keep the favor of Rome. Do not look to that bloated travesty for aid."

"Beware," Joachim warned his friend as several audible gasps were heard.

A few covert nods signaled agreement with my father, but no one wanted to be heard voicing such strong feelings. Into the almost fearful silence came the wheezing voice of old Ithmar. The man was ancient when I was a boy. Perhaps long ago he had a wife and family but for as long as I could remember he sat in the same spot in the synagogue, praying. Rarely was his old voice raised above a mumble. Many in Nazareth thought him mad. The women brought him tender morsels and wrapped the figure in blankets when the air was cold.

"The God of Abraham, Isaac, and Jacob has prepared a Deliverer for His people. Now is the time for Messiah. Beware lest you miss his arrival."

I felt a chill run up my spine. Everyone in the room swiveled to stare at the shrunken figure in the corner. Rabbi Ezra sat down next to the old man.

"What do you mean?"

The teacher shook the frail shoulder. A snore was the only response he got.

Excitedly Benoi bar Daniel jumped to his feet. "Perhaps the old dreamer is right. Now must be the time for Messiah to come. He will throw off the yoke of Rome and lead us to a free Jerusalem!"

Jacob gripped the firebrand by the arm. Roughly he reminded him, "Such talk will get you nailed to a Roman cross before any Deliverer appears."

His fierce look quelled some of the zealous fervor in the crowd. It was a sobering reminder. I turned to leave. When I passed Ithmar he leaned forward. For a long moment we stared at each other.

"It will not be what you expect," he said so softly I was not sure I understood him.

I glanced around to see if anyone else heard. When I looked back the old man had sunk into his blankets. I retreated away until I bumped into a wall. My father's hand on my wrist saved me from stumbling.

"My son, you look as though you had seen a spirit."

"It is nothing," I assured the man.

"You are not fool enough to believe the ramblings of an old crazy man, are you? Prophets and old men have been prattling of Messiah for centuries. Whenever times get rough, someone drags out the old writings," he sneered. "Even the rabbis cannot agree on who the Deliverer will be."

"I know. Some claim a warrior, others a wise teacher. Still other experts believe Messiah will be a priest or even a leader like Moses," I sighed.

"You see no man can fulfill all the requirements. There is no chance of such a thing happening in my lifetime anyway. I must speak to Tomas. He has just returned from trading north of Sidon where we parted company. Perhaps he has heard something from Damascus or further north."

It had been five months since the trader brought Mary home. Now he was on his way south to distant places, maybe even Egypt. I watched Jacob stride off toward the edge of Nazareth where the Greek was camped.

I almost envied my father's skepticism. It was not so much that he doubted the interpretations of the scriptures. Jacob felt no reason to believe. Sure that the God of Israel had abandoned him long ago, he was as unaffected by the Holy One of Israel as by the pantheon of Greece and Rome.

"Mary has a different faith," I mused, suddenly lonely for my wife. "She trusts the Holy One no matter what happens around her."

I hurried up the street to my house. My wife was waiting eagerly. The spoon in her hand rotated as she rolled the handle between her palms nervously.

I was barely through the door when she asked, "Joseph, did Ithmar really predict Messiah's arrival?"

"How?"

At my amazed expression the young woman smiled. "Mother hurried to tell me. She heard the news at the well from Hagar and Dinah."

"Well, yes," I acknowledged hesitantly. "Old Ithmar did say it was time for Messiah."

She was not satisfied until I repeated the entire conversation including Benoni's reaction and Jacob's warning.

"So you see, Ithmar was speaking in general terms," I insisted although the memory of my encounter with the old man's intense eyes made me frown.

Mary's sharp eyes did not miss my expression.

"What else?"

I paused remembering the comprehension in the aged eyes when we stared at each other. Again, I saw the old man leaning forward and heard his words. Mary's soft, slightly impatient sigh brought me back to the present.

"It is just..." I hesitated then plunged on. "Ithmar said something as I was leaving. He said, 'It will not be what you expect.' He knows."

Mary did not seem upset. Calmly she turned back to stir the stew.

"Does that bother you?" I asked.

The young woman smoothed her hands over her distended belly. There were only a few weeks left until the baby would be born. Already I had a cradle ready to receive him. Blankets and swaddling cloths were waiting in a hide trunk. Her expression was serene when she looked at me.

"The child will be born," she smiled. "How God will make him known, I do not know. I have wondered, but my part is to bear the baby and call him Jeshua as we were told. Whether Ithmar has had a vision cannot matter now. We are in God's hands."

Lovingly I drew my wife into my arms, humbled by her faith.

"You are right, Mary. We must trust God."

After dinner Mary slipped her hand into mine as we sat together in the courtyard.

"My husband, tell me what the priests expect of Messiah," she begged softly.

I turned to look at the young face in the moonlight. Gently I stroked a strand of hair from her forehead.

"Why do you want to know?"

"Ithmar said, 'it would not be what we expect.' So what is expected?"

Looking up at the stars, I slipped my arm around Mary's shoulders.

"There are those who claim Messiah as a warrior."

I felt Mary's head move against my shoulder. "No, God will not send a fighter. Violence begets violence. We do not need military might but the hand of the Living One to free us from bondage."

"Some rabbis look at the Holy Writings and claim that Messiah will be a prophet greater than those who have gone before. Greater even than Isaiah."

"I think he must be more than a prophet," Mary agreed.

"I have heard others claim that Messiah will be a priest who will cleanse and rebuild the temple. He will be a greater leader than Moses and David."

I felt her nod of agreement. "He will be holy and dedicated to God, but Messiah is not just a priest."

"Messiah is the son of David. All the rabbis teach that," I asserted.

"The angel said, 'God will give to him the throne of his father David,'" my wife mused in the night. "I wonder…"

When her voice trailed off, I turned to stare at the girl in my arms.

"Wonder what, my wife?"

"If that throne is not the obedience to the will of God that David sought." I saw her smile in the moonlight. "I know that sounds naïve."

It was my turn to shake my head. Slowly I agreed, "No, perhaps you are right. Surely Messiah must be dedicated to fulfilling the will of God to claim the promised throne."

"Isn't that what is required of us all?"

Mary's final question left me staring into the darkness for several minutes.

"Other men have risen up in the nation claiming to be Messiah. They each had their own agenda of retaliation or repentance. All have been forgotten after a brief notoriety," I mused. "You may be right. The prophets each pointed to an aspect of the Deliverer. The calling of a true Messiah must be to follow the will of the One God."

Mary and I sat together with my hand resting on her belly. I felt her confidence seep into my heart.

"All will be well," she stated drowsily.

I kissed her forehead and repeated, "All will be well."

The trust in God's purpose lingered with me in the morning as I completed several projects for my neighbors. I thought about the upcoming changes to my life.

"Soon we will have a child. Someday he will help me in the shop. Woodwork is a good trade to study God's ways," I decided. "I will teach him that it is better to work with the grain of the wood just as life is easier when we work in the will of God."

Chapter 10

Less than a week later my serenity was shattered. We were gathered at the synagogue for Sabbath prayers before the sun set when the rattle of armor and clink of swords and spears with the tramp of marching boots made each man look at his neighbor. We all jumped to our feet and rushed to the doorway. Ten Roman soldiers stood in the street. An officer looked down at us from a restive gelding. The legionnaires stared down the street unaffected by the flurry of fearful activity their arrival caused. All around Nazareth, mothers called children inside. The street was deserted by the time the captain spoke.

"Who is rabbi here?" He asked in heavily accented Hebrew.

Rabbi Ezra stepped forward. "I am the leader of this synagogue."

The officer sneered. It was not a pleasant sight. One of his front teeth was missing and the rest were stained brown from the poor food the army lived on.

"This is for you to read to your people. Heed the words and obey. The arm of Caesar is long."

Somehow his tone made it sound as if we were lower than vermin. After tossing a small scroll in Ezra's direction the man turned his horse. With no further acknowledgment of our stunned presence the troop marched on through Nazareth. The well-trained company did not even flinch when a dog rushed out to snarl at their heels. In silence we watched the leather clad men until they disappeared on the road toward the south.

"What does it say?" Joachim finally broke the seething silence.

We all turned from staring after the departing enemy to look at the scroll in Ezra's shaking hand. His fingers fumbled with the seal until Abel slid his knife under the wax.

"It is written not written in Hebrew," Samson remarked with a scowl. "How are we to read it?"

We could all see that the neatly formed letters did not resemble our alphabet.

"It is Greek," I stated. "My father taught me to read and write it when I was a boy. He said, 'we live under the hand of Rome. It is wise to learn to read her decrees.'"

The rabbi thrust the scroll into my hand. "Here, Joseph, read it to us."

Several impatient voices interrupted my perusal of the scroll.

"What does it say?"

"Augustus, by the will of our brother gods, Caesar of the known world," I read the opening line.

There were murmurs from the gathered men.

"Arrogant!"

"Blasphemy!"

"May God strike him for presumption!"

I ignored the comments and continued, "to all the people living under the gracious and benevolent hand of Rome…"

More grumbles interrupted me but I struggled on, "from the ends of the Great Sea to the farthest reaches of Syria, greetings. We have decided, for the benefit of all the people dependent on Rome as a child on his father…"

Simon spat angrily into the street and snarled, "'Dependent', more like captive."

After the growls of agreement quieted, I read on, "To conduct a census in order to more equitably rule the far flung provinces of Mother Rome."

A roar of rage and disbelief greeted my words.

"A census! Abel was right!"

"Caesar wants to count us to tax us more harshly."

"We will not allow a foreign power to number our people!"

"It is against the laws of God."

I still held the scroll open in my hand.

"Is there more?" Ezra asked.

I nodded without looking up. My heart thudded heavily and my mind reeled with the implications of the rest of the order.

"All Jews within the borders of the Empire will return to the city of their father's birth for the census. This is to be accomplished before the moon cycle of the equinox."

Everyone turned to the rabbi in a hubbub of confusion, anger, and fear.

"Father's birth?"

"Does it mean my father or my tribe of lineage?"

"What trick is this?"

"The harvest moon has just passed. Only three turnings remain until the equinox."

"It a trick to destroy our livelihoods!"

"How can every man travel to his home?"

I stood stunned and silent with the scroll clenched in my fist. A quote from Micah rang in my head. 'You Bethlehem…from you shall come One who is to rule in Israel.'

I whispered to myself, "All the prophecies are being fulfilled. Mary and I will have to travel south to Bethlehem. The very symbol of pagan oppression is obedient to the One God. By decree of the Emperor the child will be born in the city of David. Thanks be to God."

Joachim roused me from my musings. He drew me aside.

"Joseph, you must go alone to Bethlehem. Mary cannot travel at this time."

"Caesar's order does not wait for the convenience of man or woman," I replied.

"That is a week's travel under the best circumstances."

"We will travel by gentle stages," I assured the worried father.

He shook his head fretfully, "It is not right for my daughter to have her first child in a strange place."

"The baby will be born in Bethlehem," I reminded him as we walked away from the crowd still milling outside the synagogue.

Joachim continued to sputter, "Yes, away from her mother's care."

"Bethlehem is the city of David," I reminded him softly.

My companion stood still. His jaw dropped open. After a moment, he raised his hands in awe. "God of Abraham, Isaac, and Jacob, even Rome obeys the Living God!"

"My father, Mary will be safe. God will provide a place for us in Bethlehem."

Over the next few weeks I had to reassure my mother, as well as Anna, again and again, "Mary will be well cared for when the baby is born."

Both mothers packed and repacked the canvas bag of things needed for a new baby. They gave her advice, too.

"Be sure to take these soft swaddling cloths."

"Tell Joseph each day as soon as you are tired."

"Find a midwife as soon as you get to Bethlehem," Anna repeated over and over until Mary took her mother's hands between her own.

"My mother, truly all will be well. I am strong and healthy. Have not our women always tended flocks and followed their husbands? Think of Sarah and Rebekkah and Leah. Have no fear. No harm will come to me. The child is in the hand of God."

I was glad to escape to the workshop each day. Rapidly I completed the jobs that would not wait for my return. Throughout Nazareth other families also prepared for travel. Samson and his father brought me an ox yoke to repair late on the last afternoon.

"We need a new fitting so we can take the cart to Beersheba," he explained.

For a moment I was exasperated. There were many things I needed to do before leaving for Bethlehem. Samson was a good friend and staunch customer so I quickly cut the new piece and pinned it in place with a dowel. With a nod and a shake I tested the piece.

"That should see you safely to Beersheba and home again."

He gave an approving nod and handed me a piece of silver. "Good work, Joseph. We leave in the morning. When do you plan to start?"

"I too hope to leave with the sunrise. The journey must be taken in short stages for Mary's sake."

Sagely the men nodded, "We will travel together for a time, then."

"Yes, and if the repair does not hold, I will have my tools. A good carpenter can always earn a shekel or two by doing odd jobs."

Samson laughed heartily and left me alone to gather the tools I planned to take.

In the morning, the sturdy donkey that I used to drag trees from the hillsides was fitted with a soft saddle for Mary. I hung a bag of food over one flank. On the other side was the sack filled with our clothes and all the items the concerned mothers had packed. A roll of blankets lay over the little beast's shoulder. I would carry my tools on my back.

We set out with Samson and his family. Other travelers from Nazareth and even further north joined us at the fork in the road. We followed the dirt track down the mountain. Among the newcomers was a lively group from Sepphoris heading for Sebaste in Samaria. Mary struck up a conversation with the young mother. We learned that Dinah was from Jericho. Her husband, Barakiah, was a smith of the line of Dan although generations early his family moved to Samaria.

"Funny how we cling to the old tribes, isn't it?" mused the outspoken young woman.

"That is our heritage!" Samson's wife took umbrage.

Dinah laughed gaily, "I know. Have you ever thought of how many are the sons of Israel now?" When no one replied, she shifted her baby to her other hip. "The Romans will know more than we do how many consider themselves to be sons of Dan or Judah or Levi. We have become so scattered in Israel that there must be this great shift so the tribes can be counted."

"You talk too much for a woman," Samson growled and prodded the oxen ahead of the group.

Mary diverted the conversation by asking, "Tell me about your baby. How old is he?"

The two young women walked together discussing babies and birthing. I turned my attention to another member of our party.

Eliezar spoke hotly, "The woman is right. The Romans will know more about us than we do ourselves. Why do we obey this order?"

"It is better than a Roman cross," Samson threw his opinion over his shoulder.

Eliezar shuddered and frowned, "I myself am of the tribe of Benjamin, youngest born of the sons of Israel. I travel to Ramah. You, Carpenter, where do you go?"

"I am Joseph. My family comes from Bethlehem of the tribe of Judah, David's line."

I could not resist the pride in the statement. Eliezar was not impressed.

"Any of us could claim any heritage we want. You live in Nazareth. I live in Sepphoris. If Messiah is born, how will we know that he is indeed from Bethlehem and of David's line as the prophet's state? How will we know the true Messiah?"

"Messiah will be known by his deeds." Unexpectedly Barakiah spoke up. "Messiah will fulfill all that is prophesied."

"How can one man satisfy all that is written? He is a prince of the line of David yet also a man despised by all. Messiah is to be the liberator of Israel who will also bring peace to the world." Eliezar enumerated some of the attributes of Messiah while challenging the smith.

All talk stilled as we waited for the answer from the man from Sepphoris. At first his reply did not seem to be an answer.

"Look at our history. Which of the ancient leaders was as expected? David himself was a shepherd, then warrior and a fugitive outlaw before he became a king. Who are we to predict the ways of the Living God? Messiah will come at a time and in a way not expected."

I found myself looking at Mary. Our eyes met. We alone knew how near and how unexpected was the coming of Messiah.

"Barakiah, for a Samaritan, you speak intelligently about the history of our people," Eliezar admitted. "Almost, you could convince me that Messiah might be among us now."

"God alone chooses the time and the manner of revelation," the man stated. "Those who have eyes will see."

"Clear the road, Rabble!"

The shout from a Roman patrol ended our conversation. I shielded Mary with my body from the stares of the soldiers. I smiled grimly at Samson's muttered prayer.

"May God send Messiah soon to sweep that scourge from our roads."

The discussion gave me much to think about. I knew Barakiah was right to say that the Living God of Abraham, Isaac, and Jacob acted in ways that man does not anticipate. I had only to look at my wife to be reminded of that truth.

We made camp not far from the road at the Spring of Harod. The jackals calling in the night caused me to grip my dagger in the darkness. While Mary slept, I stared at the stars praying, not for the first time, for clarity.

"Lord God of the Universe, how can it be that the child growing in Mary will be Messiah? There are so many things I do not understand. God, how can I dare to care for a holy child? I am a man of but poor faith. Why did you not choose a priestly house for this infant to live in? How can I hope to live up to your expectations, my God?"

My sleeplessness was evident to Mary. As we walked together beside the donkey in the morning light, she laid one hand on my arm. Her other hand stroked and cradled her belly.

"Husband, do not fret. My love, God has chosen the perfect man to be the father of this child."

My own fear that I could not live up to her trust kept me silent.

"See," with a giggle she added, "our child rejoices by rolling over and stretching."

Through the homespun, I saw the movement and had to smile at my wife's explanation. I dropped a quick kiss on her hand.

"I pray you are right," I whispered more to myself than the woman.

Samson called, "Come, come, there will be time enough for cuddles and whispers when we are safely through this area."

Looking around, I realized that we were descending into the Jericho Valley along the Jordan.

"Those tall cliffs make a perfect hideout for bandits," Barakiah frowned. "I hope we looked imposing enough not to be attacked or too poor to bother with."

Samson explained, "We will bypass Sethopolis, long ago known as Beth-Shan. That is Mount Gilboa to the west. Over thirty miles stretch ahead of us before we reach the Roman fortress of Alexandrium. It will not be possible to reach the security of Rome's eagles today. Abel-Meholah is our destination."

"It is halfway through the valley," added Barakiah, "a perfect haven for travelers."

Mary calmly assured Dinah, "All will be well. God will protect us."

Again I wished I had her simple faith. I gripped my dagger tightly. As rapidly as possible we moved down the road. The sun was high when a movement in the bushes caught my eye. At my shout Barakiah and Samson sprang to my side.

"Show yourself," the big man commanded.

A low moan was the only response.

"Someone is injured!" I heard Mary exclaim even as she hurried past me.

"It could be a trick!"

I did not need Barakiah's warning. Already I was at my wife's side. Lifting her I backed away onto the road. Angrily she twisted in my arms.

"Joseph bar Jacob, you are not going to leave that man to die! He needs assistance. You will help him."

Flaming cheeks and flashing eyes warned me that my normally gentle wife was serious.

Dinah added, "We cannot go on. We must help."

"I…we…" Stammering, I looked around at my companions.

Barakiah avoided my eyes. A low moan from the verge made Mary stamp her foot.

"Go!"

With a shrug, a sigh, and a prayer, I strode over to the injured man. Every second I expected an attack. None came as I carried the badly beaten figure to the road. Mary dropped to her knees when I laid the unconscious man on the ground.

Dinah rushed to my wife's side, issuing orders, "Bring water and bandages."

Helplessly we watched the women tend the man's injuries.

My mumbled concern and Barakiah's order, "Come away, woman, we must be on our way," were ignored.

Finally satisfied that the bleeding was stopped and the wounds bandaged, Mary turned to me.

"Joseph, we must take him to the next town."

"How?" I asked, afraid I knew the answer.

"The donkey…I can walk a few miles. It is smooth here."

The tears that brimmed when I did not immediately reply were my undoing. Again I hefted the injured man and laid him across the little beast.

"Let's be off!" Samson urged.

He had not ceased to glance nervously around during the interlude. Now he led the way rapidly. By dusk we reached Abel-Meholah. In the morning we saw Barakiah gave the innkeeper a pouch.

"This is for the care of the stranger. When I pass this way again, I will pay you whatever else is due."

I was sad to watch the Samaritan and his wife head up the wadi to the west in the morning. With luck they would reach Sebaste by nightfall. Mary and Dinah clung together. Before they parted, the older woman pressed a small coin into my wife's hand.

"You are a brave woman for one so young. May the God of Abraham, Isaac, and Jacob bless and keep you and your baby."

After a final hug, she picked up her own son and followed Barakiah. Eliezar was already on the road, impatient to begin.

"We can make it to the Roman outpost today," he told us.

Samson walked beside me. I insisted that Mary ride after the long walk the day before.

"What do you think of the Samaritan?" He asked.

"A good man, why do you ask?"

"He alone thought to provide for the wounded man," he mused.

My friend seemed to be struggling with understanding how a despised Samaritan could have performed a mitzvah when we good Jews had not.

"A good man," I repeated, "even if he is not a Jew."

The loss of Dinah and Barakiah was offset by the addition of half a dozen men from across the Jordan. Like us, they traveled for the census. After a brief stop for a meal and rest in the shade of a few clustered acacia trees, we trudged on our way. Mary walked beside me. I drew my wife close for a brief embrace. I felt the child stir and was struck with awe.

"Soon you will hold your son," she smiled. "Walking is good and I am tired of sitting on Balaam's backbone."

Eliezar and Samson talked to the men from the east. I listened with only half an ear, more intent on watching Mary's path and helping her over any small rough places. She hummed softly to herself as we moved along the road.

The sight of tall walls topped with the eagle standard of Rome encouraged us with thoughts of security as the day drew to a close. We made camp in the shadow of the city. Other pilgrims, traveling both north and west were already camped there.

"If you want water, you'll have to pay," they warned us.

As I drew my costly ration of water from the Alexandrium well, I overheard one of the lounging guards. His comment implied we were scum to be cheated.

"Caesar is lining our pockets thanks to his census of his. Soon I'll be able to by Lydia a necklace."

"That will earn you a pleasant night," his friend guffawed. "Myself, I do not plan to wait that long. Some of the women traveling through have not been averse…"

A gesture and coarse laugh completed the sentence. I heard no more. Gritting my teeth, I strode away to Mary and my supper. The thought of Roman soldiers getting rich from our need rankled. I was angrier at the insinuation from the younger man that he could lie with Jewish women than at his friend's greed.

After my wife slept, I sat beside her trying to understand God's plan.

"God, this child is Messiah," I whispered to the night breezes and stars. "Will he be another Judah Maccabeus and cleanse the nation?"

A line from Isaiah rose unbidden in my mind. 'A dimly burning wick he will not quench.' This was followed quickly by another, 'He was despised and rejected and we esteemed him not.' A chill coursed through me. Protectively, I laid my hand on Mary's belly.

I argued in outrage and denial, "No! Messiah is the son of David—a king."

The breeze that blew across my face brought no comfort and more than a few stinging pieces of sand. Beneath my hand the unborn savior of Israel moved. Evidence of the might of Rome loomed behind me, proof of King Herod's treachery against those he claimed kinship with. I shuddered with realization of the forces massed against God's Messiah. Fiercely I glared up at the standard visible in the light of the watch fires.

I swore to the unseen enemies, "I will not let you harm my son."

Mary stirred. She must have sensed my distress. A hand covered mine on her belly.

"Joseph?"

"Sleep my wife."

I bent forward to kiss her forehead. One soft hand stroked my cheek.

Sleepily she mumbled, "Do not be afraid. God is still God."

"Yes my wise and lovely bride." Tenderly I agreed, but I did not forget my vow.

Chapter 11

Another day's travel brought us to Jericho. The highway was full of pilgrims and we did not feel as nervous about bandit attacks. Roman patrols marched regularly along the road. We had to move out of their path or risk the flat of a sword against our backs.

I sensed Mary's excitement as we neared the city. She was awed by the size.

"Just think, Joshua and the Children of Israel took this city without a fight. They trusted in God despite appearances and the walls fell."

"Joshua faced an entrenched army, but that was long ago," I replied.

"He obeyed the word of God and the city was taken and burned. God has not changed."

Her simple faith made me ashamed of my fears in the night. At the bazaar I purchased the woman a packet of sweets and received a laughing hug.

"Joseph, you spoil me," she giggled.

"The mother of Messiah deserves the best," I whispered close to her ear.

I sat with Samson and Eliezar late into the evening. The news they gleaned increased my anxiety.

"Several people have said that the roads around Jerusalem are full of many who claim to be sons of David. They are returning to either Bethlehem or Jerusalem to be counted. I do not envy you my friend," Eliezar stated. "Finding a place to stay may be difficult."

To myself I added what they did not say, "Especially with a pregnant wife."

We parted in the morning. Samson and Eliezar headed to Hebron. Mary and I turned west. My new friend's warning proved true. More and more people crowded the road the nearer we got to the capital.

"I hoped this would be the final day of travel," I told my wife. "With these crowds, we may be another day on the road. We are barely to Bethany and the sun is setting. We will have to stop here. Tomorrow, I hope that I can find lodging with my uncle or some other kinsman in Bethlehem."

Mary smiled tiredly, "You will find something."

Several helpful townsfolk were not as optimistic.

"There is no space here. There may be room in Bethlehem. It is only another hour down the road."

With a sigh, I turned back onto the highway. My wife balanced herself on the donkey. I heard a gasp when Balaam stumbled on some loose gravel and reached out to steady the woman.

"It is all right," the girl's voice sounded breathless.

I glanced at her. A wan smile only made me urge the little animal to greater effort along the road. We passed a couple of groups of travelers making camp. I barely acknowledged their greetings. My whole being was focused on arriving in Bethlehem and finding a bed for my bride.

"Tonight you will not sleep under the stars," I promised with a forced grin.

Her answering smile was short lived when Mary winced and bit her lower lip. Instantly concerned, I jerked the donkey to a halt.

"What is it?"

"Nothing, just a twinge," she insisted. "Let us hurry on. Bethlehem cannot be far now."

When we topped the next rise the city lay before us, nestled against the sheltering hills as it had for generations. I could see the sheep bedded down on the hillsides and in the last light of the sun I saw campfires being lit by the shepherds. I did not pause to look at the pastoral scene but hurried down the hill into the town. Inquiries for my uncles were disappointing.

Men trudging to their homes told me, "The sons of Mattan have taken their flocks to the fields nearer to Jerusalem. Their lambs will be used in the sacrifices this year."

"What of their families?" Desperately I caught one stranger's arm.

His answer was short and what I dreaded. "Their sons are with them."

One of the residents turned back to offer a suggestion.

"Rachel, wife of Perez bar Mattan might have room. She has opened her home to visitors during this census."

"Where is this house to be found?"

A glance at Mary confirmed that she was very tired. One hand resting on the rump and the other on the donkey's neck kept her upright. Although she tried to hide it, I caught more than one gasp or whimper from behind the veil she wrapped around her face against curious eyes.

"I will show you the way, Stranger," an elderly resident volunteered.

The remaining men wandered off to their homes. The old man who hobbled ahead of us chattered volubly.

"To think that the son of Jacob bar Mattan has come to Bethlehem. How is Jacob? I remember him as a lad. Played in these streets, he did. Odd sort of boy, though. Ran away after his mother, er…, um…, died. No one has heard from him since then. Mattan never spoke of his son again, either. He raised a whole new family with Deborah, daughter of Abijah, the smith. Perez is the youngest of that brood. He's probably about your age. I can tell you are a good Jew. Your prayer shawl is well worn. It is a shame you will miss meeting all your uncles. But there is the honor of providing the lambs for the Feast this year.

Trust the Romans to insist on this census at the New Year. That is when it is most inconvenient. And why must we be counted by Rome anyway? A new plague of taxes is bound to follow. Here we are."

I was glad when the guide stopped before an open gate. In the courtyard facing a surprisingly large home people and animals milled around. It appeared many visitors had already learned of my half-aunt's hospitality. Our elderly escort called to a youngster.

"Elam, where is your mother?"

"She is finding a place for the merchant from the Nabatea. These are his camels."

The boy was more excited about the odd beasts than the tired man and woman with a donkey at the gate. The six-year old turned to go. I caught the child's shoulder.

"Tell her that a kinsman is here," I begged.

He frowned at my hand and shrugged free.

The old man nodded, "It is true. Get your mother. She will need to find room for her nephew."

A slightly malicious gleam came into the old eyes and he grinned toothlessly at the boy. After a wide-eyed look that took in me, Mary, and the dusty donkey the child ran toward the house. Balaam lowered his head to gather a few stray scraps of hay. I left my wife for a moment to bring water to Balaam. I offered a dipper to Mary but she shook her head.

"What is it?"

Sudden fear rushed through me when her eyes closed in obvious pain and I heard her sharp intake of breath.

"Fool," a harsh voice at my back made me spin around. "The baby is coming."

The woman that stood there would have made two of my wife even now that she was large with child. Hands on her hips, the speaker surveyed me up and down.

"Who do you claim to be?"

The rough question caused me to lift my head with pride.

"I am Joseph, son of Jacob bar Mattan of Bethlehem."

"Well, and almost I could believe you are a grandson of Mattan. You have his proud look when you are provoked."

Her considering words gave no clue whether the woman believed me or not. Dropping my anger at another gasp from the girl on the donkey, I turned to the woman.

"My wife must have a bed tonight," I begged.

Almost sympathetically Rachel shook her head. "Kin or not, I have no room. Your wife will have need of the midwife this night also."

"The young man is kin and his wife is in need of a roof. Is there no room you can prepare for them?" My garrulous friend interrupted.

Irritably my aunt rounded on the old man. "Even my own room is taken by the merchant from Nabatea. Let me think."

I held my breath as she muttered to herself. "All the regular inns are full. The home of Isaac bar Ephraim is taken. Miriam, wife of Zedekiah, has filled her home as has Simon bar Dan."

"What of Uziah or Nahum?"

The old man's suggestions were met with negative movements of the woman's head. She squinted and gazed around the courtyard seeking a solution. My guide continued to offer names. Each was met with a shake of the head. Finally she turned back at a small cry from Mary.

Reaching a decision, she nodded, "It might serve. At least it will be private and quiet and dry."

Torn between irritation at our talkative guide, who still suggested fellow villagers as hosts, and concern for my wife's condition, I was less than polite.

"Yes, where is it?"

Rachel responded with a vague gesture toward the rocks at the back of the house, "It is the cave against the hill. We use it to shelter the ewes in the early spring when they are lambing. I am sure Perez has cleaned it…"

"A stable!" I interrupted angrily.

Mary placed a hand on my shoulder. "I am sure it will be fine."

Her words ended with a sharp intake of air as another pain grabbed my wife.

"It is settled then. Elam!" Turning quickly for such a large woman, she called for her son. The lad scampered over.

"This is your cousin…"

"Joseph bar Jacob." I supplied my name through clenched teeth.

Further delay was unnecessary. I wanted to get Mary settled somewhere and find a midwife. My heart pounded with fear. A brief nod from Rachel acknowledged my name.

"Take them to the lambing cave. Get fresh straw for a bed and bring water and fodder."

Orders complete, the woman turned to go. Feeling churlish, I held out my hand to stop my aunt.

"Wait. Thank you for your help."

"Yes, yes, let it never be said that Rachel, wife of Perez bar Mattat turned away a kinsman or woman," she added, glancing at Mary.

"Where can I find a midwife?"

Another gasp from my wife warned me that time was short.

"I will send for her and come myself as soon as I can."

With that assurance, I had to be satisfied. Moving away, my aunt reminded me of the ship in full sail I saw once in Tyre. She strode across the courtyard dropping orders right and left.

There was another delay while the old man patted my back. "Glad to see you settled, my boy. Knew Rachel would find you a spot. Never doubted it for a minute."

"Thank you, I must go and settle my wife."

"Yes, of course, only right, take care of the little woman. I will visit and meet the new arrival." With a grin, the elderly resident finally released me.

Elam led the way through the many animals. Camels grudgingly moved aside when the boy shouted at them. A couple of donkeys barely shifted as they eyed the new arrival walking past. Chickens scattered with great clucking and a cow decided to follow us. We went past the house and up a small incline, then back down. The path led to a round opening in the rock. With the ease of familiarity, the boy located a lamp and struck a flint. The small flame flared and settled into a steady glow.

"This way," Elam gestured and led us into the cave.

Mary leaned heavily on me and walked slowly. I had to bend to enter. Once inside I was pleasantly surprised. A decent sized room was hollowed out of the rock. Several mangers were chipped out of the walls. Low wooden partitions divided the space into separate pens.

Elam quickly removed one of the fences. He placed the lamp on a shelf carved for that purpose. With a speed motivated by the thought of the dinner awaiting him in the house, my young cousin brought arms full of straw and spread it in the space.

Mary leaned against one of the mangers while I hurriedly brought the blankets from our packs and spread them over the straw pallet.

With a sigh, the woman sank down. "Thank you." Her smile was for Elam as well as me.

The boy scampered out. I heard him call, "I'll get water and feed."

"Joseph, it is almost time."

I thought I heard a hint of fear mixed with awe in my wife's young voice. Hastily I knelt at her side to take one small hand.

"What can I do?"

Another spasm caught Mary and she gripped my hand tightly.

"It is enough that you are here," she said when she relaxed.

Elam brought a hide bucket of water, which he poured into one of the mangers. Another trip provided hay for Balaam who happily began his supper. For a third time the boy left and returned several minutes later, this time with a pitcher of water and mugs.

When he left, the child suddenly turned back to remark, "Mother said she will be down as soon as she can. The midwife is attending Naomi, wife of Hiram. She sent word that she will come later."

"But…"

My objection was to an empty space for Elam was running back to the house for his delayed meal. Mary raised herself on one elbow.

"Help me up. I must prepare the swaddling clothes myself."

A gasp shortened her planning. Gently I pushed her back down.

"Tell me what to do. You, um…, rest."

I was embarrassed by the situation. Men should not attend a woman in childbirth, but I had no choice. I had seen animals born and even helped Balaam into the world when he was too slow. The memory of the wet, spindly, weak-kneed donkey foal was not much comfort now even when the animal looked my way with big brown eyes.

"Blankets and the swaddling clothes are in the bag."

Glad for something to do, I unpacked the faithful little beast. I tossed the saddle into the corner, followed by my tools. I carried Mary's bundle to her side. When I unrolled it, she showed me which items were needed. Every time the contractions came, she grabbed my arm with surprising strength. The woman scanned the cave obviously looking for something. Anxiously I bent over my bride.

"What is it? What do you need, my love?"

I thought she flushed in the lamplight, before she met my eyes.

"When the baby comes, I will need something to balance against since we have no birthing stool."

My confusion must have shown in my face.

"I cannot give birth lying down," she explained patiently. "A woman squats to deliver a child."

"I will hold you," I declared, sure it was something I could handle.

She shook her head with a forced smile, "Joseph, my dearest husband, you will have to receive the baby."

Another, longer contraction interrupted our conversation.

I said hopefully, "Surely Rachel or the midwife will arrive before then."

"I think the child will be born very soon," my wife panted. She closed her eyes and steadied her breathing.

Silently I called out to God. "Why are you doing this? The Son of God, Messiah, should not be born in a stable with only a man to assist. Send help," I pleaded. "Mary deserves better than this!"

My inward raging was interrupted by an intense grasp on my arm.

"Joseph," through gritted teeth she gasped, "help me up."

Her whimper as I lifted the slight form tore through me.

"Let me run to the house for Rachel," I begged.

"No!"

Again her hand clutched my arm and she moaned. After a long minute she released me.

"I will lean on the manger. You must tell me when you see the baby's head."

Another animal-like cry tore at me as we moved to the manger only steps away. The woman stopped to clench both hands around my arm.

"Messiah is eager to be born. When the baby comes, you must wash him with water and wrap him tightly in the swaddling bands."

Rapidly she gave instructions leaning with one hand against the rough-hewn manger. With her other hand, she lifted her gown and tunic above her knees. I turned my head to give the woman privacy.

"Joseph, you cannot look away. You must be read…ah…"

Another pain snatched the word from her. I saw a rush of fluid pour into the straw between Mary's feet. I remembered the animal births I had attended and crouched between my wife's feet. It seemed hours but was only a couple of long contractions later I reported with awe.

"I see the head."

From the depths of the woman's throat came a cry as the newborn slipped into the world. Panting and drenched in sweat, both Mary and I admired the child. As she had instructed, I washed the tiny body, marveling at the perfection. Then I wrapped the infant in the cloths and blanket. Gently I laid the squalling baby in the straw and washed my wife before helping her back to the pallet. While she offered her breast to our son, I knelt beside my family in wonder. Mary stroked the dark tendrils of hair on the tiny head.

"He is beautiful," she whispered.

"My son," I said, still awed by the infant's arrival.

"Thank you, Joseph."

Her words reminded me of the long ago decision made in the darkness of a tortured night. I had no doubts now about calling the child my own.

"His name is Jeshua bar Joseph," I stated.

Tenderly I kissed first Mary and then the dozing baby. A movement at the entrance brought me to my feet. It was Rachel.

"It seems I am not needed." The woman bustled forward, elbowing me aside.

Elam stood hesitantly in the doorway.

Exuberantly I shared the news with my young cousin. "I have a son!"

Rachel stood up from her examination of mother and child.

"Not a bad job, for a man," she grudgingly admitted.

Laughing, I grabbed her around her not inconsiderable waist for an impromptu jig.

"My son is born!" Again I made the announcement with joyous relief.

My aunt separated herself from my grasp. With a wave she sent the boy on an errand.

"Yes, yes. Elam, bring the skin of goat's milk from the house and bring the mutton and bread, too. No doubt you will want to eat."

The large woman spared a thought for me before turning back to her newfound niece and child.

I was not really hungry. Leaving the women, I stepped outside. He trotted toward the house looming above us. Then I turned toward Jerusalem to the north. Lifting my prayer shawl over my head to shut out distractions, I began to pray.

"Thank you, God of my fathers, for safely delivering Mary. This child you have sent is perfect."

I paused as the prophetic words of the angel sprang into my mind. 'He will save the people from their sins.'

"Lord God of the Universe, he seems so normal and ordinary. How can this baby be of Your Spirit?"

A breeze wafted over me seeming to caress and comfort. I looked up and saw the stars glittering in the sky. They seemed brighter and closer than usual. The thought occurred to me that they were rejoicing with me. I shook my head at the fantasy. Reverently I committed myself to being a father.

"Holy God, I will seek to be faithful in raising this baby to be a son of Israel."

My eyes blurred as I thought of the years ahead and the many things a boy must learn. The task seemed almost too much. Then again a breeze lifted my prayer shawl.

"I will never leave you nor forsake you." The words were so clear I looked around.

There was no one to be seen. I stood in silence until the rustle of Elam's bare feet on the path roused me. In his hands he carried a plate of meat and bread while the skin of milk hung over one shoulder. Stepping forward, I met the boy at the entrance to the cave. He grinned and handed me the food. I followed my young relative inside. Rachel sat beside Mary. My wife dozed with Jeshua in her arms. She looked even lovelier than the day she became my bride. I set aside my dinner to crouch beside my family.

"Joseph bar Jacob, may your son be a blessing to Israel."

I raised my head. The traditional dedication of an infant seemed to have special meaning to me even spoken softly by my aunt. Looking at the sleeping girl and infant, I remembered the wonder of the child's conception.

"He will be," I promised.

Rachel's eyes drew together in confusion or perhaps anger at my response. Shaking her head, she hefted her body up. With a wave of one hand she indicated Mary.

"You do not need my help here. See that she drinks the milk when she awakes."

Realizing that my hostess was offended at my lack of gratitude, I stood and bent low in a salaam of courtesy.

"Thank you, my aunt. Your hospitality is only exceeded by your kindness to a poor kinsman. May God bless your house for your graciousness. We are truly honored to be your guests."

There was a slight softening in the frown. Rachel finally allowed herself a half smile.

“It is a blessing to offer lodging to a stranger,” she replied formally. “Take care of your family.”

In a more friendly fashion she patted my hand. She herded Elam ahead of her and strode from the cave. I watched her go with relief, glad to be alone with my wife and son.

CHAPTER 12

The interlude with Rachel left me suddenly tired. I leaned my forehead against the wall of the cave and patted Balaam. Mary giggled and I turned to see her looking at me.

"Kind woman, your aunt" she teased.

"Formidable," I answered with a wry smile, hurrying to kneel at my wife's side.

Jeshua slept in the crook of her arm. I was afraid to touch the child I helped deliver.

"He is well?"

"My husband, he is your son. You may hold him."

Gracefully and too swiftly the baby was transferred to my arms. I stared down at the newborn man-child in my arms.

"It hardly seems possible…"

My musing broke off at the sound of subdued voices outside. Frowning, I handed the infant to his mother. Mary drew her veil over her head and around the child. I grasped the first thing that came to my hand. It was an abandoned shepherd's crook. Thus armed, I barred the entrance.

"What do you want?"

A group of men milled uneasily just outside the door. In the bright starlight I could see that they were shepherds. Their clothing and staffs, the smell of fields and sheep were evidence of their occupation. All eyes turned to a stout man. His gray beard proclaimed him the eldest of the herdsmen. With a low salaam the shepherd approached.

"Pardon kind sir, for the intrusion at this unseemly hour." He coughed and glanced nervously back at his companions.

Their eager nods urged him to continue. The man seemed tongue tied in my presence.

"Do you…that is…are you…" he stammered.

"Tell him, Jediah."

"Get on with it."

"Ask him."

Encouraged by his assembled friends, I saw the petitioner heave a sigh before he took a step closer to me.

"Was there a child born here this night?"

I know I looked amazed. A young man pushed through the crowd.

"We saw a vision of angels," he panted excitedly. "They said 'The Savior is born.'"

Suddenly several voices spoke at once. I heard only bits of their comments. My mind was still reeling with surprise at Jediah's question and the young shepherd's statement. Finally I held up my hand. Focusing on the spokesman, I tried to sound calm.

"Tell me…" My words came out hoarsely and I swallowed a hard lump of anticipation that threatened to choke me.

"We were tending our sheep," the stout man explained. "You know how it is. The night is calm and you are not quite awake but you are not asleep. The slightest sound rouses you to check for danger."

I nodded encouragement when he paused as though expecting a response.

"We all heard something. I sat up. We all did."

A wave of his hand included the men now vigorously nodding agreement. For a moment the speaker appeared to forget us in his memories.

"Go on," the youngest man urged his friend.

"It was faint at first. We looked at each other. The sound was like nothing we ever heard."

"Sweeter and clearer than a bell."

"Sparkling like a spring brook."

"So alive I wanted to dance."

One by one the shepherds tried to explain the sound. Their metaphors were astonishing from such rough-hewn men.

"Truly it was like the song of a flock of larks," Jediah agreed. "It grew louder and then there was light. We heard words."

Again he paused while each man remembered the vision.

"'Fear not,'" the younger man took up the recital. "The first thing we heard was 'Fear not.'"

"And we were afraid," someone admitted.

I could nod in understanding. "I know the feeling."

Respect came into several pairs of eyes as we each recognized a shared experience.

"What then?"

"From the light came a proclamation."

Jediah glanced at his friends. Encouraging nods urged him to continue.

"From the light we heard 'This day is born the Savior who will be Messiah'. I did not know what that meant. I still do not know what it means."

The shepherd stood silent, shaking his head in confusion. His young companion blurted out a final exclamation

"Before the vision vanished we were told 'You will find the baby in swaddling cloths, in a manger.' This is the only stable big enough. So we came here."

Stunned, I stared past the shepherds. Here was the confirmation of my son's parenthood. The visitors took my silence as a rebuff and started to shuffle away.

Jediah lowered his chin to his chest and turned away. "I knew it was not true."

"Wait!" I reached out to grasp the man's arm. "Jediah, the child you seek is here."

With a lift of his head the old man eyed me skeptically.

"You did see angels. The God of Abraham, Isaac, and Jacob has revealed Messiah to you."

Almost holding their breath, the men crowded around again.

"Come and see."

Slowly and reverently my companions tiptoed after me. Mary greeted me with a composed smile. It was obvious that she had heard the conversation. With a shy look, my wife held the infant toward the now kneeling men.

"His name is Jeshua," I told our visitors.

"It means 'God saves,'" Jediah whispered with awe.

"Blessed be the God of our Fathers," another shepherd sighed a prayer.

"He has revealed his salvation to the lowly," a gruff voice rumbled.

At that moment, in the cave owned by my uncle in Bethlehem, I understood that God does not deal in might but in love. Those who expected Messiah to restore the splendor and power of King David were destined to be disappointed. I rejected the thought that flashed through my mind—that God might even love the Romans.

"Blessed are you, Lord God of our Fathers, Ruler of the Universe!" A slender, graying shepherd moved forward to lay his own sheepskin blanket at Mary's feet before backing out of the cave.

We could hear him repeating his praises to God. The gift freed everyone from the awestruck spell that seemed to grip us. Each man sought to honor the child. They piled other offerings onto the blanket. There was a gourd drinking cup, carved in the long hours of watching the flocks, a chain of silver from around a tall shepherd's neck, the last piece of copper in a young lad's pouch, a finely woven cloak of dyed wool.

Mary thanked each man with a smile and nod. Her gracious acceptance stopped my instinctive aversion to taking their prized possessions. My wife understood the need for each man to leave an offering for Messiah. In the lamplight her face had an almost ethereal radiance.

At last only Jediah remained. In his hand he held a shepherd's pipe. I could imagine the old man playing a gentle tune to calm the flocks. The shepherd was clearly torn between giving the instrument and keeping it for his use. For the first time Mary spoke.

"Will you play a tune for my son?"

Raising the pipes, the old shepherd began to play. The sound would have been at home in the Temple courts themselves. I was sure the ranks of musicians in Jerusalem could have done no better. The melody lifted me out of the cave and up to the sky. Mary's eyes closed. The smile on her lips expressed her enjoyment. Gently she swayed and rocked Jeshua in rhythm to the song. Too soon the last note died away.

"Now I can give this." Prayerfully Jediah bent to add his offering.

I was surprised when my wife leaned forward. She pressed the pipe back into the old man's hands. "No, you must keep this. Your gift was the song. Keep the instrument to make many more songs of praise to God."

Tears stood in the shepherd's eyes when he turned to leave. "I had lost the joy of playing after Tamar died. Now I have music again."

The awe in the old man's voice brought tears to my eyes. Jediah gripped my shoulder and then with a last thankful look at my wife and son he hurried into the night after his companions.

"Joseph, that man has found God again."

Mary's soft words were filled with delight. Gazing after the departed shepherd, I nodded abstractedly before returning to the girl's side.

"Yes, my love. You should rest."

"Dearest Joseph, you are so good to me."

I could make no response except to kiss the dark curl on her forehead and tenderly tuck the blankets around her figure. Jeshua slept in the crook of her arm. For a long time I crouched there, watching the pair. So much had changed this night.

Finally I moved away to sit against the cave wall near Balaam. The donkey dozed with a hoof cocked at rest. He opened his eyes when I sighed and closed them immediately upon seeing that no hay was forthcoming. Leaning my head back I thought of the shepherds' words, 'We saw a vision of angels'. I remembered my own night of agony on the hill outside Nazareth that ended with an angelic reassurance, 'Fear not to take Mary as your wife.'

"Why did you choose me, a humble carpenter of Nazareth, to be father of this child? What can I give him? Messiah should be clothed in purple and live in a palace." I whispered my nagging question into the silence.

Eventually I drifted to sleep no closer to an answer than any time in the past nine months. Voices roused me. For a moment I was disoriented. Then I remembered the stable, the birth, and the visit of the shepherds. They were back, joyfully celebrating and praising God. Somewhere a skin of the local wine had been obtained.

"To the father!" The tall shepherd, a little unsteadily, raised the skin to his lips and then offered it to me.

The rest gathered around me with more congratulations as I took a drink.

"God truly is wonderful!"

"Messiah is announced to shepherds!"

"Always it is to the humble and lowly that God reveals His works," Jediah announced.

He was not drunk except with peace and joy.

"What did you say?" I stared at the man in amazement.

"It is not the proud or mighty who see the Hand of God. We who are poor and humble are the ones who know God."

There was no time for further conversation. Rachel, hostess of the compound, appeared at the top of the path. Like a storm she advanced. Her robe and veils billowed around her. The tempest burst around us.

"What is this noise? You will disturb the mother and child as well as my other guests!"

The real reason for her concern was apparent in the way my aunt glanced back at the dark house she left. Singling me out the woman glared at me.

"Some husband you are, carousing with the locals when your wife is just delivered of a son!"

I opened my mouth to explain. She forestalled me by turning on my companions. They cringed away from her rage.

"You, Hiram and Asher, should be with your flocks! Joab, do you think sheep watch themselves? What will your father say when he returns from Jerusalem?"

They youngest of the shepherds lowered his head and shuffled his feet.

"Jediah, I would have thought you would set a better example."

When she paused for breath, I interrupted, "My aunt, these men heard of the birth and came to offer congratulations."

Disbelief and scorn were clear in the twisted mouth and squinting eyes confronting me. "And how did these erstwhile shepherds hear that a baby was born here in my stable?"

Several pairs of eyes turned to Jediah. No longer the hesitant petitioner of earlier in the night, the man confidently addressed my aunt.

"Rachel, do you believe Messiah will come?"

His question took the woman off guard. Irritably, she nodded. "Of course, what does that have to do with this?"

"We left our flocks and came here," He paused to bite back a grin of anticipation, "because we saw a vision of angels."

"Angels! Of all the lame excuses for drunkenness…"

My aunt was enraged. The rest of the group nodded eagerly.

"It's true!"

As though my aunt had not spoken, Jediah continued, "We were told that the Savior of Israel was born."

"A son was born to Naomi and Hiram this night. He has as much chance of being Messiah as anyone." Disbelief and scorn still dripped from Rachel's words.

The old shepherd ignored her doubts. "Rachel, the angel said that the baby was born in a stable."

"Messiah will be born of high estate, not in a stable." Shaking her head, the woman looked past us to the dark opening in the hillside.

Jediah continued persuasively, "Who knows the mind of God? Was Gideon a warrior when he was called to lead Israel against the Philistines? David himself was not born a king. Joseph spent time in jail and Moses was a murderer. Messiah will be born in Bethlehem."

Rachel shook her head emphatically, "Not in my stable. Such things do not happen any more. Maybe they did in the days of King David or the prophets, but not now."

"I know it is hard to believe." Jediah smiled sympathetically.

My aunt shook her head. "I have seen the baby. He's an ordinary newborn."

The old man glanced toward the cave. He hesitated and then blurted, "I played my pipes for him and found a peace lost with Tamar's death."

A murmur from his friends and Rachel's open-mouthed astonishment told me that his confession was unexpected. Jediah motioned to his companions as the silence grew.

"We have been celebrating the birth of Messiah, but we will be quiet and leave now."

With a salaam to me, the shepherds headed back to the fields and their flocks. The starlight was dimming with the approach of dawn. I stood watching my new friends depart. The wineskin hung forgotten from my hand.

I heard Rachel's muttered imprecation. "Fools! They'll find their flocks scattered and regret the wine they consumed."

"I do not think so. God sent them here and God will have kept their flocks safe." I stated confidently.

She spun and faced me, puffed up with rage. "You are an idiot, too, if you think anyone can be born to free us from Rome. Tend to your carpentry and your family. Do not fill the child's head with dreams of the throne of David. That will only end on a Roman cross."

Before I could respond, the woman stamped away back up the path to her home. I was left with much to ponder.

"Joseph."

Mary called me from my reverie. Hastily I entered the cave. My wife sat on the bed of blankets and straw Elam and I had prepared the night before. The baby slept in the food trough carved in the cave wall. More straw and blankets made a cozy nest. With her hair loose around her shoulders, Mary looked more like a child than a woman who had recently given birth.

"Yes, my love, did we awaken you?"

A warm smile softened the young face even more. Then she looked serious. Mary leaned over the infant and kissed his cheek, gathering the little body into her arms.

"Your aunt is only the first to doubt that Jeshua is Messiah. You and I and Jediah have the words of angels to reassure us. But, he is so ordinary, just as Rachel said."

When the woman looked up, I saw disappointment and even doubt in her eyes. Tears brimmed and threatened to spill over. Dropping to my knees beside my wife, I gathered her reverently and gently into my arms. My lips touched the baby's forehead. I held my family in silence trying to find an answer. Jediah's words came back to me.

"I think the old shepherd was right," I faltered, trying to explain my insight. "The God of our Fathers reveals himself in unexpected ways. Yahweh uses the ordinary to show his power and glory. Jediah mentioned Gideon, David, Moses and Joseph as examples of ordinary men used by the God of Abraham, Isaac, and Jacob. This stable is perhaps the most fitting place of all for Messiah to be born, among the people where God has always sought to dwell."

"Yes, my husband. It is in the commonplace that God is present." Confidence was back in Mary's voice and she smiled up at me. "Stars and sand were signs of the promises to Abraham. Esther was not born to be a queen, yet she was raised up and saved her people. This child is indeed the Son of the Most High. The shepherds were sent to affirm that to us so we would not doubt."

"Truly God has blessed us," I agreed.

I held my wife and child as the darkness outside the stable lightened into day. When the baby stirred and whimpered, Mary roused from her doze to offer her breast. I rose to say my morning prayers from the entrance of the cave. My heart was full of praise.

"God of Abraham, Isaac, and Jacob, blessed are you, awesome and mighty are your deeds. In the common is found the holy. In the ordinary is your hand, Creator of the Universe. Praise to you, O God."

CHAPTER 13

I half feared that daylight would bring more visitors drawn by the shepherds' report of angels and the birth of Messiah. Jediah and Hiram returned, bearing fresh goat milk and cheese but the people of Bethlehem went about their daily routine, unaffected by the miracle in their midst.

Elam appeared at midmorning with a tray of freshly baked bread and a bowl of humus.

"Mother said to tell you that when the merchant leaves tomorrow, you can move up to the house."

"My aunt is most kind."

The boy missed the slightly ironic tone in my voice as he hurried back to his chores.

Mary chided me for my petulance. "Your aunt is doing her best. This is a difficult time. So many people have descended on Bethlehem that everyone is called upon to open their home. I am sure that Rachel is finding it impossible to get everything done. I will be happy to help her."

"You need to rest and care for my son," I argued.

"Joseph, I am fine. Childbirth is a normal thing. Women have cared for children and for their homes and husbands since time began."

When she reached for the tray to prepare my meal I stopped her.

"Today you will rest," I insisted. "I will prepare the meal while you care for our son."

Clumsily I spread a blanket and arranged the platters. In our bags I found the wooden bowls we used every day and the cups I had taken such care to carve and polish. I felt Mary watching me curiously when I hurried from our cave home. In a moment I returned with a small bouquet of late blooming flowers from a sheltered niche to put at her place. Only then did I look at my bride. With a salaam as to a queen, I gestured to the meal.

"Come, my love."

"This is beautiful!" She kissed my cheek and smiled as she accepted a cup of the watered wine from me.

After the meal we walked together into the early afternoon sunlight while Jeshua slept. From the not so distant hills, we heard an occasional baa from the flocks or a sharp bark from a sheep dog. Mary looked toward the sound.

"How strange that God would use a carpenter and a village girl to be parents of the Son of David. Jediah and his friends do not have an easy life, but it was to them that the birth of Messiah was announced. They willingly left their flocks to see if the word of angels was true."

Her voice trailed off and she tilted her head considering the wonder.

"Those who will find God must be willing to leave all behind," I said slowly as if figuring out a puzzle.

A slight chill rippled over me as I wondered what that meant for my carefully planned life.

It was late when Elam brought a packet of the mutton I could smell roasting all afternoon. Carefully wrapped in grape leaves by Rachel, the meat was seeping through the wrapping before the six-year old presented it to me. Still, it tasted delicious. Mary smiled her thanks to the boy when he arrived.

"I would have been here sooner, but there was a lizard on the rock." He scrubbed his toe against a rock and looked down.

With his vague gesture up the path we understood that there had been a side trip to investigate a potential pet.

"Tell your mother thank you." Mary ordered with a stifled giggle.

I chuckled to myself at the relieved expression on my young cousin's face. That night I slept across the entrance to bar any roaming dogs or other marauders from entry. The spot was worn smooth by generations of shepherds doing the same thing. I felt a kinship with my father's family and wondered if my grandfather had ever watched the sheep here.

Morning light was just touching the hills and rooftops with gold light when the racket of the merchant's departure drifted down the hill. I peered into the cave hoping the noise had not awakened my family. The small room looked quite cozy since Mary insisted on hanging the few extra blankets on the walls. She and Jeshua still slept soundly. I had heard her tending the baby in the night. As quietly as I could, I untied Balaam and led him outside. On a slight rise, the little donkey found a patch of grass and began to graze. I brought the animal a bucket of water.

"Enjoy your rest, my friend," I told the shaggy beast with a pat on his neck. "After Mary's purification, we will return home and there will be much to do."

The Roman census faded into the background as I thought of all the work that would await me in Nazareth after over a month away. I set aside a passing thought of returning to Nazareth before the thirty days of purification were over.

"We must do all according to the Law," I informed the small animal who twitched his ears. "My son will be circumcised on the eighth day and presented in the Temple when the time is right. That will be when the moon is new again. We will stop in Jerusalem on the way home to Nazareth."

Returning to the cave, I cleaned out the stall occupied by Balaam. Mary repacked our simple baggage despite my protests. My aunt arrived while I was carpeting the floor with fresh straw. Elam trotted at her heels pushing a small cart.

"Joseph, you and your family will move into my house," Rachel ordered brusquely.

I felt irritation at her tone, then remembering Mary's comment I offered, "If there is anything I can do to help while my uncle is gone, you must tell me. I have brought my carpenter's tools. Your hospitality is generous."

The woman's face relaxed even more when Mary rose to embrace her. "Aunt Rachel, we are truly blessed to have found in you a generous welcome. Please let me help you with such things as are fitting."

Wrapping an arm around her niece, Rachel led her out of the cave. Over her shoulder she gave final instructions. "We women will go up to the house. Elam will help you bring your things. The donkey can have a place in the stable near the house."

I watched my wife walking up the path beside Rachel with Jeshua cradled in her arm. My aunt bent close to see the baby. I was sure the conversation centered on child care.

Together, Elam and I loaded the small cart with the blankets and small bundles Mary packed. Balaam followed us readily. When I offered to help push the cart, the boy shook his head, intent on proving his strength.

"I can do it."

"Your mother must depend on you a lot. I can see that you are a great help." My words brought a glow of pride to the childish face. Then I changed the subject. "Is there a rabbi in Bethlehem?"

"Of course!"

The amazed look on the boy's face made me smile.

"I must speak to him about circumcising my son."

Nodding as if he was a man of many years, my guide pointed vaguely toward the town. "Rabbi Barach bar Barach will be happy to do that. He just took over from old Barach who is too blind and old to do anything."

I led Balaam to the stable when we reached the courtyard. Stoically the small animal accepted his new lodgings. The cart sat near the door to the house. After carrying one load of the blankets into the comfortable home, my young helper disappeared. I gathered up the remaining bundles and entered the open door. Mary sat shelling beans while Jeshua dozed on a soft goatskin nearby. She smiled and pointed the way to our room. Later I asked my aunt for directions to the rabbi's house.

She repeated her son's information. "That would be young Barach bar Barach. Old Barach bar Barach is unable to see to perform any rituals, especially circumcision. He still bears the title of Rabbi and is a very learned man, but be sure to ask for Barach the younger."

Early the next morning I sought out the rabbi. He was nothing like Rabbi Ezra in Nazareth. This was a tall young man with a habit of standing up on his toes and teetering there while talking.

From his enhanced height the teacher peered down his nose at me. "So you are the young carpenter, Rachel's nephew."

I tried not to bristle at the tone, which made me sound like a boy. I was a few years older than this man.

"Old Jediah had quite a tale to tell about the birth of your son. When was it? Four days ago?" He frowned at me.

"Yes, that is why I have come. We will need your services for the circumcision." I forced myself to be civil even in the face of the derision implicit in the conversation.

Through pursed lips, Barach proceeded to give me a lesson. "Ah, circumcision, it is such an important time in the life of a Son of Israel. The covenant of Abraham has been kept from generation to generation. Even in exile, we have not forgotten to mark our sons as heirs of the Promise." Rocking on his toes, the young rabbi narrowed his eyes when I made no response. "You would, I assume want to present a thank offering…?" The rising tone helped me understand what the man wanted.

"Of course," I mumbled through gritted teeth, hoping this stranger did not hear the mounting rage inside me.

"Good. I will come to circumcise the boy four days from now." He rubbed his long thin hands together and sniffed through his nose before granting me the boon of his services. "As the Law demands, 'every male that opens the womb shall be holy to the Lord and circumcised on the eighth day.' A fine lamb would make a worthy offering for such a 'special' birth."

Not daring to answer his presumption, I left the rabbi with the briefest of nods. Rather than return to my aunt's house until I was less angry, I strode out of Bethlehem. Almost immediately I found myself climbing toward the fields. Soon I could hear the sound of the flocks. The shepherds were talking or singing to the animals. Every so often a low baa was heard in response. Topping a small mound I saw a mass of woolly bodies. Some were grazing but most rested under bushes or near the water. The men, too, lounged in the shade. A dog barked to announce my arrival and immediately all the shepherds were alert. Each man leapt to his feet with staff in hand. At first I did not recognize anyone.

Then Hiram stepped forward and called to his comrades. "It is the carpenter from Nazareth."

Everyone relaxed. Several returned to their interrupted naps. Jediah hurried toward me.

"My friend, is anything wrong? The baby…?" He was clearly concerned and gripped my arm.

Glad to reassure the man I laid a hand on his shoulder. "All is well. My aunt has installed us in her home."

Grimly the old shepherd nodded, "As she should. Rachel is not a bad woman. Many concerns make her distracted and forgetful of the duties of hospitality."

"I do not fault her. We arrived unannounced and she did the best she could. The cave offered warmth and privacy. We are grateful for her welcome."

My calm statement made Jediah and Hiram nod.

"It was a blessed place." Jediah's eyes took on a faraway look as he remembered the events of less than a week before.

"What brings you to the hills?" Hiram asked.

His question reminded me of my interview with Barach bar Barach. My face must have betrayed my frustration.

"Something has happened," Jediah stated. "Tell us."

The way the strong hand gripped the shepherd's staff reminded me of a man preparing for battle.

"I spoke to the rabbi."

Even away from the young religious teacher I could recall his contempt of the reports of these honest men and most of all his greed in requesting a lamb as payment.

"Young Barach is too full of his consequence," Hiram frowned. "His father has been a good and honest rabbi. The boy must learn humility in order to be a true teacher."

"He laughed me from his door when we tried to tell him Messiah was born," Jediah admitted, his earnest face reddening at the memory.

"Old Barach would have been delighted to hear such news," Hiram noted.

"My son what did he ask for?" Jediah inquired.

When I did not reply immediately, Hiram frowned and stated, "It is well known that our new rabbi is enriching himself on the fees he charges."

With a rueful smile I told my companions, "I thought he was taking advantage of a stranger. In Nazareth there is no fee for circumcision. To be honest, I did not expect one here. Barach bar Barach mentioned that a lamb would be acceptable payment."

I felt my fists clench and jaw tighten as anger mounted in me again.

Hiram and Jediah looked at each other. Hiram spoke first.

"A lamb for circumcision! That is absurd. His father should be told!"

"Old Barach is too deaf and blind to understand what is happening in his own home," Jediah sighed sadly. "It is a shame."

We stood silent for a moment then the old shepherd turned to me. "Joseph, my friend, if it is a lamb that is needed you must have the pick of my flock."

Overwhelmed by his offer, I stared at the man. With a low salaam, I made an offer that I quickly revised when the shepherd started to shake his head almost angrily.

"You must let me pay. At least I can do some carpentry work for you."

With a nod Jediah admitted after a moment, "Now, that you could do. I have a gate that needs a bit of work."

"Show me. I will bring my tools tomorrow."

Our bargain was sealed with a handshake.

"I will pick the best lamb for you. Not because the rabbi deserves it but to honor your son."

"Thank you, my friend."

I felt humbled by this unexpected friendship.

Mary was waiting for me. Her sleeves were rolled up and from the dampness of her gown I guessed she had been washing clothes. The array spread to dry confirmed the guess.

"All is settled." I said.

"You were gone so long, I was worried," she said with a frown.

"I had to arrange for payment of the fee."

My explanation made her brown eyes open wide. Mary's astonishment was as great as mine.

"Fee? For circumcision?"

"It is the custom here." I shrugged.

"It is a recent custom. The young rabbi will be a rich man soon. He hopes to obtain patronage and a position in Jerusalem. For that he needs money," my aunt commented acidly as she walked toward us carrying a basket piled with clean clothes.

I hurried to help but she set the load down on a convenient bench before I reached her side.

"Why would he want to leave here? It is so lovely and peaceful," Mary asked.

The older woman shrugged. "Some men are not satisfied with what they have. Barach bar Barach wants the power and prestige of serving in the Temple in Jerusalem."

"It is hard to think that God can be served any better in Jerusalem than here."

Mary's innocent comment caused my aunt to raise her eyebrows in surprise before turning to me.

"What did he ask for?"

Again I felt my face turning red with embarrassment and anger.

"A lamb."

My short answer was met with a hoot of laughter, "The man raises his fees daily!"

"What will we do?" Mary's worried question silenced Rachel's laughter.

"Jediah will provide a lamb. I will do some work for him."

My answer brought a smile to my wife's lips and a nod from my aunt.

"Well done, my boy," she applauded.

A slight breeze began to ruffle the drying clothes. Both women hastily gathered and folded them. I carried the now overflowing basket to the house. Mary walked beside me with Jeshua nestled in the blanket slung across her chest. She handed the baby to me after I set my load down near the door where Rachel indicated.

"I will help your aunt with the food. Go and put him to sleep on our bed," Mary instructed.

Looking down at the tiny boy I was overwhelmed with love and awe. It was the first time I had actually carried the baby. Somehow he felt perfect in my arms.

I pushed aside the curtain to the small room in the upper level of the house. The lattice over the windows kept out the sun but let in any breezes. In the filtered light I saw our clothing neatly stacked near the sleeping mat. A Roman chest and leather trunk under the window were obviously my aunt's and reminded me that my Uncle Perez was a wealthy man, well thought of even beyond Bethlehem.

Without lighting the oil lamp, I crouched next to the mat to place the baby on it. He stirred in my arms and I glanced down. Dark eyes, like Mary's, stared at me. A mewing sound came from the infant's lips. Instinctively I rocked back and forth gently.

"Hush, my son. You are safe, Jeshua my son."

The movement seemed to soothe the baby. After studying me for another moment, long black eyelashes rested on the round cheeks and the child slept again. Afraid that any movement would disturb and waken the baby, I held him while he slept. Forgotten was my irritation with Barach, my confusion about my place in the infant's life, even my discomfort at accepting my kinswoman's hospitality. With my son in my arms, I could believe that all would be well.

CHAPTER 14

Early the next morning I tramped up the hillside to Jediah's sheep pen. I barely noticed the weight of my tools and the lumber I carried to repair his gate. A smile lingered as I remembered Mary's astonishment the night before when she found me in our room. I had fallen asleep with Jeshua in my arms. My aunt's amazed exclamation brought me groggily awake.

"Here you are! Supper is eaten." Her sharp voice woke the baby. At his wail she lowered her tone. "Do not expect me to fix a special plate."

"No aunt, forgive me," I mumbled sleepily. "I did not want to leave Jeshua."

"You have held him all this time?"

Mary's surprised question from behind Rachel made me nod sheepishly. Only then did I notice that my arm was numb from the weight and also damp. Mary hurried forward to take the baby while my aunt continued to shake her head. I noticed she was no longer frowning in the light of the lamp she carried. The baby squirmed and cried as Mary unwrapped the swaddling cloths to change them for dry wrappings. Then she offered her breast to his greedy mouth. Contented suckling replaced the whimpers.

"Nephew, perhaps you will be a good father after all."

Although still sharp, the tone held what I thought might be respect. The woman gathered some items from the chest and left us.

"My love, he is our son." I nestled beside my wife and placed my cheek against hers as we watched the baby nurse.

Mary smiled, "God shows us grace."

I could only nod.

Now, walking up the path to the sheepfold I remembered her words and said a brief prayer, "Thank you, Gracious Lord God, Creator of the Universe, and bearer of good things to your people. Truly you do look out for your people!"

I constructed a new gate swiftly. Jediah arrived when the sun was high.

"Done already!" The shepherd was amazed. When he looked more closely he frowned. "You have built a new gate. All I asked was that you repair the old one."

He gestured to where the broken and patched wooden object lay on the ground.

I grinned and shrugged. "My friend, for your kindness, a new gate. Besides, it was easier to build new than repair the old."

The man looked at me with narrowed eyes. Shaking the gate he grinned in response. "Perhaps, it was easier. This is sturdier than what we had. Will you stay and share my meal?"

Happily I accepted the bread he held out. We quenched our thirst from the nearby stream. After the shared bread and cheese, I gathered my tools and Jediah prepared to return to his flocks.

"I hope you will come to the ceremony," I told my friend.

"I will," he nodded, "if Hiram agrees to watch my sheep."

The next day was the Sabbath. Only the essential feeding of animals was done. Mary joined me for prayers. Facing in the direction of Jerusalem I recited the Shema and added thanksgiving for my son. My wife's fervent Amen warmed my heart. We stood together for a long time. Ever so gently I touched a lock of black hair on the baby's forehead. Already he was looking at the world around him with interest. A butterfly fluttered past distracting the baby from his study of my face. A lump formed in my throat as I thought of all the dangers that might beset this family of mine should Herod learn of Jeshua's birth.

The day passed quietly. Even Rachel's sharp tongue seemed subdued on the holy day. In the evening I walked with Elam the short distance to the stable. The boy stroked Balaam's nose and offered him a carrot.

"He's a nice donkey."

"Yours looks like he'll grow into a sturdy beast."

Elam grinned in response to my compliment. The little black animal was the boy's pride and joy.

My young relation straightened so he stood taller. "Father says I may train him to carry the water jars to the fields and to drag brush wood for the fire. As soon as he returns from Jerusalem we will start the lessons."

The longing on the boy's face reminded me of lonely weeks during my childhood waiting for Jacob's return from some trading trip.

"Would you like to help me oil Balaam's saddle?"

"Could I?" Elam jumped up and down with excitement.

I smiled at his eagerness. "We must ask your mother, but if you have your chores done, I am sure she will agree."

I was right. Rachel welcomed anything that kept her son occupied.

"I only hope you will not regret the offer." She barely looked up from her work of slicing and chopping. "It will keep you both out of the way."

Mary smiled at me. "We will have a feast to celebrate the circumcision tomorrow."

A storm threatened to the west on the morning of the ceremony. Mary's eyes glistened with the hint of tears as she tenderly washed the baby.

"My dearest son," she crooned before handing the baby to me, "this day you will become a true Son of Abraham. All will be well, my child. Your father will be near."

Elam ran in to report breathlessly, “The rabbi is here!”

Mary followed me to the lower level with her hands gripped together. She stood with Rachel and several other women. A table was spread with a clean white cloth. The flint knife lying on the material looked stark and dangerously sharp.

“Welcome rabbi.” Courteously I inclined my head to the young man. “This house is honored by your presence.”

Elam proudly picked up the lamb Jediah provided and held it close.

“Today a son of this house is made an inheritor of the promises made to Abraham, Isaac, and Jacob.” Ponderously and with only a slight inclination of his head, Barach acknowledged my greeting and the lamb.

When he gestured for the baby to be placed on the table, my hands started to shake. I heard someone clear his throat and looked up to see Jediah give me an encouraging grin.

Steadied, I unwrapped the cloths. Jeshua wiggled and flailed tiny arms and legs, glad to be free of the linen. His hand latched onto one of my fingers. He tried to focus on his prize. I barely heard the rabbi intoning prayers. Automatically I responded “Amen” with the group.

A thousand memories flashed through my mind. There was Mary in my shop, the night on the Nazarene hillside, my father’s disapproval and the wedding day as well as the dark night in the stable. My heart was pounding with anticipation of one question, but when Barach bar Barach asked I was unprepared and he had to repeat the words.

“What name is given to this child?”

The rabbi waited and I felt all eyes on me. “He will be Jeshua son of Joseph, carpenter of Nazareth and son of David.”

The young man raised his eyebrows at the last phrase but he only replied “Amen” before picking up the knife. The cut was swiftly and neatly done. Before my son could begin to cry, the closing prayer began. Then the men of Bethlehem surrounded me.

“Congratulations.”

"Blessings on you and on your son."

"May Jeshua grow to be an honor to your house."

"A fine son, Joseph, carpenter of Nazareth."

Rachel spoke above the hubbub to announce the feast. Mary hurried forward to soothe her son who still sobbed in my arms. Only Jediah remained behind.

"Why did you add 'son of David'?" The old shepherd stared at me.

Shaking my head, I shrugged, "I do not know. The words came without thought."

"Yet Messiah is the son of David. It is fitting," my friend mused to himself and nodded.

Mary tugged my arm and there was no time for further conversation.

The feast prepared by Rachel was lavish. Piles of meat and bread, fruit and sweetmeats made my eyes open wide. It was a banquet fit for a king.

The woman bustled over to urge me forward. "Nephew, the guests are waiting."

Voices quieted when I began to pray, "Blessed are you, Lord of the Universe. You give freely of your bounty. May all who eat be fed and find your blessing. May your sons be strong in the ways of the Living God."

Looking across the group at my wife and son I smiled. As host, I took one of the breads, broke it and began to eat. The guests surged forward and the table was surrounded. I fought my way through the crowd to bring Mary bread layered with fruit and meat. She sat in the shade rocking Jeshua. The light filtering through the trees lit her face. I marveled at her serenity in the midst of the noise of many voices. Dropping to one knee, I offered her the food.

"My wife, Mary, my love."

With a tender smile she took my offering. I looked down at the baby. Exhausted from the morning's experience the child slept.

"The covenant is fulfilled."

"Yes, Jeshua is an inheritor of the promise made to our father Abraham," she agreed.

Rachel did not allow us further time. Almost irritably she herded me back into the midst of the many guests I did not know. I noticed that Barach the rabbi not only replenished his food many times but also returned several times to refill his cup. My aunt's servants carried jugs of the local wine through the crowd. Over and over I nodded thanks to congratulations from the men present. At last people began to leave and then we were alone in the courtyard. Little remained of the feast. Elam chased a dog away from the table.

With a contented sigh my aunt sank onto a bench and leaned against the wall. "That was a fine celebration! No one can say that Rachel, wife of Perez, was not generous to her kin."

I had to smile to myself even as I bowed before the woman. Crouching beside her, I took one hand in mine.

"My aunt, you have exceeded the bounds of hospitality. Surely this banquet will be spoken of for a long time. It was a feast fit for a prince."

"You are too kind, my boy. It was nothing, a mere trifle." Her words were deprecating but her eyes were pleased.

Mary added, "My aunt, you have been more than generous. We are grateful. Let me clear away what is left."

"No, no, my servants will do that."

In the morning I approached my aunt. "Tell me what is needed, that I, a humble carpenter can do for you."

"I do not take payment from my kin." Her affronted look bordered on anger.

"No, my aunt, for I could never repay you for your hospitality. However, in thanks I would do some kindness in return."

"Is Mary finding you too bothersome in your attempts to help?" With a raised eyebrow the woman nodded when I lowered my head to hide a grin at her perception. When I did not reply, Rachel nodded. “Very well. There are some things that need repair. Have Elam help you. It will give the boy a new interest.”

So it was that I spent two weeks repairing furniture and farm implements. Elam became adept at knowing which tool I would want next. He also learned to whittle the pegs I used to anchor pieces together. The iron nails of the Romans were too expensive to use except on the finest woods for royal palaces. When word spread that I was a carpenter, many people arrived bearing items for repair. I found myself almost too busy, since the local carpenter had recently died.

Mary was eager for her month of cleansing to be complete.

More than once she reminded me, “We must take Jeshua to the Temple to present him as the firstborn. It could be a stop on our way home.”

One evening we walked together down the path to the stable. The baby slept happily with Rachel and the serving girls nearby in the house. The night breeze felt good after a day sweating in the sun while building a cart for Achish, the wine merchant.

“Would you be sad to not return to Nazareth?” I asked. It was something I had been considering for several days.

“What do you mean?”

“Many have urged me to remain here in Bethlehem,” I explained. “There is much work to be done. Should not the son of David grow up in the city of David?”

The woman’s voice was thoughtful when I stopped talking. “Our parents will be saddened if we do not return.”

We walked in silence for several minutes. I was ashamed to admit that my mother and father had not entered my thoughts. Anna and Joachim would indeed be devastated if we did not return. Even Sarah and Jacob waited to see their grandson.

Mary interrupted my thoughts, “Joseph, you are right. Messiah should grow up in Bethlehem. It is prophesied, ‘You Bethlehem are by no means least for from you shall come a ruler who will govern my people Israel.' My husband, we will raise our son here."

The woman took my hands and looked up trustingly. I drew the gentle girl into my arms. A lump of emotion made it hard to speak.

"I love you, Mary, my wife."

My lips buried themselves in her hair. For a long time we held each other.

Rachel was delighted to hear the news. She starting making excited plans, "I know just the house for you. I have some furniture you can use. Your skills, nephew, are most welcome. Surely God sent you."

In a very short time we were installed in a small house just around the corner from my aunt. There was a large yard where I could work. The first thing I did was erect an awning as protection from the sun. Elam came daily to help me and my uncle visited on his return from the capital. His booming voice filled our small house. My uncle was a short, stocky man but you forgot his size when he spoke.

"Joseph bar Jacob, you are welcome. Rachel has told me of your son."

Perez gently, with the ease of much experience took the child from Mary. Jeshua reached out to grasp the bushy whiskers around the smiling mouth. The man handed Jeshua to his mother and grinned at me.

"A fine boy. You should be very proud. May God bless him with long life and you with many more sons. It is good that you have decided to stay in Bethlehem." Almost without taking a breath he changed the subject. "I have seen the work you did for Rachel. Finer workmanship I have rarely seen, even in Jerusalem."

"Thank you, uncle."

I inclined my head at this praise, but he continued to talk as if I had not spoken. "When do you go to the Temple for the presentation of your son?"

"We leave after the Sabbath, the day after tomorrow."

"That is good. A day's journey away will not harm your business. We will celebrate when you return. I have much to give thanks for. The year has brought me good sales, my nephew with a fine addition to the family, and the end of the census. If the Romans would leave all of Judea as they have left Bethlehem that would be a true miracle from God. For now though, we take what peace we can get. One thing I will say for the Roman legions, they can keep the peace."

With a hearty slap on my back that made me stagger, the man left. He turned at the gate to offer his blessing.

"May God grant you safe journey to the Temple and back. I leave you to prepare for your Sabbath."

We heard him calling Sabbath greetings as he strode up the street.

"My uncle is a good man."

"Yes, but one can hardly carry on a conversation with him."

I turned and saw the laughter dancing in my wife's eyes. Together we burst into giggles, then gales of laughter. Even Jeshua seemed to enjoy the joke for he smiled and gurgled.

"But he is a good man." I repeated when at last we caught our breath.

Mary nodded and turned to spread the Sabbath cloth. I hurried to tend Balaam before the sun set.

Chapter 15

We set out for Jerusalem in the hazy morning light. With Jeshua snuggly wrapped and cradled in her arms, my wife gave me a bag of food for our journey. I tied the leather pouch to my belt and lifted my family onto the donkey.

A few new friends called greetings as we traversed Bethlehem. Once on the road to Jerusalem, we joined other early morning travelers. The camaraderie helped make the short journey pass quickly. Soon we were in sight of the royal city. The haze of the morning was gone and the sun turned the walls to gold.

"Is that the Temple?" Mary gasped, pointing to the brilliant white and gold walls visible over the battlements.

"Yes, a grand edifice," a more seasoned visitor than myself commented in a lowered voice. "Herod outdid himself building the Temple. Too bad he is not really a Jew. We might let him be king just for that."

I did not have a chance to respond, even if I wanted to. The road dipped downward through the valley and then we plodded up to the gates. Roman soldiers stood at their posts. They barely gave our little group a glance.

The crowds, noise and bustle of the city were deafening. Mary could not help the look of disgust and choking gasp when a particularly dreadful stench drifted by. Bewildered by the bustle, I stopped a decent looking man.

"Excuse me, how do we get to the Temple?"

Although his brows drew together briefly in irritation, the stranger pointed down the street.

Noticing my wife and child, his demeanor softened. “Just follow this road. You cannot miss it. Presenting the boy as your firstborn?”

I nodded, “Yes, he was born in Bethlehem during the census.”

“Then may God be with you and grant you the blessing of many more sons.”

“Thank you. Blessings on your house, also.”

Mary leaned forward, eager to reach the Temple and complete the ceremony. When we arrived at the center of Jerusalem I stopped short. A mountain of white marble stairs rose; it seemed, to the sky. At the pinnacle, gold shone in the sun and jewels added color. A ragged boy materialized from the shadows.

“Watch your donkey?” His singsong request was half request, half demand.

When I hesitated, my wife slipped off Balaam’s back. Without a qualm she took his rope from me and placed it in the boy’s hand.

“What is your name?” She asked with a gentle smile.

Surprise etched itself on the child’s face. “Joshua bar Abbas,” he finally stammered.

“This is a special donkey, Joshua. His name is Balaam. I want you to take extra special care of him. Can you do that?”

I wanted to stop my wife when she crouched to look the boy in the eyes. Adoration shone from his brown eyes in the dirty face.

He nodded vigorously. “Yes.”

“We will not be long,” I stated, although the boy did not hear.

Already he was leading Balaam to a nearby trough full of water. The beggar boy petted the animal. He kept glancing back at Mary.

"The boy would have jumped off the wall for you." I whispered in a teasing tone to Mary as we ascended the myriad steps.

She frowned and reprimanded me fiercely, "He deserves a better life."

An officious scribe directed us to a side chamber where a bored old man sold us two turtledoves for the sacrifice. The price seemed overly high but I made no comment. A Temple guard pointed the way to a Levite who could accept the offering.

"This is my firstborn who opened the womb of his mother." I recited the words generations before had used. "I have come to offer for his life this gift to the Giver of all Life that the boy may be a blessing in Israel."

A sense of unreality settled on me as the priest took the birds and sacrificed them on a small altar. He mumbled some words and sent us out with a blessing. There seemed to be no recognition from the man that the child before him was the promised Messiah. We hesitated uncertainly near the altar.

Irritably the Levite turned back to us after washing his hands in a nearby basin. "You may go."

I drew Mary close when I saw the brimming tears in her eyes. She too expected something more. My steps dragged as we retraced our path. Before I could voice my disappointment an old man and an even older woman confronted us.

"This is he. Blessed be the God of Abraham, Isaac, and Jacob who keeps his promises. Behold the Redemption of Israel is here. Simeon, the Lord is gracious." The old woman's voice was a croaking whisper, but her words stopped us.

Mary let her veil drop from her face to stare at the prophetess. The old man addressed as Simeon stepped forward and held out his arms. Unhesitatingly my wife handed Jeshua to him. For a long time the stranger looked down at the child in his arms.

"Yes, Anna, it is he."

The woman had not stopped praying. In a surprisingly graceful movement she raised and lowered her hands in silent adoration over the infant. "Blessed be the Lord, Ruler of the Universe, the Holy of Holies."

I stared at the pair and felt a lump of emotion grow in my throat.

Simeon began to rock with the baby. "Lord, now you are dismissing your servant in peace, according to your word; for my eyes have seen your salvation, which you have prepared in the presence of all peoples, a light for revelation to the Gentiles and for glory to your people Israel."

Reverently the old man kissed my son on his forehead and handed the baby to his mother. I stared from Simeon to Anna and then looked at Mary.

"This child is destined for the falling and the rising of many in Israel, and to be a sign that will be opposed so that the inner thoughts of many will be revealed." Looking directly at my wife Simeon stated, "A sword will pierce your own soul too."

The pair bent over Jeshua together and raised their hands in blessing, "Go in peace and may the God of our Fathers be with you."

No one noticed the brief by-play. It was easy to continue toward the exit. With awe in my heart we wandered out of the Temple. When I glanced back the two old people stood together watching us with hands still raised in blessing.

I saw that Mary was crying. Tears ran down her cheeks but I was not sure if it was joy or fear that caused them. Simeon's words made a shiver of fear ripple along my spine. What did he mean by 'light to the Gentiles' and what of the old man's threat to my beloved, 'a sword shall pierce your soul'?

"God is wonderful. He has confirmed his word yet again in the midst of the holy Temple." Mary's soft words jerked me from my reverie.

The woman stopped on the stairs to look upward. A radiant smile greeted me when I looked from the Temple to my wife. Her joy was more brilliant than the light reflecting from the walls in the bright sunlight.

"Truly God is generous and has heard the doubts of my heart," she announced.

I could only nod. She scampered down the remaining steps lightly. I was left to follow with my questions unanswered.

Joshua bar Abbas waited where we left him. I gave the boy a silver coin but he seemed almost happier to receive Mary's smiled thanks. I felt him watching us until the street turned and hid his wistful face.

I wanted to ask Mary about her words on the Temple stairs but when we reached the road to Bethlehem a noisy group of young men was nearby. Their constant chatter distracted me on the journey home. Rachel had another lavish feast waiting when we arrived late in the afternoon. Mary, full of peace, smiled and answered questions about our trip.

Perez drew me aside. "How do you like the Temple? Quite an edifice, is it not? Old Herod's a builder. Been over two decades in the construction and still he is adding things to the Temple. Every time I go to the city I see some new, grand decoration."

My uncle paused for breath.

"It is a wonder."

The man chattered on, "You know of course that the tower next to the Temple was built especially for our Roman conquerors. The great Herod knows how to appease our oppressors."

"I did not notice it," I replied.

Leaning close Perez winked. "It was touch and go when Mark Anthony was defeated in Egypt. We all expected the Emperor Augustus to remove the king, but somehow he remains."

I nodded. The history of Herod's reign was not unknown even in Nazareth.

"How ever much we may despise him, Herod has given us a symbol that of our religion and identity, even in the face of pagan Rome herself." Perez paused and his eyes took on an unexpectedly fervent light. "The Temple is a sign that God still resides with the Chosen People. Messiah will come and sweep Rome into the sea. Israel will again be the nation she was under King David. The people will rally to Messiah when he comes. As in the days of Joshua, we will conquer!"

His passion took my breath away. I had not expected such words from my kinsman.

"Uncle, I…"

"I am sure the time is soon. Surely the Almighty will not allow the Queen of Harlots to trample our holy soil for long. You and I will see Messiah, my boy."

With these final words of assurance the man gave me a hearty slap on the back.

A moment later he recalled us to our duties. "We are neglecting our guests. Rachel will be looking for us."

My aunt's frown greeted our return to the gathering. I sought Mary. She sat quietly in her favorite spot under the tree. Protectively I laid my hand on her shoulder. Perez's words troubled me. My son would not lead an army, of that I was sure.

The distress I felt must have communicated itself to Mary. She lifted her head to look at me with a slight frown between her eyes. I forced a smile but the girl was not convinced.

Later as we lay next to each other in the cozy house she said, "Joseph, my husband, you are troubled."

"It is nothing."

I heard an exasperated sigh in the darkness. She shifted to lean on one elbow and stare at me. "Ever since we left the Temple you have been silent. After you spoke to Perez you became more troubled. Tell me, my love, what is wrong."

It was my turn to sigh. Her soft hand touched my cheek. I caught her hand and brought it to my lips before I spoke.

"Mary, who do you think our son will be?"

"He is Messiah," she answered unhesitatingly.

The question that tortured me burst out. "Who is Messiah? Will Messiah lead the men of Israel against Rome as my uncle believes? Messiah is spoken of as a suffering servant by Isaiah. What does that mean? The old man in the Temple today spoke of Messiah being a light to the Gentiles. How can that be? Yahweh is only God of the Children of the Promise made to Abraham, Isaac, and Jacob."

My wife gathered me into her arms. Her cheek rested against my head. Soft unbound hair rippled around us both like a curtain. Mary held me and rocked gently for several minutes.

Finally she admitted in a whisper, "My husband, I do not know what the future holds for Jeshua. The angel said, 'he will be the Son of the Most High and reign over the house of Jacob forever'. Could it be, as Simeon said today, that as he is a revelation of God's love to the Jews, the Gentiles will also be shown the same grace? Did not the One who created all things form all nations? Surely God cares for each person, not just for those who are inheritors of the Promise. Perhaps it is our duty, as Jews and chosen, to teach all peoples of the Living God. Maybe we have failed and Messiah must show the way. I do not know. All I can do is trust God."

Awed by the woman's perception, I shifted so that she lay in my arms.

"Mary, you are wise as well as lovely. Teach me to trust and wait for God like you do."

"We will learn together."

Her promise was sealed with a kiss. A flood of desire rose in me. Tentatively I deepened the kiss and drew my wife closer. I felt a brief hesitation before she slid her hands inside my clothing. My hands shook as I slid her tunic off the slender shoulders and caressed the soft body. As gently as I could, I made love to the woman for whom I had waited so long. Her warmth and responsiveness enflamed me until we lay contented in each other's arms.

I lay awake thinking about our conversation. Beside me, Mary slept like a child. A vision of the Temple, built as Herod's masterpiece, and the adjacent Fortress of Antonio lingered in my mind as a reminder of the authorities that would destroy any perceived threat.

"All I can do is trust God," I repeated Mary's words until I fell asleep.

CHAPTER 16

Soon the little house in Bethlehem became a home. Mary found wonderful bargains in the marketplace. New woven rugs replaced the worn ones borrowed from Rachel. My wife took delight in her small garden. We soon harvested some onions and carrots.

Jeshua seemed to grow bigger every day. One evening he reached out baby arms to me. Mary smiled when I snuggled the infant into my arms. Later my son fell asleep there.

"Is he not the best child in the world?"

One of her radiant smiles lit the young woman's face. "Yes, my husband, he is."

"Hush," I frowned when she spoke in a normal tone.

Mary giggled at my concern. "Jeshua will not wake now. He is soundly asleep. You can lay him on his bed."

I shook my head, enjoying the weight and scent of the baby in my arms. Mary seated herself on a nearby low stool and began to card a basket of wool. The bright moon through the narrow window added light to the small oil lamp burning in the niche. I reveled in the peace and contentment that seeped into my heart.

Neighbors in and around Bethlehem brought work to me. Men came from as far away as Hebron when it was learned that I knew the art of inlay. I was glad of the hours my father spent teaching me the craft learned in his travels among the Gentiles. Although I was not as skilled as he, the customers did not seem to mind.

Sometimes payment was in the coin of Israel with Herod's imprint or in the copper *lepton* of Rome. More often I received a bundle of wool or soft skins as payment. During the harvest many baskets of wheat, barley and vegetables were given as payment for my work. Mary was always grateful for the bounty.

Perez proudly advertised my skills to visitors. I overheard his praise once. "My nephew is the finest carpenter in Judea. Whatever you need, from simple work to the finest of furnishings, Joseph gives the same care and precision. Just look at this box he made for my wife."

The object on display was a small box for Rachel's necklaces and bracelets. I made it from scraps of many different woods all polished to a fine sheen. I was proud of the finished product. My aunt's amazement was payment enough for the hours spent cutting and fitting all the pieces into a lovely design.

"Elam, my son, is learning from Joseph," my uncle added. "Perhaps he will become a carpenter not a shepherd."

The boy was a great help and a fast learner. Already he could be trusted to measure and cut boards to the correct length using the marked measuring rod I made. I incised my hand spans and cubits on a straight stick to help the child. Sometimes I let the boy use the drill to make holes for the dowels to joined sections of a project.

One Sabbath evening I stood with Mary gazing at the darkening sky.

"We are truly blessed," I exalted. "My work is sought after, Jeshua is growing strong and will be walking soon, and you my bride, are the loveliest of all the women in Israel."

I sealed my words with a kiss. Mary leaned against me relaxed and content. The day's work was done and Jeshua slept on his little mat in the house.

"We made the right decision to stay here. Someday we can return to Nazareth. Perhaps in the spring we will journey there so our parents can see our son."

I felt the woman's head move against my shoulder in assent. "Yes, Joseph, God has blessed us. Truly Jeshua will grow to be a great son of David as was foretold. It is right that he live here in the ancestral home of the great king."

The days shortened to winter. Yom Kippur, the new year, came and went. The days began to lengthen after the solstice and Hanukkah.

Before it seemed possible, Jeshua was a year old. I invited Jediah and his friends to the celebration. Reverently they remembered the amazing night.

"I'll never forget the angels," the old shepherd insisted, "but the baby is the real miracle."

His eyes followed the boy who toddled a couple of steps before sitting down on the floor suddenly. Undeterred he crawled over to the chest in the corner. Arriving at his destination, my son pulled himself to a standing position and tried to get the vase that was just out of reach.

"A fine strong boy," Hiram stated.

It was all he said. The shepherds seemed shy and out of place in the house. Mary tried to put them at ease by offering some treats. Very carefully the tall man took one. Uncomfortably he shifted from foot to foot seeming afraid to move for fear that he might break something.

"Come outside," I suggested.

With relief the shepherds followed me into the sunshine.

Jediah nodded in approval looking around the courtyard. "God has blessed you."

A cart tilted on its axle by the door. The missing side was evidence of the reason for its presence. Pieces of wood leaned against the wall.

I nodded toward my workshop and the many jobs waiting there. "Yes, we have been blessed. I am busier than I was in Nazareth. This has become our home."

For a moment I thought of the small sack of coins accumulating in the trunk. Someday I planned to build Mary a real house. It would be larger than my uncle's, as befitted the residence of Messiah.

Soon my friends took their leave. When I returned to the house, Perez was playing with Jeshua. One the floor the man and boy rolled a toy cart between them until the child tired of the game. He crawled away to tug at his mother's skirts. She did not immediately respond and he set up a wail. Immediately Rachel scooped the baby off the floor. She selected a sweetmeat from the platter.

"There, there, here is a treat for this fine boy."

"Aunt," both Mary and I protested together.

"It is a special day. Jeshua deserves something special. Don't you?"

"You never allow me to have sweetmeats," Elam complained.

Perez shrugged and tousled his son's hair. "Jeshua will only have this birthday once. I am sure you had treats when we celebrated your first birthday."

Then he turned his attention to the birthday boy. A small morsel of honeyed fruit was selected for the child. Happily the baby devoured it. Before Rachel and Perez left, Jeshua was sticky from head to foot. When the shadows lengthened, Perez returned the boy to his mother.

"It is growing dark. Come wife, we will return to our home. I have packing to do for I must travel to Jerusalem after the Sabbath."

After many kisses for Jeshua and a hug for Mary, Rachel followed her husband. Staring after my kin, I could only shake my head.

"They mean well," I sighed.

When I picked up my son sticky hands tangled themselves in my beard. Mary moistened a cloth in the basin of water near the door.

Shaking her head over the messy face that squirmed away from the damp cloth, she smiled. "They look on him as a grandson. Your cousins have not yet found wives. It is a great sorrow for Rachel."

"Elam is too young."

"True, but Uriah and Nathaniel are of an age to find brides. It will be hard to find a husband for poor Hannah because of her squint. There you are. Come along, my son, it is time for bed."

My wife held out her arms. Jeshua fussed while Mary changed his clothes. Only when she offered her breast did he quiet. Very soon the child slept, worn out from the excitement of the day.

Mary cuddled against me when we sought our bed. I kissed her soft hair and then her lips. Every time I held my wife, I gave thanks to God. After our lovemaking, we fell asleep in each other's arms like newlyweds.

Only a few brief weeks later everything changed.

"Elam, Elam, come and see!" shouted Ezra as he came running into the shop. "There are kings on camels coming toward Bethlehem!"

My young assistant's eyes grew huge with astonishment.

I stopped my work to frown at the tale. "Camels and kings?"

My question was answered with vigorous nods.

Ezra tugged Elam's arm. "Yes! Three camels with kings riding them! There are guards, too. It is a whole caravan! Come and see."

"Go on, see the grand sight." I waved the boys away with a smile.

For a moment, I was tempted to follow them. However, there was much work to finish. The plow lying on the workbench was urgently needed by Omrah for his fields. Dismissing the kings and their retinue from my mind, I bent to the task. I had just finished the repair and was leaning the plow against the wall when Elam returned.

"Joseph…" He sounded almost fearful, but underneath was a hint of excitement.

"Yes." I turned to face the boy who stood just inside the door.

My cousin glanced back outside, swallowing nervously. Dirty fingers twisted his rope belt. Elam looked over his shoulder.

"The kings…they…I…"

Concerned by the uncharacteristic behavior, I moved toward the boy. "What is it?"

"They want to see Jeshua!" He blurted.

My breath felt suspended. Surprise was followed by anger and then amazement was erased by fear.

"They are waiting in the street," Elam added.

I swallowed the dread in my throat and straightened my back. For a moment I turned away.

A prayer left my lips on a whisper of air, "God of the Universe, protect my son."

Turning back, I saw the anxiety in Elam's face. Gripping the boy's shoulder, I smiled and nodded before striding into the courtyard. "All will be well."

Beyond my gate were indeed three richly saddled camels. Servants held the ropes and well-armed guards stood at attention. Beyond them all of Bethlehem, it seemed, was arrayed. A buzz of speculation rose from the populace. At my appearance, three figures stepped forward.

"They *are* kings," I whispered in awe to Elam.

His wide eyes were looking at me, not my visitors. I know he wondered how I would greet such regal guests. In desperation I fell back on an old nomadic greeting my father taught me long ago. The salaam I greeted the kings with was low and subservient.

"Welcome, my lords, to your servant's humble home. You honor your servant by your presence. May the Living God bless you."

One king answered in heavily accented Hebrew. "It is we who are honored. We have come from Syria to pay homage to the one born King of the Jews."

Elam's gasp spoke volumes. The crowd seemed to be holding its breath. I felt my throat tighten in fear.

Cautiously I responded, "Surely a king is born in a palace."

A younger king stepped forward. "So we thought. May God forgive our foolishness. The Lord who created all things does not act as man expects."

"That is true." The first visitor seemed to be addressing his companion and a look of impatience crossed the aged face before he turned to me. "We are not royalty as you suppose."

I tilted my head in confusion and my gaze traveled to the retinue in the street.

"We are Magi," the man elaborated. "For centuries our brotherhood has studied the stars. Their courses and alignment tell us of great events before they happen."

"Yes, I have heard of such things," I nodded. "My father told me long ago about the sages of the East."

"A son of the captive Israelites in Babylon was trained in our schools. We called him Belteshazzar. You know him as Daniel. His actions brought him favor with Nebuchadnezzar, king of Babylon."

"God saved him from the lions decreed against him," the impetuous young Magi interrupted.

"Caspar!"

He lowered his head in obeisance when the leader swung around with irritation visible on his face. "Forgive me, my father."

"My brother Magi is over-eager. He will learn patience with age," the third member of the trio spoke in defense.

"Balthazar, what you say is true." The older man bowed slightly in agreement before turning back to me. "Our studies foretold the rise and fall of Alexander of Macedonia. In the spring of last year a new star appeared in the constellation of the lion. Such an unexpected event could only mean a great one would be born into the house of Judah. A king to rule Israel, greater than David has surely been foretold even by your own prophets. The one you call Daniel himself shared the wisdom of such prophecy with his fellow Magi."

When I did not respond, the man called Balthazar stepped forward. "Do not be afraid. We do not come to harm the child."

His words did not reassure me. I realized that Elam was holding my hand, whether from fear or as reassurance I was not sure. My eyes traveled from the face of the speaker to the young man, Caspar. His eager and open expression was comforting.

"We seek to honor the child," he insisted softly.

My head swiveled to look at the spokesman. His nod indicated Elam. "The boy told us that the only unusual birth recently was your son."

My cousin tried to hide behind me when attention shifted to him.

"I am sorry, Joseph," he whispered in a contrite tone.

There was no evil or malice in any of these men, I decided.

"It is all right, Elam," I reassured the boy. Bowing again to the Magi, I explained, "my son was born in a stable because we were visitors newly arrived for the census of Rome. If that is unusual and what you seek…"

Almost, I hoped that the men would be disappointed and leave.

"I think there was more than that," Caspar stepped forward and looked at me. "The hand of God is upon you, Joseph of Nazareth. I can see it in your eyes. The child is of the One True God. The star we saw rising has led us here."

This time no one silenced him. I could only stare at the men.

"You fear for the safety of your child. In this you are wise. There are those who would harm any perceived threat to their power."

"Herod," I barely breathed the name.

The nod from three heads was unnecessary. Fear gripped me. The king had spies everywhere. Such a visit to a humble carpenter would not go unnoticed. Sensing my disquiet, the leader of the Magi snapped his fingers. A servant ran forward to kneel. He issued an order in a foreign tongue. Immediately the man hurried back to the retinue. Everyone moved up the street toward the outskirts of Bethlehem. In a few moments the street was empty. The crowd trailed after the camels and guards to see the show. There was silence. I could hear my heart beating in my ears. Awe of the Magi and greater fear of Herod held me tightly.

"May we see the child?" Humbly the oldest man made his request.

My heart was torn. I glanced toward the small home where Mary and Jeshua were safely out of sight. Then I looked back at the Magi who were waiting for my decision. The hope in their eyes convinced me of their honesty even before Balthazar spoke.

"Your son will be a light to all nations. That is why the star has burst forth in the heavens."

I remembered Simeon's words in the Temple and nodded assent. "Follow me."

Almost on tiptoe the three men fell into line. I was not surprised to find that Mary had food and wine waiting on a small table just inside the doorway. I offered water to our guests. Each man rinsed his hand in acceptance of my hospitality. We broke bread and shared a cup of wine before I drew back the curtain separating the entry from the main room. Mary looked up from her play with Jeshua.

"We have visitors."

"Yes, my husband." She inclined her head.

As propriety demanded she had her veil draped across her lower face. Her eyes turned apprehensive when she looked at the three men who came forward to kneel in the center of the small room.

"I am Melchior." The spokesman introduced himself. "We are Magi come from Syria to honor the birth of the One sent by the Living God as a Light for all nations."

He drew a gold box from the folds of his robe. Bowing until his forehead touched the dirt floor he lifted the gift in homage before placing it at Mary's feet.

"I bring gold to honor the King."

Elam gasped and Mary's eyes opened very wide when he lifted the lid. Gold coins glistened in the afternoon light. Jeshua cooed and reached for the shiny objects. Melchior smiled, satisfied that his offering was accepted.

"I am Balthazar." The man placed a second small casket on the floor and prostrated himself before lifting the jeweled lid. Frankincense scented the air. "Here is incense for the Priest born to make restitution with the One God and return harmony to the world."

Jeshua sneezed and everyone laughed, nervousness forgotten momentarily. From his robe, Caspar brought out a sealed alabaster jar of purest white.

He spoke softly looking directly at Mary with pity in his eyes. "I am Caspar, youngest of the Magi. My gift is myrrh, the most precious of all oils. A sacrifice will be required."

My heart stood still in agony when I thought of the symbolism. Myrrh, the priceless oil used to anoint kings at their crowning and at their burial was only for priests to use. Mary stared intently at the young man. Tears stood in her eyes and I remembered Simeon's pronouncement a year earlier, 'A sword will pierce your soul'.

The almost oppressive silence was broken when the child squirmed out of his mother's arms to toddle over to the three gifts. He selected a coin then dropped it to touch the bright jewels. When he reached for the alabaster jar, I scooped it out of his reach.

"My lords, I have food prepared." Mary gestured gracefully to the low table none of us noticed when we came in.

A simple offering of fresh bread, fruit, and sliced mutton was set out. I bowed my guests toward their meal.

The men were delighted to find that Jeshua and his mother remained in the room. The child toddled from one man to the next. His bright eyes and ready smile enchanted them. Melchior fashioned a toy from a piece of papyrus he found in his robe. Caspar gave my son his medallion and Balthazar produced balls from thin air to delight us all.

Eventually the baby grew tired and fretful. Mary picked him up despite loud protests from the child. My face flushed with embarrassment at Jeshua's cries and struggles.

Melchior chuckled. "All children hate to leave a party. I have seen my sons do the same thing."

He rose. Balthazar and Caspar also got to their feet.

Ruefully Melchior shook his head and announced, "Night has fallen. We must leave your hospitality and seek our camp. Before dawn we will be gone. Our visit may linger in the legend of the town. For that I am sorry. Yet we have seen the Savior of the world."

I smiled when the man gave a contented sigh.

"Blessings on your house, Joseph, carpenter of Nazareth," he continued. "May your son grow and prosper in the knowledge of the One Living and True God. The Jews brought teaching of the God of Abraham, Isaac, and Jacob to Babylon. Those of us who have kept the wisdom have been blessed to see the rising of the Redeemer."

Balthazar bowed low to me. "Thank you, Joseph for your welcome. We followed the sign from God to your door. See the star is setting." I looked in the direction the man pointed. Low and brilliant in the dark sky hung a star unnoticed before. "Now we have seen the child for ourselves and can return to our home in peace."

After another low bow, the man joined Melchior by the gate. Caspar lingered at my side. He seemed to be deciding whether or not to speak.

At last he nodded decisively. "We may have brought danger with us." The young man lowered his head almost in shame. Guiltily he glanced toward his comrades.

I waited, wondering what the man meant.

"When we reached the border of Judea clouds hid the star from us. We argued." He rubbed his brow in distress. "I insisted that the one we sought would be a prince and must be found in Jerusalem in the royal palace."

I felt my heart lurch.

Slowly he confessed, "Despite their wise counsel to wait for the clouds to clear and follow the star, I insisted on proceeding to the capital. 'Where else would a prince of the house of David be born?' My foolish words will haunt me forever." Looking toward his waiting companions, the young man seemed to draw courage. "We reached Herod's palace. 'Where is he that is born King of the Jews?' My question sent courtiers scurrying, I must admit. We were ushered into the king's throne room. In that moment I knew how wrong I had been. We were in the presence of sheer evil. Herod questioned us closely."

The man paused to remove his turban and run fingers through thick curls. Then he stood turning the head covering in his hands.

Caspar's eyes begged for understanding when he raised them to mine. "After a while the king pretended to be interested in our talk of a promised redeemer. He sent for several of the priests and scribes. One old man had an immediate answer to the question 'Where will Messiah be born?' He quoted one of your prophets and named Bethlehem. Herod turned to us then, 'Behold your answer, Magi. Seek for this child and bring me word that I may worship him.' He does not plan homage but harm."

Some inarticulate sound came from my throat.

"We will not return to Herod," the young Magi assured me, "but that may not do anything more than delay the king slightly."

"Yes." The strangled word barely sounded like my voice. "Thank you."

"May the One God who is Light protect you and your family."

Caspar bowed low to me. The last I saw of the Magi was three shadows moving up the street behind Elam. I stared for a long time at the glowing star low on the horizon. My mind refused to concentrate.

'We went to the palace.'

'There are those who would harm any perceived threat.'

'He does not plan worship but harm.'

'We may have brought danger with us.'

All of Caspar's warnings rang over and over as I watched the star disappear. When the night sky was normal again, I turned to the house. Mary slept soundly, secure in her innocence. I lay stiffly beside my wife. Caspar's words still replayed in my soul. Finally, I must have slept. Into my fitful dream came the figure of light I had seen two years earlier on a hill outside Nazareth. This time the voice commanded rather than comforted.

"Joseph, son of David, get up now! Take the child and his mother. Go to Egypt. Remain there until I send for you."

Then the presence was gone. I sat up straight on the mat. Gently but urgently, I awakened Mary with a touch and kiss of apology.

"Mary, we must leave."

Drowsily she stirred and opened dark eyes. "Leave? What do you mean? Are we going home to Nazareth?"

The slight eagerness in her last question struck me with the realization that my beloved was homesick.

Sadly I shook my head. "No, I am sorry. It would not be safe."

I was already gathering clothing and blankets. Sensing my urgency, Mary scrambled to her feet. She removed a bundled blanket from my inept hands and folding it neatly.

"Get Balaam ready and your tools."

I slid my carpenter's tools into the carrying bag quickly. Balaam complained by tossing his head and grunting when I led the donkey from his pen. The animal snorted in disgust when I cinched a saddle on his back. Mary had a bag of food and a second bag with clothing and blankets already packed. Hurriedly I strapped them onto the back of the saddle.

I heard a muffled sniff from my wife when she turned back to the house. In two strides I was beside the woman.

"I am sorry." My arm slipped around her waist. Desperately I tried to soothe her sorrow. "We dare not stay. An angel came…"

Her finger on my lips interrupted my babbling. A quavering sigh completed her thought, "I understand. It's just…"

In the fading moonlight I saw tears on her lashes. My eyes grew damp at the young woman's distress.

"We will return, someday," I promised.

Gently Mary stroked my cheek. "As God wills. I will get Jeshua."

The slender figure slipped out of my embrace, returning a moment later with the baby in her arms. Together we stood in the doorway staring into the home we had made together. I wanted to linger, to pretend that we were a normal couple. It was Mary who tugged my arm and urged me from the house.

Balaam waited, head drooping to the ground as he dozed, unaffected by the human emotions tormenting me. Gently I settled my wife and child on the animal's back. Then we slipped out the gate and through the quiet streets. Not even a dog barked at our passing. The eerie silence made me hurry faster. At the edge of the city, I looked back. To the north and east I caught a brief glimpse of a camel silhouetted against the stars. The Magi, too, were on the move.

"God be with them, and protect us."

By the time the sun rose to awaken Bethlehem we were halfway to Tekoa on the road to Hebron. I was grateful that we passed the fortress of Herodium in the dark even though the edifice was not on the trail we followed.

In the shade of a cluster of trees I finally stopped. Stiffly, Mary slid to the ground. Together we fixed a brief meal of flatbread covered with goat cheese. Jeshua explored the area, discovering fascinating rocks and twigs, which found their way into his mouth. Mary wiped the dirty little face with the corner of her veil before giving the boy a piece of bread. Balaam found a patch of grass, which he happily devoured. Then we set out again.

My wife shook her head when I offered to lift her onto the donkey. "I will walk for awhile. Give the poor beast a rest from carrying so much."

We took turns carrying Jeshua or letting him balance on Balaam's back.

"Where are we going?" Mary asked finally.

"Mary, I am sorry. We must leave Judea and go to Egypt."

"Oh, so far?" Her face mirrored my emotions of fear and sorrow.

I sought to console my wife. "The angel that came to me in my dream ordered us to go to Egypt and wait until God says it is safe to return."

"God will not fail us." The woman nodded slowly, almost as if convincing herself.

Jeshua wiggled in his mother's arms and pointed to the ground. Mary put him down. The boy toddled a short distance before plopping down to play in the dust. I drew my wife close.

"It will be all right. This is God's plan."

With her arms around my waist, Mary leaned against me for a long time. I rubbed her back and watched the child in his play.

"God of Abraham, Isaac, and Jacob, you protected your servants in their wanderings, be with us now as we follow their footsteps to Egypt."

My prayer was spoken softly, but Mary heard and lifted her head.

"I will not be afraid. God walked with Abraham, Isaac, and Jacob. How much more will the Living One be with us? Come, Jeshua, my son, we have far to go. You will see great wonders."

The young woman left the security of my arms to pick up the child. As a family we faced south and started down the deserted road. It was not until midday that I realized that the reason we saw so few travelers on the road was that it was the Sabbath and travel was forbidden. I was grateful for the solitude although I could not suppress the twinge of guilt at breaking the commandment.

"God's angel ordered it," I reminded my conscience. "There is no one to report our passing this way."

By the end of the day we had passed Hebron. By keeping to the hills we skirted the town like outlaws. The sun was setting when I dragged Balaam up the last incline and we could look west to the sea. To the south I saw a Bedouin encampment and turned the donkey toward it.

"Pray that the desert welcome extends to fugitive Jews," I muttered to myself.

CHAPTER 17

I saw a child race away to announce our approach. An old man, who could only be the sheik, stepped out of the largest tent. I stood beside Balaam at the edge of the camp. Happy to stop, the donkey lowered his head and sniffed hopefully for some stray grass or hay. Mary sagged in the saddle almost too weary to raise her head at the man's approach.

"Peace to you, Sheik," I addressed the man with a low salaam.

His answer was bowed in return. "Peace to you, Stranger."

The sheik took in our dusty appearance and obvious exhaustion. I saw compassion enter the old man's eyes as he looked at Mary and the child she held.

"You have traveled far. Come and rest in my tents. Let it not be said that Sheik Abram bar Esau turns away any weary traveler."

"I am Joseph the Carpenter and this is my family. We are honored by your hospitality, great Sheik. Your kindness to the poor and homeless will be rewarded."

Bowing slightly with a hand on my heart I made the expected response. If the chieftain noticed that I did not designate lineage or home, he was too courteous to comment. With a clap of his tanned hands our host summoned servants.

"Come then. Ishmael, take the donkey and see that he is fed." He did not even watch to see if his order was followed. Carefully not looking directly at my wife the sheik gestured to a young woman who hurried to his side. "Dinah will see to the needs of your family."

With a glance at me, Mary followed her escort across the camp.

"Caleb, see that a kid is prepared for our guest." His final order sent a young man running toward the flocks not far away. With a friendly hand on my shoulder, the sheik escorted me to his dwelling. "Joseph, come, enter my humble tent."

A servant stood waiting, stiffly holding a bowl and pitcher of water. Gratefully I splashed the cool liquid on face and hands.

"Greatest of Sheiks, your kindness is beyond that of kings." I bowed ceremoniously toward my host as he gestured toward a comfortable mound of pillows on the floor of his tent.

With a sigh of contentment, I seated myself. At a snap of his fingers, a procession of servants appeared, bearing pitchers of wine and platters of bread.

"Blessed be God who gives us the fruit of the vine and grain from the fields," The sheik intoned a brief blessing before handing me a goblet. The man grinned at my surprised expression. "We may not worship at the Temple, but we are closer to the God of Abraham than many who do."

"Forgive me. You are right. It is not the Temple but the heart that determines true faith."

It was Abram's turn to look surprised. "What manner of Jew are you to say such things?"

"Only a humble carpenter," I replied carefully. Thinking of Jediah and Barach, I added, "I have seen greater faith in the offering of a shepherd than the actions of a rabbi."

"Each man's path to God is determined by God," the old man agreed.

We sat quietly enjoying the delicious food. I was impressed by the quantity of the feast prepared for chance visitors. The fine workmanship of the pottery and wood utensils, prosperity of the camp, and size of the flocks proclaimed the wealth of my host. Despite the mountain of food, the man motioned to the servants bearing in more trays of food.

"Here is freshly roasted mutton. My sons will join us, now."

Three young men entered. The eldest, tall and serious with a thin string of a beard, which he stroked incessantly, was introduced as Ezra. Next in line was Onan. He was a younger image of his father with the same intelligent eyes and thick hair, although his was black and not sprinkled with gray. Abram introduced a jovial young man barely sprouting a beard. His short, round body and perpetual enthusiasm made him seem to bounce when he talked.

"This is my youngest son, Abner."

"I am Joseph the Carpenter." Bowing with my hand to forehead and heart I greeted the men.

"Joseph has traveled far this day and is welcome in our tents," the sheik stated briefly.

Abram reached for the meat, signaling the start of the meal. Perhaps the man hoped I would give further explanation. Instead I took a bite of the food.

"Mighty Sheik, this is a grand feast. The mutton is so tender it melts in your mouth."

"You are most kind. My flocks have prospered this season. There has been rain enough and plentiful grazing."

The rest of the meal was occupied with discussion of the merits of Bedouin grazing practices. Abram was quite critical of the habit of pasturing flocks conveniently near towns.

"As you are not a shepherd," he apologized, "you no doubt cannot understand the problems of such a practice."

Then he proceeded to elaborate. Ezra and Onan added comments until I was dizzy. Only Abner remained silent. I tried to ignore the curious looks he directed my way. I found myself stifling a yawn, only realizing how tired I was when my hunger was satisfied.

"I know nothing except what I have observed. It is true that I have never feasted on meat as fine as this. You are gracious in your hospitality Sheik of the Nabatea."

"I do what I can and the One God gives the increase." The sheik tried to sound humble, although his satisfied grin told me he was pleased with the compliment.

Ezra and Onan stood up. Abner followed slowly.

As if he could no longer restrain himself, the question I dreaded burst from the young man. "Tell me how it is that you, a Jew, are traveling on the Sabbath. You must have urgent business to break the Law."

His father frowned. I was silent, searching for an answer. The sheik and his sons would not understand an angel's command, I felt certain.

A portion of the truth might satisfy the man. "We are sent to Egypt."

I astonished when my host reared to his feet angrily. "Egypt? Who is your master to send a man with his wife and son on such a journey? Abner, you should not inquire into such things."

I was bewildered by the Bedouin's rage until I realized it was directed at his son on my behalf.

"It is necessary." I sought to defuse the tension with the simply stated truth.

"We should not interfere in your business. Forgive my son's presumption." The old man frowned again at his son.

Abner lowered his head in chagrin. "Sir, I meant no harm. As my father says, it is your business and I should never have inquired. Forgive me."

I took pity on the embarrassment evident on the round face. "It is an honest question. My journey could not wait another day."

Abner flashed a broad smile of relief before following his brothers out of the tent.

"My friend, I beg you will not hold my son's impetuosity against him. He is young and thoughtless."

"Great sheik, the only thing your son is guilty of is a curious heart. I have taken no injury."

Somewhat mollified the old man grunted and nodded, although he still frowned.

Servants quietly began to remove the empty platters. My host stood with me at the entrance to his tent. The flap was pulled back to allow the cooler evening breezes in. Stars glittered in the desert sky. I thought briefly of the Magi and their strange star.

"You have a long journey ahead of you."

"Yes, I hope to join a caravan at Gaza. We will need someone who knows the water holes and the route."

"Hmmm…" The man gazed off into the distance lost in thought.

I smothered another yawn and wondered what my host was thinking. His next words drove sleep from my mind.

"Most of the traders will have already left for the Black Land."

"God will provide." I tried to sound more confident than I felt.

"Caravan leaders will charge you to join," Abram added, to my dismay.

"I have some money," I admitted cautiously. "My carpentry work has prospered."

"You planned to save the coin for Egypt," my host guessed without looking at me.

I nodded with a slight incline of my head.

"I may have a suggestion which may solve both your needs and my concerns." When I did not respond immediately, he elaborated. "You have met my youngest son. Abner is a likable boy. However, the boy tends to speak before he thinks. You have seen that. Certainly he is always good humored and no one can stay angry with him for long. However, compared to Ezra and Onan the boy has no common sense. He would as easily give away a horse as sell it for a fair price."

"Yes?" My brow furrowed in confusion.

"I am sending Abner to Alexandria with a load of fine wool rugs and several horses to trade."

"I still do not understand..." I stared at my host with a bewildered frown.

"If you travel with him, perhaps my son would listen to wisdom from a stranger. He appears to ignore everything his brothers and I tell him." Although he sounded exasperated, the father's concern and love were evident. "I do not want him to fail on this first expedition."

It only seemed fair to point out the obvious. "I am a carpenter, not a merchant."

"A successful businessman, be he carpenter or merchant uses the same skills. Joseph the Carpenter, you are wise in the ways of the market. No one who owns a donkey and such tools as I glimpsed is without knowledge of the secrets of trading."

His compliment was accompanied by a slap on the shoulder. He gestured toward the nearby sleeping tent.

"Come, my friend, we do not have to make a decision tonight. Let us seek our blankets and talk more in the morning. Think on what I said. Perhaps the True God has provided your solution."

"Abram, Sheik of the Nabatea, thank you for your hospitality. I shall indeed think on your words."

We bowed slightly in farewell and I entered the tent. It did not surprise me that several, already snoring men occupied the space. The servants of the sheik did not stir as I searched for a spot. Mary was safely asleep in the women's tent because Bedouin men and women slept separately. I found an available blanket and rolled up in it. Sleep was far from me when I lay down. I missed my wife's comfortable softness and Jeshua's nearby baby noises.

I considered Abram's proposal. "Traveling to Egypt with the son of a great sheik will give us the protection and anonymity we need. The young man is obviously curious about our mission yet I do not think he will question me further," I mused. “The sheik’s concern for his youngest son has touched my heart. It could be the perfect solution.”

I decided to accept the offer and fell into a short-lived sleep. The stirring of my companions at sunrise awakened me. Stretching on my pallet of skins and blankets I sat up. A few curious glances came my way but mostly the other men just yawned, scratched, and stumbled out to greet the day. Abner’s cheerful round face peered in.

The young man grinned happily when he saw me. “You are awake! Father bid me take you to see your wife, if you want, before we eat.”

The thoughtful offer was welcome. Abram must have seen my longing glance toward the women’s area the night before. Scrambling to my feet, I donned my turban and followed my young guide.

“Thank you.”

“Why is it you have only one wife?” The potentially rude question was obviously asked out of curiosity not malice.

I shrugged, “It is the Jewish way.”

For a second the young man frowned, then he nodded and grinned. “Then it is good.”

I was not sure what my guide meant but seeing Mary I hurried forward. Conscious of many eyes I only gave her a brief hug and light kiss.

“Did you sleep well?”

We asked the question simultaneously.

I had to smile when my wife blushed and admitted softly, “I missed you beside me.”

“And I you.” My whispered response made her face grow even rosier.

Turning away she held out her hand to Jeshua.

He toddled over and lifted chubby arms to me. “Abba.”

The child’s newly learned word made me gasp in astonishment. The nearby women tittered behind their veils at my expression. Mary laughed in delight. For a moment my family was an island in the midst of the bustle of the awakening Bedouin camp. I held both wife and son secure. The boy babbled his new word happily and tugged my beard.

"All is well?" Abram's booming voice brought me back to reality.

Mary stepped back and covered her face.

"Abba," Jeshua repeated as I gave him a kiss and lowered the wiggling child to the ground.

"Go to your mother."

"Abba," he insisted, holding my leg.

"Abba must go, my son. Stay with Mama."

"Jeshua, come and see the lamb." Mary's promise attracted the boy and he toddled to her.

I could not stop my proud boast, "He just learned to say 'Abba'."

"I remember how that was with my first. Makes you feel like you can do anything, does not it?" The sheik grinned and clapped me around the shoulder. "There is nothing to compare with your own flesh and blood calling you 'Abba!'"

We reached his tent in a few steps.

"My sons are with the horses, picking which ones to send to Egypt. Have you considered my suggestion?" The sheik peered at me out of the corner of his eye while slathering rich camel cheese on a piece of fresh bread.

"Yes, your generosity is greater than I can hope to repay."

"Then you will accompany Abner? You will see him safely to the markets at Alexandria?"

"If my meager skills can be of any use, I am at your service Sheik of the Nabatea."

The man settled back with relief. He gazed steadily at me. "It is good. My heart can be at ease. The God of Abraham will be with you. You will leave after the coming Sabbath. By then the preparations will be complete."

"So long?"

Abram raised his eyebrows when my question slipped out. "It is less than six days. Surely your business can wait that long. You might have to wait even longer in Gaza."

"Forgive my impatience, Great Sheik. Your wisdom is greater than mine."

Good humor restored, the man stood up. "It is settled then. Come, we will tell my son the news."

We strode across the camp. His three sons and several servants were gently coaxing certain of the horses into a rope and wood enclosure not far from the camp. Three horses already pranced impatiently inside the ropes. The men worked on foot and with great patience.

"It becomes too great a contest if the men are mounted," the sheik explained. "Watch how Abner handles the horses."

The high spirited beasts seemed to be playing with the humans. As I watched, a handsome mare allowed herself to be urged by hands and voice almost to the pen. Then with a toss of her black mane, she spun away. The animal did not go far, but seemed to be waiting for Abner to circle around to start the process again. Finally, she consented to enter the enclosure. Only then did Abner acknowledge our presence.

"My father and honored guest, we are gathering the horses to take to Alexandria for sale."

"Fine animals," I murmured appreciatively.

Although I knew little about horses, I could enjoy the obvious breeding, beauty and strength of the sheik's herd.

"Few and poor," the sheik insisted modestly. "Likely they will bring but small profit."

"Surely, my host, such fine animals will sell for many pieces of gold. Abner will find rich patrons to purchase such well-bred and handsome beasts."

Abram looked at the young man. "Joseph the Carpenter will be traveling with you to Egypt."

"Wonderful!" The young man replied cheerfully.

"He will help you in Alexandria. His experience and wisdom are greater than yours. Truly, with your assistance, my son will not utterly fail."

"I welcome your guidance, Joseph the Carpenter." The slightly hurt expression that crossed Abner's broad face at his father's insinuation was quickly gone. "My father is right, I have no knowledge of trading. Your company will be welcome."

With that, the young man returned to the task of choosing the horses for the journey.

"He has the instinct to know which animal is best for a desert trek," admitted Abram. "Abner can tame the wildest of animals. It is with business matters that he is ignorant and gullible."

"Surely such a gift with animals is rare and a God-given talent," I suggested.

My opinion was greeted with a grudging nod. Then my host motioned heavenward.

"The sun is rising high. I will retire to my tents. Later, we will visit my flocks. They are kept on the other side of the camp."

For a little longer I watched the sons of the sheik work among the horses. Despite his size, Abner was quick on his feet. As his father said he seemed to know just how to approach each animal. Then his brothers and servants would help urge the horse into the pen. When the men paused for water, I wandered back to the camp.

Mary hurried to meet me. "Joseph, when do we leave?"

"My wife, all is well." My hearty assurance did not erase the frown of concern from her face. I slid my hand around the slender waist and drew the woman close. "We will leave after the Sabbath."

"So long?" Mary interrupted me with my own words.

"God has provided a way for safe travel into Egypt. All will be well."

The woman stepped away. My wife faced me with hands on hips and a stern look.

"Tell me," she ordered.

"Sheik Abram is sending his son on a trading trip to Alexandria. In exchange for my knowledge of trading, we will accompany Abner and travel in the security of the caravan."

"Knowledge of trading?" The slight lift in Mary's voice told me she doubted my marketing skills.

I shrugged sheepishly, "I tried to explain that I am but a humble carpenter."

"Will we be safe here until then?"

As much to reassure myself as Mary, I nodded firmly, "God will not remove his protection."

Suddenly the young woman smiled, "How foolish of me to doubt. The One who is manifest in Jeshua will not desert his son."

At her faith-filled words, I glanced around. We were alone some distance from the tents. I had not realized we had walked so far. Seeing my look, Mary took my arm.

"Your son," she amended. "In the eyes of the world and by the Law of Moses, Jeshua is your son for you have named him so. For that I would love you, even if I had not already adored you."

I could not resist a kiss on her upturned face. My lips found hers. Worries and the desert receded. After a minute I drew back, slightly embarrassed lest we be noticed. We were still alone.

"We should return to the camp. Jeshua will miss you," I said, turning back toward the tents.

Mary stumbled a little in the sand and I swept her up into my arms.

"I am not hurt!" The woman giggled when I tightened my grip to carry her the remainder of the distance to the tents of the women.

Their chatter stilled at my arrival.

"I am fine." The girl called out, laughing. "My husband wants to impress me with his strength.

A ripple of laughter answered her. The oldest woman present stepped forward to look searchingly at me.

"You are a good man. This is a strong woman. She will bear you many sons. May your name live long, Joseph the Carpenter."

Unsure how to respond to such a statement, I stood holding my wife until she slipped from my arms. Jeshua toddled forward and held out his arms to me.

"Abba."

I caught the boy to my heart, delighted by his trusting embrace.

CHAPTER 18

The next few days were busy. Abram's sons chose fine horses for the Egyptian market. Elaborate rugs made on the women's looms were rolled in preparation for the journey and bales of soft wool were wrapped in coarse material. Food, saddles and tents were added to the supplies.

I saw my wife and child only briefly each morning and evening when I accompanied my host to the women's tents. Mary seemed content to wait and we had little time for discussion.

Early on the sixth day I stood with Onan while he oversaw the final preparations.

"It is a propitious time to begin a journey," he commented. "This Sabbath we will offer prayers for the journey."

I nodded in agreement. The faith of the desert tribesmen was not so different from my own. As the sun descended and the Sabbath began, I pulled my prayer shawl up over my head and faced north toward Jerusalem. Shutting out the nearby bustle, I committed myself to the future.

"God of my Fathers, send your protection on our travel and your blessing on Sheik Abram. In his kindness he has provided safety for your son. Bring us to Egypt to await your will."

Abram courteously allowed me time for my prayers. Only after I removed the prayer shawl from my head did he step forward and join me.

"It is good to remember the command of God. Tonight you will join us in our festival. From the time of Father Abraham, we have celebrated the longest day as a time of new blessings. Betrothals are announced and marriages consummated. That it falls on the Sabbath and the eve of a journey is especially significant."

We had a grand feast that night. A calf and a kid had been roasting all day on the spit. The young women danced and everyone clapped. Across the fire, I smiled at Mary. Like me, she sat amazed at the tambourines and bells the women used as they danced. It was late when the tribe sought their beds. Newly betrothed couples watched enviously as husbands and wives strolled to the tents together. A full moon lent light to the warm night.

"Joseph." Abram stopped me before I sought my bed.

His serious expression made me instantly alert. Mary caught my arm, sensing the change in tone. We were alone near the fire. Servants finished banking the coals for the night and hurried off to their own beds. One remained behind.

"Ishi has just returned from Jerusalem. I thought you would want to hear what he learned there." The old man gestured to the young man waiting in the shadows.

The stocky servant stepped forward and bowed in our direction. "My master sent me to the capital when the moon was new. In Jerusalem I heard rumors of a dreadful thing done by Herod."

Mary's grip tightened on my arm.

Through suddenly dry lips, I croaked, "What did you hear?"

"It was so awful that I doubted my ears. No one could do such a thing. I had to see for myself."

Impatiently I waited, hoping no one could see my fear. The speaker peered at me, trying to see in the deepening darkness.

"My master tells me that you came from Judea recently," he stated.

"Yes."

I slid one arm around my wife. She was trembling.

"Perhaps you heard of the kings from Syria who visited Herod. Jerusalem was still talking about the news when I arrived. Three grand men traveling with a great retinue went to Bethlehem after they left the capital. Then they vanished without a trace. That would have been a Sabbath ago."

"Tell my guest what you told me," gruffly Abram interrupted.

"It was whispered that Herod was livid with his spies for allowing the kings to slip out of the country. It was said that the men died for their failure. That was bad enough, but the rest…" The man passed a shaking hand over his brow.

"Go on." My voice was harsh with dread.

"I heard the rumors of tragedy and took my journey through Bethlehem on my return. There is great mourning in the city of David. What I heard was true. It is awful."

Mary stifled a gasp behind her hand. Ishi paused to regain control of his voice. Again he rubbed his forehead.

Taking a deep breath the man finished in a low, cracked voice, "Herod ordered the slaughter of every boy in the town two years old and younger. There is not a household unaffected. The silence in the streets is only broken by sobbing. There are so many new graves."

My wife would have fallen if I had not been holding her. Her wail of sorrow was buried in my robe.

"God have mercy," I cried out. Tears ran down my cheeks. Too well I remembered toddling children in the streets and the babies in their mother's arms. Brokenly I recited a line from scripture, "A voice in Ramah, Rachel weeping for her children, but they were no more."

Mary clung to me and wept desperately.

"Tell them what else you heard," my host ordered sternly.

"The rabbi told me that the kings had visited a carpenter recently arrived from Nazareth. The man and his family were thought to have gone with the kings for they vanished the same night with their son. The rabbi claimed the carpenter had cursed Bethlehem and brought Herod's vengeance on them all."

I was aghast that Barach would have said such a thing. "God have mercy," I repeated.

Abram dismissed the messenger with a nod. He gestured us into his tent. The moon cast light into the dimness when he tied back the flap.

"Joseph the Carpenter, I do not ask why the king of the Jews would massacre children or why you flee ahead of him. You are under my protection," the sheik assured us. "Herod's arm does not reach this far. Tomorrow, as planned, you will start for Egypt. My people will forget that you were here. For now, rest and comfort your wife."

For a moment the man stood straight and proud, then he turned and left us. We were alone and clung to each other in sorrow too deep for words. Mary continued to weep until exhaustion claimed her.

All night I held my wife in my arms and silently raged at God. "How could you have allowed such a tragedy? Where were you when the soldiers of Herod struck down the innocent? What did Bethlehem do to deserve such grief?"

My questions received no answer. When the sky began to turn gray before dawn the camp stirred to life in preparation for our departure. Gently I awakened Mary. When she saw my haggard face, memories of Ishi's message brought tears to her eyes.

"Joseph, the One who gave us this child has not abandoned us." She touched my cheek tenderly. "We will be safe in Egypt and return to our home some day. I know that is true."

Amazed, I stared at my wife. "Where does such faith come from? My heart is still heavy from Ishi's news."

She sighed, "God weeps with the mothers and fathers in Bethlehem. It was nothing done or not done by our friends that caused the horror. A mad king, driven by fear lashed out to protect his power. The God of Abraham, Isaac, and Jacob will protect his own and bring us out of Egypt just as he led the Children of Israel to freedom ages ago."

"Why must the innocent suffer?" I whispered angrily.

Mary reached out and drew me into her arms. Tears ran down her cheeks. For a long time we wept together.

"My husband, who can know what will come of evil?"

"How can any good come from so many children…so much sorrow…?" I groaned.

"Joseph, I believe that the God who gives life can bless every circumstance and in the end bring good. Our father Jacob thought his son lost to him. Yet through the vicious betrayal of the favorite son, the world was saved from famine and a nation born."

"Beloved, I will pray that the One God can ease the sorrow of the parents of Bethlehem." Awed by the wisdom and faith of my wife, I held her tightly, wishing that I could feel as confident.

"Amen," she murmured against my cheek.

Abram cleared his throat to make us aware of his presence. We turned in simultaneously to look at our host. He inclined his head briefly. I saw understanding in the old man's eyes.

Rising to greet our host, I helped Mary to her feet and sent her to the women with a kiss on her forehead. "Get ready for our journey."

"Yes, I will get Jeshua."

The sheik did not say anything. With a heavy step I followed him to the fire. Despite my lack of appetite, I took the offered bread knowing that I would need strength for the travel ahead. After the rapidly eaten meal, I saddled Balaam and started loading my tools and our belongings on the donkey.

Onan approached me, gesturing to the tall beasts he led. "Here are camels for you and your wife. It will be easier for the donkey to keep pace if he is not heavily loaded."

Obediently I helped transfer our luggage to the waiting camels. My mind refused to function beyond obeying instructions. I kept replaying Ishi's words. Each time horror swept through me.

The sun was just cresting the horizon when we set out. Abram laid his hands on my shoulder in blessing and farewell. "May the God of Abraham bring you safely to Egypt."

"Abram, Sheik of the Nabatea, may the God of Abraham, Isaac, and Jacob bless you and reward you for your hospitality to the homeless and stranger."

We embraced as friends. The man turned to his son with another hug and blessing.

I lifted Mary onto her camel. She clung tightly to the saddle with one hand. The other held our son on her lap. The boy laughed with joy when the beast heaved to his feet. Clumsily I mounted my own camel. Abner was the last to join us. With a final wave at the camp, the young man led the way south away from the familiar and into the unknown.

It was an impressive caravan. One camel carried food supplies and several were loaded with the rugs and wool for sale. Balaam trotted among the horses. I was amazed to notice that only one of the horses wore a rope loosely looped to Abner's saddle. The rest followed her lead tamely. Ishi was among the armed servants on horses who completed our group. Their bright curved swords were reassuring.

"May the Living Lord be with us," I whispered my prayer into the breeze that met us.

Mary too, seemed to be praying. Jeshua dozed in her lap. We stopped in the heat of the day to rest the animals at a small water hole. Jeshua toddled around under his mother's watchful eye. As the sun began its descent and the shadows lengthened the air-cooled and we set out again.

"We will travel in the mornings and afternoons, resting during the hottest part of the day," Abner explained. "There is no hurry. In easy stages we will cross the Lowlands of Judea toward Gaza and the Great Sea."

Three days later we topped the last of the rolling hills that lined the coast. Abner pointed to the city whose walls were lit by the afternoon sun.

"There is Gaza. We will camp by her walls tonight. The new town on the harbor is called Agrippias. To the north you can see the historic port of Ashkelon, the city despoiled by Samson to obtain payment for a wager."

I looked where my guide pointed but my gaze was drawn to the expanse of blue stretching to the horizon. The Sea of Galilee was broad but it could not compare to this body of water.

"From Gaza we will follow the trade route to Egypt." The young man directed my attention to the road traveled by generations of traders, conquerors, and refugees.

A caravan entered Gaza from the south as we watched.

Recalling his responsibilities, Abner gave the signal and urged his camel down the incline. "Come, we must arrive before the gates are shut at sunset."

The sheik's son rode ahead with his father's trusted servant, Ishi.

"They will make arrangements for camping and inquire about the conditions of the route," I told Mary when she looked at me curiously.

The city grew taller as we approached the walls. We were directed to an area not far from the main entrance. The horses were tethered for the night within a rope enclosure. Abner's servants bought hay from a wizened old man who pandered his wagonload of dry grass to needy travelers. Mary set to work making a meal while I found myself beside Ishi erecting tents. It was the first time we had spoken since he delivered the news from Bethlehem.

"Did you live in Bethlehem?" The man asked diffidently.

"We came for the census. My son was born soon after we arrived. The people urged me to stay. My skills were needed." Although I did not want to appear rude, I tried to give as little information as necessary.

"Did you see the kings?"

The man's open face convinced me that honest curiosity prompted the question.

"I think everyone in Bethlehem saw them," I answered truthfully.

"It must have been amazing. I wonder why they came and where they went."

It did not appear that my companion expected a response, so I shrugged and tightened the last rope. We were interrupted by the arrival of Abner. The young man was ecstatic.

"There is good news! We will join a caravan from Damascus. The leader is known as an honest man. There is greater safety in the larger group."

In the morning I was amazed to learn that it was Tomas, my father's friend, who managed the Damascus caravan.

Joyfully he gripped my wrist and arm in greeting. "Joseph, I have not had word of you since my last trip to Nazareth before you were married. How are your father and your wife?"

A wave of homesickness flooded me. "My father was well when I left him. My family is with me. You may remember my wife, Mary. This is my son Jeshua."

The boy held out his arms to me. Happily I took him from his mother. From my arms the child surveyed the clean-shaven stranger. Then he reached out to Tomas.

"It is difficult to think of you as a father!" The trader chortled and tossed the child into the air. Jeshua giggled with delight. "We will talk more on the journey. It is a long road to the bazaars of Alexandria."

With that promise and a grin, the boy was returned to my arms.

"How do you know the trader?" Abner asked the next morning.

He reined his horse close to my camel as Gaza receded behind us. I had been expecting the inquiry. Still I could not stop my grin at the astonishment in the young man's voice.

"He is a friend of my father. Often he brought special woods for us to use. He sometimes sells finished pieces from our shop."

The days in Nazareth when my father and I worked together seemed another lifetime. I was a different man before the hand of God changed my life. Now I fled before the wrath of the king to save the life of my son. Staring ahead, down the dusty road to Egypt, I felt very inadequate.

"Then it is fortunate that we have met the Greek," Abner stated. I forced myself to concentrate. My companion shifted in his saddle to face me. "Tomas is experienced in the ways of the road. He knows the best water holes and places to camp. We will travel more swiftly, I think. Ishi says the Greek is in a hurry to reach the markets. You will be glad that you are riding."

I shifted a bit uncomfortably in the camel's saddle. My body was sore from the unaccustomed mode of travel.

"I am more comfortable walking," I admitted.

The young man nodded in understanding. "I prefer a horse, myself. You will find it gets easier. Your wife is doing well."

I glanced in the direction he indicated. Mary did seem relaxed. Urging my mount forward I drew up beside her.

"Are you comfortable, my love?"

"Yes, Joseph. We are fine."

Jeshua slept across her lap, lulled by the rocking of the camel. In his hand he clutched a frond pulled from a palm tree we passed outside of Gaza. I reached out and brushed a smudge of dirt from the boy's face. Here was my son, named so by my own word and by the affection I bore him. Looking at him lying in his mother's lap with grubby hands and face I found it hard to remember that this was the Messiah of God.

Our convoy was swallowed up in Tomas' many animals and servants. I wondered what treasures he carried in the many packs on the donkey and camel backs.

By the time we stopped for a rest, the day was hot. Sweat ran down my back. As soon as his feet hit the ground, Jeshua began to toddle about, exploring the area. He ignored his mother's call as he attempted to climb an unstable looking pile of boulders erected long ago to mark the small well.

Ishi rescued the child from his precarious perch. "I have something for you." He held out a small branch. "See how you can draw in the sand with this smooth stick?"

Delighted and distracted Jeshua toddled back to show Mary his treasure. When she turned away to stir our supper, he headed toward the camels.

"Jeshua!" Mary's cry caused heads to turn.

The big animals lay quiet, chewing their cud, but I feared their reaction to a baby in their midst. I took a running step in his direction and breathed a sigh of relief when Abner swung the child up to ride on his shoulders.

"I'll be your horse," he offered.

The sheik's son pranced while Jeshua bounced up and giggled. I slipped a hand around Mary's waist.

"Every man in the camp has become a nursemaid," I chuckled in her ear.

Each day took us closer to Egypt and further from the familiar hills and people of Israel. That we were still under the hand of Rome was evident by the occasional imperial messenger racing by on a fine horse and the intermittent guard posts along the route. Bored Roman soldiers questioned us about our destination. Tomas was well known to nearly all the guards from his many previous trips.

It seemed that each day Jeshua learned some new word or activity. From Tomas he gained a few Greek words. Abner and his servants taught him Syrian names for the animals. Mary was appalled to hear certain Roman words on his tongue after we camped for three days at the outpost near the Brook of Egypt, ancient boundary of the empire while a severe windstorm raged outside the walls.

"It is lucky that we are here," Tomas noted. "This sandstorm would be dangerous if we were on the highway without the protection of the walls here."

The men and animals enjoyed the rest even though the wind drove stinging sand into every opening. When he learned there was a Jewish woman in the caravan, the commander made Mary comfortable in his own quarters.

"It is my honor," he insisted in a mixture of Latin and broken Hebrew. "We rarely have women visit. You remind me of my daughter. She has recently given birth. Actually, I just got the scroll so the baby must be six months or older by now."

"Is the child a boy or a girl?" I was amazed at the ease with which my shy wife responded to the old soldier.

Proudly the grandfather grinned, "A boy, named Marcus Timotheus, for me. You must all join me for dinner."

In the Roman fashion, Mary too was included in the invitation. At first she hesitated until Tomas pointed out that it would be rude to refuse.

"He is a kind man. I will come if you agree," she conferred in a low tone with me.

Only too happy to spend time with my wife, I nodded. Shyly the young woman walked with us into the atrium of the commander's quarters. A lavish feast was set out.

There was succulent mutton in a special herb sauce, grapes and dates prepared in an extravagant tart, greens from the garden beside the house, and bread piled high. Honeyed wine completed the display.

"Nearly everything is grown here at this post," bragged our host. "I am fortunate to have been stationed where there is water. Growing things and trying new recipes has become my hobby."

Carefully I watched Tomas and Marcus. They reclined on the couches set around the table. Abner plopped his bulk cheerfully on a third couch. Mary clung close to my side. We shared the fourth couch. Jeshua sat beside his mother briefly then slid to the floor to explore the room.

When his mother reached for the boy, Marcus laughed. "Let him go. There is nothing here he can harm."

I kept one eye on my son while I ate and listened to Tomas discuss the state of the emperor's health with Marcus. Toddling from Abner to Tomas, the child eventually clambered up beside the Roman soldier. He seemed fascinated with the bronze broach that held the man's toga in place. The man was enthralled by the trust of the child.

"You are a fine boy," he smiled.

Unable to remove the ornament, Jeshua settled down beside his new friend and accepted a piece of bread. The boy's bright eyes watched everything. After the meal, Mary left us, although Marcus tried to encourage her to stay.

"It is time Jeshua was in bed," she insisted with a slight smile.

The conversation turned serious. Marcus looked from Abner to Tomas to me. "I have heard troubling reports from Jerusalem. A recent dispatch mentioned a rumor that Herod, king by the favor of Great Caesar, ordered the murder of children in some town. If that is true, I am sure Caesar will not hesitate to remove him. A madman cannot be allowed to reign, even in…"

The man stopped abruptly and looked abashed.

Tomas winked at me and completed the thought wryly, "Even in Judea?"

Abner looked at me briefly before he spoke. "My father, too, heard of the massacre. No one seems to know why, although there may be some connection to a visit to Bethlehem by mysterious kings."

"All I know is what I heard in the tents of the sheik," I added in a strained voice.

I hoped the Roman would not ask anything further.

Tomas sensed the tension and changed the subject. "Will Caesar allow the sons of Herod to reign?"

We discussed the possibilities and problems of either Philip or Archelaus assuming the throne of Judea.

"I doubt Caesar will allow a Jew to rule. A procurator will be appointed to keep the peace," Marcus stated. Almost apologetically the Roman looked at me. "There will be more troops in your country."

Soon we separated for the night.

"Now would be a good time for your God to send the Messiah," Tomas commented to me in a soft tone as we walked out of the room.

I stumbled and gasped.

My friend laughed, "Do not worry I would not say such a treasonous thing in our host's hearing."

For a long time, I lay beside Mary. My thoughts were a jumble of all the discussions. When I finally slept it was to dream of Roman soldiers inexorably marching forward toward my wife and child while I was powerless to protect them.

Chapter 19

"We are halfway to Egypt," Tomas announced when we set out the next morning.

"The animals seem more eager," Abner noted. "The sandstorm gave us time to rest the horses."

I felt more energetic, too, despite the greater heat we encountered as we traveled further south. Mary also appeared more relaxed with the journey.

"Many heroes of our history have walked this same road," I reminded her when she brought me a gourd of water and some flat bread with humus at midday. "From Abraham with his lovely wife to Joseph sold into slavery and Jacob driven to Egypt by famine, each man sought to find God. Countless armies have marched across this desert in search of earthly fame and power. Now, Messiah travels the same route."

She smiled and rubbed my neck, "Yes. I was thinking the same thing. Again the prophecy is fulfilled."

Jeshua wandered away a short distance before returning to crawl into my lap.

He reached up for my food. "Abba, mine."

I tore off a piece to share. The boy put his arms around my neck.

"Abba, love you." His loving lisp brought tears to my eyes.

I held my son close, promising myself that neither Herod nor Roman armies would harm the child.

"We are safe among friends here." I told myself, recalling what Tomas told me when we were a day out of Gaza.

"Only an army could stop us. Between my guards and the sheik's servants, we could defeat anyone else."

I was glad to get reacquainted with the Greek trader and even more thankful that he agreed to help Abner learn some secrets of wise merchants.

"The sheik asked me to help his son learn the ways of trading," I told my friend. "My meager suggestions are nothing compared to your knowledge."

"Perhaps your God sent me to meet you so that you would be spared embarrassment in the markets," Tomas joked.

I chuckled in response, although his words did make me pause to consider the idea. When we neared Egypt we all benefited from his knowledge.

"We will reach the Delta tomorrow," Tomas announced one evening several days after we left the Roman outpost. "We will be expected to give an accounting to the border guards. There are ways to minimize the cost."

Abner leaned forward to learn how to pay the least tax. "How is that possible?"

"There is no sense in lining the pockets of the border patrol at our expense. You do not have to lie," the Greek explained. "For instance, if the horses are ridden, rather than led, they are not considered merchandise. Who is to say that you cannot sell them after their usefulness is done?"

The young man listened and nodded. I sought my blankets beside Mary in a small tent leaving the trader and his student to their plans. In the morning, Abner and several of the sheik's servants rode horses. The packs had been redistributed among the camels, which were tied together in a train. I was amazed at how smoothly the ruse worked.

Mary and I passed almost unnoticed through the checkpoint as one family among the many that came into the land along the Nile. Abner and Tomas took longer. We were all relieved to make camp on the Egyptian side of the border.

"Two or three days to Alexandria," Tomas stated early the next morning.

I felt the same spirit of anticipation that ran through all the men. We made swift time along the Egyptian road to a boat landing. Here all the goods and animals were loaded onto barges for the trip down the river to Alexandria.

The horses balked at stepping onto the narrow gangplank. It took Abner and a couple of strong servants several minutes to encourage the first horse to cross. Most of his companions seemed to take courage and followed behind. Some still reared and pulled on the ropes but eventually all were settled on board.

"The camels must be driven overland," Tomas told Abner. "I know an honest man."

The camels' packs were unloaded and a second vessel was piled with the sheik's rugs and Tomas' trade goods.

I paid for passage for my family and myself. We climbed into the boat with the merchandise. Abner chose to ride with his horses and servants. When the boats were poled out into the current, I held my breath. It seemed impossible for such fragile looking and heavily loaded craft to float.

Mary did not need my urging to keep Jeshua far away from the low sides of the boat. She held him tightly despite his squirming.

"Let's count those funny animals," she suggested pointing to some huge gray beasts in the water.

"Those are called hippos," Tomas explained when joined us.

We all started trying to spot hippos along the riverbank, always making sure that Jeshua had a chance to see them first.

"You will find welcome among the Jewish community in Alexandria," Tomas remarked. "There have been Jews in Egypt since Abraham first journeyed here."

"Yes," I nodded.

My heart lightened at the thought of meeting with the learned rabbis at Alexandria. There was so much I hoped they could explain about Messiah.

"Jeshua!"

I heard Mary cry out and turned to see my son toddling toward the front of the boat. My heart clenched in fear. I started for the boy when he decided to climb on the piles of bales and boxes. Our stern looking captain caught the child even as a small box clattered to the deck. The Egyptian's frown vanished when the child laughed and grabbed for the beads around his neck. I hurried forward, followed by Tomas.

"Forgive me." I held out my arms for the boy, hoping my intent was understood even though I spoke stumbling Greek, not Egyptian.

"A fine boy," the captain responded in heavily accented Greek.

Gratefully I took the child, trying to frown at him. A smile crossed the smooth-shaven Egyptian face when Jeshua waved his goodbye.

"You must stay with your mother," I scolded.

I walked back to Mary. It was only when I sat down beside my wife that I realized I was shaking. The woman stroked the boy's hair to reassure herself that he was safe. I knew she was as frightened as I when she scolded the child and gave him a small shake.

"Jeshua, that was bad."

"Abba…" The boy turned to me with his lip quivering.

"It was bad. You could have been hurt," I informed him, trying to look angry. My heart melted at the pout on his lips.

"Mek-mah is a fine captain," Tomas told us from his comfortable seat on a bale of cotton. "He has two grown sons of his own and a number of daughters. Some are married now but I believe there are at least three still at home."

I laughed. "Do you know everyone and everything?"

The trader grinned and shrugged. “I have had dealings with many people over the years. It is good to develop a relationship with those who can be of assistance. It is an added blessing when associates become friends. I count your father among those I consider as friend.”

“He is fond of you, also.”

Tomas looked embarrassed so I turned my attention to the passing scenery. The elaborate buildings along the shore amazed me.

“There is fresh paint on the walls of some of the ancient buildings,” I commented to Tomas. “I thought the old monuments would be in disrepair.”

“Some are still in use to worship the ancient Nile gods. Many are now used to honor the gods of Rome. Belief in the old gods merged with the Greek gods brought by Alexander. The Roman leadership has given them new names and new life.”

I shook my head, not understanding how people could change their beliefs.

Mary was more outspoken. “How odd. The children of Israel still worship the same God that Abraham did. I think it would be confusing to change the god you follow.”

“There are many names for the same gods. Horus, god of the sun is the same as Apollos who drives the Greek chariot of the sun. Ra, chief of the gods becomes Saturn. Of course, the highest god is the Roman emperor himself,” Tomas winked at us.

My wife’s aghast expression at such blasphemy caused me to intervene. “It is what the people have been taught.”

“How sad,” the woman sighed softly before turning away to play with Jeshua.

I mused to my friend, “We Jews claimed that the One whose Name was too holy to speak is the only God. The Roman pantheon is perhaps only another expression of the endless human search to explain life and find meaning for eternity.”

He shrugged without responding. I looked at my young wife and the son who was Messiah.

"Tomas, you know the Jews expect Messiah to come?"

He nodded and looked slightly interested. "Is not Messiah the One who will restore the Kingdom of David and lead the nation to victory over their oppressors? The entire world knows that your people wait for this deliverer. He is supposed to be greater than Moses. Of course I've heard some say Messiah is to be a great warrior, like David or Joshua to raise and army and defeat your enemies."

"Most in Israel would agree with you."

The man stared at me with one eyebrow raised in curiosity. "Why are you concerned?"

"What if Messiah is not like that? Could Messiah be like the prophets of old, preaching the will of God? Is Messiah only for the Jews or for all nations?"

I stared at the everlasting temples as I stumbled through my questions. Clearly I remembered the magi, the shepherds and the angels.

The trader grimaced wryly and clapped me on the shoulder. "I would say a lot of people would be disappointed or even angry. Fortunately you and I do not have to worry about that."

His hearty words did not help. There was no further time to talk or even think. Boat traffic increased as we drew close to Alexandria. Shouts and curses between boatmen all around made it impossible to concentrate. Mary looked worried by the noise and confusion. I sat with my family until our craft was safely docked.

Dark-skinned bearers wearing only loincloths swarmed aboard to unload the cargo. Tomas calmly directed the disposition of the goods. In a very short time all our crates and bundles were piled on shore. The dockworkers began to load a new shipment onto the vessel for the return trip.

Protectively I guided my wife across the gangplank onto solid ground. After a brief word of thanks to our captain I started to look around for Abner and the horses.

Mek-mah surprised me by holding out one of the beaded neck chains he wore. “For your son. He was fond of the colors.”

Half embarrassed the man shrugged off Mary’s shy thanks.

“May Horus protect you.” The blessing seemed to be directed at Jeshua when the gruff man gently touched the boy’s cheek before hurrying away.

“That is as close to emotion as I have ever seen the old scoundrel.” Tomas shook his head in surprise. He pointed to Abner standing on the deck of an approaching boat. “Here comes the other barge.”

The young Arab raised a hand in salute before turning his attention to the horses. As soon as the plank was in place, the restive animals were led ashore. They seemed quite anxious to get off the strange moving platform and stamped their hooves on the solidly packed sand. Ishi and the sheik’s servants led the prancing animals out of the crowd. Abner watched intently until all the animals were safely away.

I stepped forward as soon as Balaam was led off the boat. Unaffected by the bustle, he looked around in a bored way. A slight shifting of his weight was the only evidence he gave of being aware when I tied my tools onto the saddle. Mary held the little animal’s bridle. Jeshua perched proudly on the donkey’s back. From his vantage point my son could see nearly the entire dock area. Bright eyes observed the colorful and ever changing pageantry of people, animals and commodities.

“Follow me to the Trader’s Camp.” Tomas led our group to a spot where his men had already erected our tents amid many others.

The horses were rapidly penned using ropes and stakes to create an enclosure.

Mary began to prepare the evening meal with Jeshua balanced on her hip. The boy squirmed. Disaster seemed imminent. A moment later, one little hand pushed the jar out of his mother’s hand. The milk spilled into the fire and the pottery shattered.

My wife burst into tears. “No! Bad boy!”

A wail from the baby pierced the low din of men preparing for the night. Heads turned in astonishment and curiosity at the sound. I rushed to my family.

"You must let Mama make the food," I said gently while I rocked the sobbing child. Mary's tears soaked my robe. I tried to calm both son and wife. "Do not worry. Everything is all right."

"I am sorry," the young woman mumbled. "I did not want Jeshua to get lost and…"

Tomas and Abner moved to intercept a curious surge of fellow travelers interested in our minor household drama. Eventually the comments penetrated my concentration.

"Is that a baby?"

"My son is about that age."

"I would not bring a baby here."

"Why would anyone bring a family?"

"He does not look like a trader."

"A Jew, it appears."

I looked up when I heard Tomas intervene. "The young carpenter is a friend of mine. He and his family have business in Alexandria. How are you Belial? Still peddling pottery from Nubia? And Keshra, old friend, I thought you no longer came this far. I have not seen you in years."

I was grateful for the way the trader diverted attention from us.

Abner gestured to the nearby fire where a pot of something savory simmered. "Eat with us tonight. If you prefer, I can bring you a portion here."

"Thank you for your kind offer, my friend. It would be easier to eat with you this night, if Mary is willing."

I felt my wife nod against me then she turned to look at the young man. "Thank you, Abner, you are most thoughtful," she mumbled.

Mary sat in the shadow of the tent with her stew while Jeshua happily toddled from Abner to Ishi to Tomas until he was tired and crawled into my arms. Still he strained to see everything until sleep overcame him.

I stood to carry my son to his bed. Mary rose and joined me when I laid the child down. Gently she tucked blankets around the boy.

"It is strange," she said suddenly.

"What is, my love?"

"This land, the people, the fact we are here at all." Vaguely my wife gestured at the scattered tent city huddled beside the walls of Alexandria.

I rested my hand on her slender shoulder. "We will grow accustomed. This has been difficult for you, I know. I will seek lodging in the Jewish section. It will be more familiar for us."

"I know everything will be well. We are in God's hands. I was just afraid in all the strangeness and you were not here and I did not feel well."

At the tiny quiver in the woman's voice, I drew her into my arms. My conscience pricked me. I brushed a strand of hair from the smooth forehead I loved.

"Mary, I have neglected you, I am sorry."

"My husband, there is a reason I did not feel well," she interrupted. "You will be a father again."

"A father? Are you sure?" I heard my dumbfounded voice asking foolish questions while my mind spun.

"This will be your own child," she confided. "I have known since we left the camp of Abram."

"I would have made it easier for you," I stammered.

"There was no need. All is well."

Later I held my wife in my arms. Soft breathing told me that she slept. I thought about her announcement.

"It will be difficult fitting into this new culture," I mused. "Another child will mean many changes. Mary will need support of other women. I must find a house where she will be comfortable."

Eventually, I slept with my hand nestled in Mary's. My last thought was a fervent prayer. "God be merciful. Do not leave us refugees here forever. Surely your Messiah must grow up in the land of Israel."

CHAPTER 20

The sun was not even visible over the rim of the world when shouting men, braying donkeys, and camel complaints wakened me. Tomas' servants had already loaded several of the crates onto camels. Ishi directed the sheik's men to do the same.

"Stay here. There is no need for you to get up," I told Mary tucking the blanket around the woman.

Throwing on my robe, I joined Abner and the trader.

Tomas issued firm instructions, "We must be in position and ready to enter the city when the gates open. Have your documents and the fee ready for the Master of the Market. The less time wasted in bureaucratic details, the better spot we can acquire."

I wondered if I looked as amazed as the young Arab beside me. With Tomas' prodding we were able to obtain a position in line fairly close to the Traders' Gate. When the trumpet blast welcomed the day and the great wooden doors swung open, we were carried into the city on the surge of energy.

We were fortunate to have followed the trader's advice. I watched others digging through bundles or their garments to produce the necessary documentation from the border. When our turn came, money changed hands and a scribe for the Master of the Market noted our names in a scroll.

"Abner of Nabatea, Joseph of Nazareth, and Tomas of Damascus," the man repeated in Greek. "May the gods prosper your trading this day."

Immediately he forgot about us to summon the next man in line.

I relaxed and began to look around. Alexandrian merchants were already opening their booths. Everyone else had to jostle for a position. Because of the horses Abner was selling, we were actually able to claim one of the more favorably located booths near the entrance to the market. The bustle and unaccustomed noise made the animals prance.

"Be still my beauties," Abner soothed them. "You must not fret and be nervous. All will be well."

"You have a gift." Tomas watched for a minute admiring the way the horses calmed under their master's voice.

He then turned to his own products. "Put the spices there and the ivory near the pottery," he directed. "Dyed and woven goods from Damascus and Greece can be draped behind them."

The man carefully unpacked inlaid jewelry and cosmetic boxes. He held up one for my inspection. "Joseph, do you see whose mark this bears?"

I did not even have to look closely. "Jacob bar Mattan. My father made those boxes."

"He will be delighted to see your son."

It was the closest my old friend came to questioning me about our presence in the company of Abner.

"I pray that the God of Abraham, Isaac, and Jacob will bring us safely to Nazareth again," I agreed.

The strange sights, smells, and sounds of the teeming city reminded me that I was far from home. I turned away to hide my longing for the familiar things we left behind.

Abner turned out to be a natural salesman. His gregarious personality was an asset in the market. Ladies paused to glance at his wares and lingered for his compliments and gentle jests. I was even more amazed to watch the Arab barter with an Egyptian official for one of the horses. When the money finally exchanged hands both sides were satisfied with the price.

"That young man has the makings of a master trader," Tomas commented after the sale was complete. "I doubt I could have done better myself. If he can sell the rest of his father's herd for equal profit, I believe our friend will be considered quite the success."

I could only nod, astonished by the confidence previously unsuspected in my friend. It was mid-morning when I remembered my duties as husband and father.

"I should return to the camp. You do not need me here. There is more business savvy in your little finger than I have in my whole body," I told Abner. "Perhaps I can do some carpentry work for our fellow traders."

"I find that I am enjoying myself," the young man confided, with a grin at my compliment.

"You father will be pleased."

The young man frowned slightly at my assurance. "Perhaps, although I fear that I will always be 'little Abner, the easy-going'. I think that my manner helps disarm arguments though."

I hid my smile with a cough and turned away with an encouraging pat on the shoulder.

Briefly I explained to Tomas, "I am returning to camp. Mary is likely wondering what is happening. Perhaps she will want to visit the market later."

My friend nodded and waved. As I walked back through the city that stretched along the Great Sea, I was amazed by the architecture. The famous lighthouse in the harbor was not the only wonder. Pillars carved from native limestone held up porticos in front of the official buildings. Some even had marble columns. I marveled at the expense of bringing the rock to this city, named for Alexander the Great. Vaguely I remembered hearing that he never actually saw this city that he so carefully planned even though it was dedicated to his grandeur. A fever killed him far to the north. Now Rome claimed his prize as her own.

I shivered, thinking about the brief and turbulent history of the city. Mark Anthony and his beloved Cleopatra attempted rebellion from these shores. Doomed to fall against the might of Rome, Cleopatra took her life after her lover was killed.

Curiously I peered down streets wondering where Jews of Alexandria lived. Almost before I knew it, I was walking out the city gates. It took me a moment to reorient myself for I had come out a different gate. Looking around, I spotted the many tents of the camp. A few minutes later I was in their midst. Some traders or slaves worked around the area. They looked rough and vicious. I quickened my pace to reach my family.

Mary sat placidly spinning while Jeshua played peek-a-boo with Omri, one of the sheik's servants. I noticed a couple of Tomas' men lounging in the shade of a nearby tent playing a game of knucklebones with two of Abner's servants. They were not the only men in camp but I was relieved to see them. I understood that my friends had taken thought for Mary's safety even though I had not known the need.

My wife looked up. Her veil covered her face, but her eyes smiled a welcome. Immediately the woman laid aside the spinning whorl.

"Joseph, is all well?"

"So well that I left Abner and Tomas happily bartering and came to see my family," I nodded. "I thought I might set out my tools in case someone needs a carpenter."

"Oh," she sounded disappointed, although she turned away quickly to pick up the yarn.

"Unless you want to see the city," I amended.

"Could we? I have been wishing I could just see the market. Is it very large? Are the women very beautiful? What are their clothes like?" Like an excited child my wife clapped her hands.

Jeshua sensed that something was happening. He left the game with Omri to trot to my side.

"Abba?" The child tugged on my hand. I swung my son up above my head.

Mary hastily put away her work while I informed the lounging men nearby, "My wife and I are going to the city."

They barely nodded, intent on the game and the pile of money in the center of the blanket.

Omri set out behind us. It took me a moment to understand that he was doing his duty. None of the sheik's wives would have ventured anywhere without a full vanguard of servants for protection and to carry purchases. I was glad to have Omri's company when some of the men in camp stared at my wife. His hand casually resting on the curved sword discouraged any interruption.

"We will have to use the main gate," he stated. "The Trader's Gate will be closed."

The Roman guards at the gate barely gave us a glance before continuing their conversation. Mary's eyes opened wide in astonishment as we entered Alexandria. It delighted me to watch her enjoyment of the sights. Her first glimpse of local women made the girl gasp. The linen tunics were not quite transparent but they clung to the voluptuous forms in a most revealing way.

Mary gripped my arm tightly and whispered. "They are indecent."

"It is the Egyptian style," I commented, trying not to stare.

My companion found her voice as the pair disappeared around the corner. "I'm sure it is very cool."

I heard Omri chuckle although he tried to cover the sound by clearing his throat and looking up at a nearby house.

The further into the city we strolled the more people we encountered. Slaves seemed to wear nothing more than a loincloth or short tunic. Mary averted her eyes from every man we passed. Officials were identifiable by the Roman togas they sported. Townsfolk appeared to prefer tunics in varying lengths. Most of the women wore their hair uncovered. I saw my wife covertly studying the hairstyles. Beads, braids, and ribbons seemed to be favored.

"I like your hair just the way it is," I whispered in her ear.

"Oh, I would never..." Mary's voice trailed off as we reached the market.

Booths stretched for blocks. I was amazed myself since I had not ventured away from the booths of Abner and Tomas earlier. The smell of the fishmonger mingled not unpleasantly with the spice merchant's wares. Shimmering lengths of a cloth called silk hung in a tantalizing display near the linen draper. A sign proclaimed that togas of all styles could be completed in a day. Further along, leather goods hung beside a small booth with woolen cloth for sale. They were not busy. I thought the rugs that Abner brought were a better quality than the ones in a booth at the end of the market. Mary paused at a small shop. The sales woman was a thin girl who looked a couple of years younger than my wife.

"Great lady, we have the finest lotions and perfumes," she called in Greek. Her voice was a lilting singsong of a well rehearsed sales patter.

My wife giggled at being called a great lady. We would have moved on but the seller caught Mary's hand.

"Smell the perfume, feel the smoothness of this fine lotion. You can use it for your hands and body." With a coy glance toward me the girl confided, "The men say it makes them wild with desire."

"Oh!" The young mother at my side was shocked speechless.

Her face flamed with embarrassment even as she rubbed the cream onto her hands. Jeshua squirmed in my arms pointing to the colorful bottles just out of reach.

"Would you like some?" I asked.

Mary glanced up. Although she immediately shook her head, I saw the longing glance as she returned the pot to the owner.

"It is too expensive," she protested.

"Not for the wife of my son." I grinned when she sighed in delight.

We haggled briefly over the price before the girl filled a glass jar with some of the sweet smelling lotion. Wax sealed the stopper in place.

The girl smiled as she handed the container to Mary. "Great lady, you have a kind husband."

My wife cradled it against her chest and nodded, "Yes, Joseph is the best of men."

We moved on. Jeshua wanted to explore the enticing and exciting displays. I was kept busy sifting the child from arm to arm and pointing out distractions whenever the boy spotted an especially desirable item.

Eventually we completed our circuit of the market and arrived at Tomas' booth. Mary had acquired some fresh fruit and a fish for dinner as well as the lotion and a little metal chariot horse for Jeshua.

The Greek looked pleased with his day's sales. Abner, too, spoke happily of success as we walked together back to camp.

The unsold horses trailed behind us in the care of servants. Other merchandise was loaded onto the camels and returned to the camp. Part of the evening was spent sorting and preparing the goods for the morning.

"I mentioned to a few customers that the son of the craftsman who work I displayed was available for small jobs," Tomas announced as we ate a delicious meal made by Mary.

The fish was a welcome change from the beans and mutton we had eaten on the journey.

"Thank you, my friend."

Abner added, "I told at least two men of your skills also. They were complaining about the lack of skilled carpenters in Alexandria. Perhaps you will be able to find enough work to keep you busy until you decide to return to your home."

"God will it is so," I responded almost as a prayer.

CHAPTER 21

The morning bustle of traders hurrying into the city at the first hint of daylight roused me. I smiled at my family. Mary dreamed beside me. Jeshua slept on his mat with his small bottom in the air and a thumb in his mouth.

Facing east I drew my prayer shawl over my head and bowed toward Jerusalem so far away. "Blessed are you, Adonai Elyohim, Ruler of the Universe for you bring light to the world. Preserve me in your service this day and bring us safe again to your home."

I had barely finished my devotions when a supercilious slave confronted me. He held himself stiffly as if afraid to come in contact with the dust still settling from the departure of all the traders.

"Are you the carpenter from Nazareth?" His tone indicated that he doubted the truth of such a claim.

Suppressing a smile I inclined my head. "I am Joseph of Nazareth. I am a carpenter."

"You are to come with me," the man ordered as he turned to pick his way back to the main gate. When I did not move the slave looked back with a frown. "My master commands you to come. He has an important commission for you, perhaps."

"Very well," I nodded.

"Come, come. It will not do to keep the master waiting."

A little reluctantly I followed my guide across the camp. The soldiers at the main gate greeted the slave with surprising deference.

"This man is with me. He is summoned to my master."

His brief explanation was enough to grant me entrance without question. Once inside Alexandria his pace increased until I was almost trotting to keep up with the long strides of my escort. We came to a wide street with many elegant houses. Without pause I was led through a side door into the largest home.

The man hurried ahead of me down the hall. "This way."

He spoke briefly to the steward at the door before I was ushered into a wide room. The size and magnificence of the furnishings almost took my breath away. A wizened old man and his middle aged son approached. From their dress, I could tell they were wealthy Egyptian nobles.

The younger of the men addressed me in surprisingly good Hebrew. "Are you the carpenter from Nazareth?"

Wondering why such important persons sent for me, I bowed low. "I am Joseph bar Jacob."

"We have a fine jewel box that needs repair. It was my mother's and I want to give it to my daughter as part of her dowry." The man picked up a leather wrapped object from a nearby table as he spoke.

Gently he unfolded the soft skin to expose the inlaid lid. Some of the pieces were missing and the lid was warped from contact with water at some time in the past.

"Can you repair it?" The old man wheezed when I did not immediately respond.

I took the box from the son to examine it more closely. Although the sheen was long since worn away and the lining was tattered it was not beyond repair.

"Yes, the bottom seems to be in fairly good condition. I will have to make a new lid. This one is warped. Many of the inlay pieces can be saved, but I will need to get wood for the lid and for the pieces to be replaced."

"How much?" The Egyptian waited for my reply with his eyes narrowed.

The new lid would be the work of a morning although the inlay itself would take a couple of days. I stated a price. The two men drew away to consult. I easily overheard their conversation since the young man had to speak loudly for his father to hear. My imperfect Egyptian caught the gist of the argument.

"Camptah or Silas the Greek would charge twice as much."

"Neither one does decent inlay work."

"We do not know this carpenter's work."

"Tomas the trader says he does good work. I trust him."

"Very well, Father," finally the son agreed.

They turned back to me.

"How long will it take you to complete the work?"

"Less than a week, if I can find the necessary woods," I replied.

"Very well, we will expect you to return in a week with the box. I am Antonius and this is my father Ptolmey. If you do a good job, we will speak to our neighbors."

An unspoken threat hung in the air. I knew I would find no further work if the job was not approved.

I offered a low salaam to my first customers. "Until then, my lords."

"Sekt will show you out." Antonius dismissed me with a vague gesture toward the door.

I bowed again and left the room with the precious box in my hand.

The same slave awaited me in the hall. He led the way to the side door and gave me directions to the market when I asked. Although I searched the shops for a piece of mahogany wood there was none to be found. I was able to find a piece of oak for the lid and soft silk for the lining. With my purchases, I made my way back to the camp.

"I have a job," I told Mary, holding up the box. "Some of the wood can be salvaged. I think all the rosewood and ebony will be usable. Perhaps Tomas knows of other sellers of wood where I can obtain a small piece of mahogany. I know there is a perfect scrap in the woodbin in Nazareth."

It felt good to hold the adz and saw in my hands. By afternoon the new lid was ready for the inlay work.

As I worked, Mary sat sewing nearby. "I am making a new tunic for Jeshua. He is growing so quickly, his clothes do not fit for long."

The boy toddled back and forth between us playing with the little metal cart and digging in the sand. When he stopped to watch, I gave him a smooth block of wood.

"If you rub this with the fine sand here, it will shine," I told him.

Very seriously the child set to work on the wood. It kept him entertained for several minutes. I set aside my work when the shadows began to grow. Soon Abner and Tomas arrived.

The Greek was angry. In his hands my friend carried pieces of a cosmetic box. It had been one of the larger pieces brought from Nazareth. Now he laid it in front of me.

Through gritted teeth he growled, "Can this be repaired? A doting mother let her overweight child do as he pleased and he smashed this chest."

One side was shattered and the top was cracked in two places. My father's work was ruined. I felt a twinge of rage at the inconsiderate woman in the market.

"It would be easier to start over," I stated sadly after surveying the damage. "Some of the wood can be salvaged and used to make a new box but the joints are broken on this side and weakened here."

I pointed out smaller cracks on the edges. The trader cursed long and vehemently. I glanced anxiously toward Mary. She hurried Jeshua into the tent, away from the man's fury. Finally my friend calmed enough to speak coherently.

"We took such care getting that piece here safely. To have it broken by a thoughtless child is..." Tomas sighed heavily and stamped off in frustration still shaking his head.

Later I sought him out. "Thank you, for speaking of my work to Antonius and Ptolemy."

"So they have come to see you. Ptolemy is very important here in Alexandria. He is related in some distant way to the old dynasty. You can tell from his son's name that he also sought Mark Anthony's favor. However, like Herod, he smoothly changed sides when the rebellion failed. His daughter is named Julia Octavia in honor of the new power. I have heard that it also cost a pretty shekel to keep in the Emperor's good graces. Be that as it may, Antonius is an important man in the city. He retained his father's position as mayor. If you do a good job on whatever they have commissioned you will be established here."

"It was a small jewel case. I plan to visit the market tomorrow and try again to seek out some mahogany to complete the inlay that is missing."

"I doubt you will find any at a reasonable price. Neither of the local carpenters is likely to sell to you, either," the man mused. "Isn't the broken chest made of mahogany?"

"Yes," I nodded, my mind leaping ahead of my friend. "With your permission I can use some of the broken wood for the small pieces I need."

"Then make me a smaller box from the rest." The trader saw a way to recoup some of his loss.

I spent the next day shaping and attaching the inlay design to the lid of the jewel case. Jeshua toddled over to watch my work. I was surprised that he did not reach for the project but watched me quite seriously.

"Tomorrow I will sand and oil the wood," I told the child.

A passing lizard distracted the boy and he left my side to chase the creature.

In the afternoon I measured and cut the broken mahogany chest into smaller pieces to make a dainty cosmetic box. It was almost finished by the time Tomas and Abner returned at dusk.

Abner reported happily, "The last of the horses are sold. My father will be pleased with the profit. I still have a few rugs and woolen goods. Then I can be on my way back to my tents. This city is too busy for my liking."

Later I showed Tomas the box. He was amazed at my progress.

"There is a small tray inside that lifts when the lid opens." I demonstrated my innovation. "This will be ready for you in the morning. All it needs is another coating of oil to give it a soft sheen."

"How clever! This will be a fast selling item," he grinned.

The man tried the lid again and again, fascinated by the device. I showed the Egyptian's box to Tomas.

"Here is the jewel chest I repaired for your friends. I used a hinge my father developed. When I dismantled his broken box I remembered how it was done."

The trader examined the jewelry box in the firelight.

"Joseph bar Jacob, you do fine work. You would never know that this piece was damaged. I am sure that Ptolemy and Antonius will be pleased."

I spent the cool morning hours finishing the Egyptian's box.

Mary came to stand beside me. "It is good to see you with wood in your hands, my husband."

"I have missed it," I admitted.

I set aside my work to draw the woman onto my lap.

"Where is Jeshua?" I inquired after a lingering kiss.

"Sleeping."

The woman snuggled close to me. I wrapped my arms around her, grateful for the time with my wife. We were alone in the camp except for a few servants here and there busy with their duties. I knew Omri was nearby, but he would not intrude on our privacy. My wife rested her head on my shoulder and played with my beard until her ears heard Jeshua waking.

"I must go," she said softly and softened her departure with a kiss.

I watched her move away gracefully to tend our son, filled with gratitude and love. "God of Abraham, Isaac, and Jacob you bless me greatly."

As the shadows lengthened in the afternoon I looked up and saw the approach of what could only be my Egyptian customers. A retinue of armed guards accompanied a pair of litters carried by burly slaves.

Sekt trotted ahead of the group to announce, "My master has come."

Antonius dismounted from his litter and turned to assist his father. Together the Egyptians approached. Mindful of their rank, I bowed low to my visitors.

"I know it has not yet been a week," Antonius stated. "We came to see how the work was progressing."

"The chest is just finished." I turned away to pick up the box, biting back a smile at the astonishment on the two dark, narrow faces.

Sekt took the wood box from me and handed it to Antonius with a bow. Both men bent to examine the workmanship. Ptolemy ran his finger across the inlay. His son lifted the lid and opened the delicate drawers. They slid smoothly in and out. A lining of silk replaced the old, torn cotton cloth. Finally Antonius ran his fingers across the smooth lid again.

"You have restored the piece better than I anticipated," he admitted. "It will make a fine wedding gift."

Slowly Ptolemy nodded in agreement. "My wife would be pleased."

The old man turned to leave. Sekt hurried to assist his master into the litter.

I rested one hand lightly on the lid of the box to prevent Antonius from following his father. "My fee?"

"I have heard that you did not have to buy as much wood as we thought." The Egyptian frowned and squinted at me.

We began the inevitable bargaining over the price. When we eventually reached an agreement, it was more than I anticipated receiving although less than my original bid. Antonius counted the Roman coins into my hands.

"May your daughter be a blessing and may you be blessed with many grandsons." I bid my customers farewell with a salaam.

The procession moved back across the camp toward the setting sun and the city gate. Tired traders plodding from the city gave the wealthy equipage surprised looks. New arrivals from the south and east stopped jostling for campsites to stare.

Mary hurried forward with Jeshua on her hip. "They were pleased?"

The woman did not really have to ask. She could tell the answer by my smile.

I showed her the coins. "Yes, my love and they have paid well. If they tell others of my work, we shall be secure here."

"Until we can return home," she added in a whisper full of longing.

"God will let us know when that time is."

CHAPTER 22

Antonius and Ptolemy did tell their neighbors. By the time Tomas and Abner left the Trader's Camp Mary and I were established in a small house amid the other craftsmen of Alexandria. Already my workshop was taking on the smell of sawdust and fine wood. When Antonius' daughter was wed, he requested a small table for the girl.

"It must hold her lotions, brushes, and cosmetics," he explained. "I think it should compliment the jewel box you repaired."

Together we labored over a design. When the man was finally satisfied I set to work. Jeshua often kept me company by playing in the corner of the workshop with scraps of wood.

"Ho, Carpenter," Antonius summoned me a few days later. His voice echoed in the street.

"Come in, Antonius. See how your gift is progressing," I invited.

A frown appeared on the smooth shaven face. I half expected my visitor to refuse. Instead he gathered the folds of his toga tightly to keep from getting them covered in sawdust and crossed the threshold. Jeshua paused in his play to watch the stranger.

"See, here are the drawers for cosmetics. This lid lifts to reveal a mirror and a place to keep her brushes and hair ornaments. It is just as you planned. See how the inlay work is similar to the jewelry box she received from you."

Proudly I showed the man the smooth inlay and demonstrated the various openings. It was my best work.

"Very good."

I could not tell if my customer was pleased or not. Out of the corner of my eye I saw Jeshua start across the shop. He carried a block in each hand.

"Abba, look," he called.

Distracted by watching me, he tripped over a piece of lumber on the floor. The blocks flew out of his hands and my son began to cry. Antonius turned in surprise while I picked up the child and started to dust the sawdust from the little face, hands, and tunic.

"There, there, nothing is that bad." Bending I retrieved the prized pieces of wood. "Here are your blocks."

My eyes met Antonius' as I stood up. There was a longing and sorrow in the Egyptian's face that shocked me.

"I had a son," the man said hoarsely. I could feel his undiminished anguish. "He was about that age when a fever swept through the city. We went south but it was too late. Marcus died in my arms less than a week later."

"I am sorry."

Instinctively I clutched my own precious son to me. The boy squirmed in my arms. He reached out his chubby arms to the Egyptian. Hesitantly the man responded. Jeshua cuddled into his new friend's embrace. Tears slid down dark cheeks as the father wept for his lost child. I wondered how many years the grief had been held inside. Jeshua's little hands played with the medallion around Antonius' neck and his grubby fingers wiped at the tear tracks.

His toga dragged forgotten through the sawdust as my visitor walked up and down talking to the child. "You are a fine boy. Already you are helping your father. You will be an honor to your family."

I watched in silence, bemused by the way my son turned the stiff scion of Egyptian royalty into a gently, tender man.

Eventually Antonius looked at me. "It has been twenty years since I held my son. With Julia married my home will be empty. You are wise to enjoy this time with your son. We never know what the god's will send."

When the man left, I stood for a long time holding my son, lost in thought. Antonius' words reminded me that I planned to seek out the rabbis in Alexandria and learn from them the prophecies of Messiah.

"What sort of man will you be, Jeshua my son?" I asked.

Bright eyes looked into mine, then the boy squirmed. When I set him on the floor he resumed his play.

"After the table for Antonius is complete, I will visit the rabbis," I promised myself.

Over the next few days Antonius visited regularly. He no longer inquired about his daughter's gift. Instead he spent the time playing with Jeshua and telling me about his family.

"Tomas, the Greek, told me your family is related to the line of Pharaohs," I mentioned one day.

"The line dies with me," shrugged my friend. "Rome is queen now and the world is at her feet. Egypt will never rise again to greatness."

I could not think of a response to the statement. Instead I concentrated on sanding the table.

Antonius changed the subject. "Your people anticipate and hope for one called the Messiah."

I stared at my guest, wondering why my friend brought up a subject so close to my heart.

"The prophets have spoken of one who will restore Israel," I answered.

"What will he be like, this Messiah? Will this Deliverer be just for Israel?"

I hesitated before answering honestly, "That is what we have always been taught, 'A branch shall rise from the root of Jesse.' But I wonder…"

My voice trailed off as memories of the Magi intruded.

When I did not continue, Antonius prodded. "Do you doubt your own holy writings?"

For a minute I sat silent.

In the quiet I heard Mary shout, "Jeshua, bring that back!"

There was a patter of little feet as the toddler scampered through the door with a piece of fruit in his hands.

"Abba, fruit." He held out a smashed plum as evidence. Juice dripped between the small fingers.

"Let him have it," Antonius grinned at Mary standing nearby with hands on hips.

I chuckled and agreed, "Yes, my love, you may as well. The fruit is beyond using now."

Sighing and shaking her head, Mary turned back to the house, calling over her shoulder to me, "You watch him, then, since you are not working. I am trying to prepare your dinner."

Happily the sticky child clambered into my lap to enjoy his treat. Conscious that the naughty boy in my arms was the subject of our discussion, I bent to kiss the rumpled black curls.

"Perhaps Messiah will be for more than Israel," I said slowly. "Perhaps he will come in a way that is not expected."

Looking up, I saw my friend draw his eyebrows together in confusion.

With a proud lift of his chin the man asked a bit scornfully, "How could that be? Do you think the world will rise up in revolt against Rome and follow a Jew?"

"No…I think that Messiah will not be a warrior and may not bring a kingdom like we expect," I mumbled uncertainly. "I plan to visit the learned rabbis and talk to them. You may come if you want."

I set my squirming son on the ground. Immediately he toddled over to Antonius and held up his arms. The Egyptian smiled at the boy and tousled his curls.

He looked at me and shook his head. "I never expected to have such a conversation with a fugitive Jew from Israel. Maybe I will go with you. You are an unusual man, Joseph of Nazareth."

Our visit to the rabbis was delayed when Julia returned from the south with her new husband.

"The young man has a promising career," Antonius told me when he returned to the shop. "It will probably take him to Rome one day. I hope that promotion is a long time coming. May the gods grant I hold grandchildren on my knee before Julia goes to the capital. Surely a father must yearn to hold his grandson."

The man's eyes followed Jeshua as he played in the courtyard under Mary's watchful gaze. My wife looked up at the words. Even across the area, I knew her eyes held longing. My throat tightened with yearning for the hills of Galilee. Joachim, Anna, and my parents seemed far away.

"Let us go to the rabbis after the Sabbath," I suggested as much to divert my thoughts as for a response from the Egyptian.

It was not as easy as I expected to speak with one of the learned teachers.

An officious young scribe blocked the doorway to the compound. "No one may disturb the Rabbis."

"I only seek to speak to someone about, um, certain, um, questions I have," I stammered.

"Do the learned rabbis not have time for a seeker of truth?" Antonius seemed to gain height as he assumed a regal demeanor.

The scorn in the Egyptian's voice made me cringe. Although no taller than the scribe, he gave the appearance of looking down on the hapless young man.

"I am Joel," blustered the guardian of the door. "It is my duty to keep importunate travelers from disturbing the rabbis. They have important matters to meditate on."

The heir of the Pharaohs looked at the young man as if he were of no consequence. "I am Antonius, son of Ptolemy, last of the royal line of Egypt."

Joel's attitude underwent a dramatic change at the announcement. He bowed low while directing a venomous glance at me.

"Mighty Lord, I had no idea that it was a personage as noble as yourself seeking entry to address the Rabbis. I am certain that had your servant made that clear from the start; there would have been no confusion. A member of the royal house is always most welcome in the humble apartments of his servants. Great one, forgive the seeming insensitivity of this most lowly of your tenants…"

The young man seemed intent on babbling on interminably, while bowing up and down until I was becoming dizzy.

"Joel, is it?" Antonius interrupted with a raised hand.

"Yes, most exalted Prince." The young man began his bobbing bows again.

"Then, Joel, you will announce to your masters that our *friend*, Joseph bar Jacob of Nazareth in Galilee, seeks to speak with the Rabbis of Alexandria in order to learn from them more about the prophecies of Messiah. It has become a matter of interest to us also."

Joel immediately favored me with a low salaam as he glanced from the implacable face of the descendent of the Pharaohs to me.

"Masters please enter and favor this humble place. I will see that food and drink are brought. Great one, I will inform the Rabbis of your desire."

Still bowing, the scribe ushered us into a comfortably furnished room. Rich hangings covered the walls and mounds of cushions surrounded a low table. With a final low bow the man disappeared. We heard him shouting for the servants as the curtain dropped into place over the door. I looked at my friend in astonishment.

"What happened?"

Antonius chuckled. His grin was broad and almost boyish. "My friend, the Rabbis of Alexandria were given this dwelling by my great grandfather. They pay no rent and no taxes. However, they are very aware that they only hold possession as long as the house of Ptolemy allows it. In return they translate not only your Holy Writings but any official documents from or to Israel."

"You can be very intimidating, Great Prince," I stated, glad that we were friends and not enemies.

Before we had a chance for further conversation, a procession of servants entered with platters of fruit, sweets and breads. Others followed with jars of wine. Antonius nodded to indicate one of the wines. After accepting a silver chalice filled with the ruby liquid, the man signaled for the hovering servants to leave. Impatient, I set aside my cup after only a small sip.

"Drink up, Joseph, I am sure the wine is perfectly kosher," urged the Egyptian, draining his own cup.

Although I picked up the vessel I simply turned it around in my hands. I stared at my work roughened hands gripping the polished silver. Amid the expensive silk hangings and soft cushions I felt out of place. Even my best robe, donned for the occasion at Mary's urging, looked coarse and uncouth. Antonius leaned back, perfectly at ease. I wished I had his confidence.

"Will the Rabbis see me…you…us?"

I felt the older man staring at me and heat rose in my face.

"You have every right to speak to the Rabbis of Alexandria."

As if in response the curtain was pushed aside. Joel bowed himself forward into the room.

"Great one, if you are ready, the Rabbis await your presence."

The Egyptian inclined his head and rose to his feet. I followed, trying to ignore the slight look of irritation I noticed on the scribe's face. The man led the way down several halls to a large airy room. Low tables, covered with scrolls, were placed around the room. Scrolls filled the shelves that lined the walls below windows close to the ceiling where light and air entered. I was surprised at how comfortable the temperature was. Ten men sat on chairs and benches against the far wall. I knew they were the Rabbis and felt my mouth go dry. What could I say to explain my presence or my need to understand the Messianic prophecies? The idea had seemed simple when I pictured myself discussing scripture with someone like old Ezra of Nazareth or even Barach of Bethlehem. These intimidating men in black robes with wide phylacteries and perfectly oiled hair intimidated me.

Lost in my anxious thoughts, I only caught the end of Antonius' introduction. "...and so, wise Rabbis, I have come with my friend, Joseph of Nazareth. We decided to seek your wisdom on this subject. Joseph has suggested that the Messiah is not only for the Jewish nation but for all people. I seek to understand if your god proposes such a thing. What is within your Holy Writings?"

I cringed when ten pairs of eyes focused on me. My heart began to thud almost painfully as the silence stretched out. I felt sweat beading on my forehead. At last, the youngest of the rabbis shifted.

He leaned forward slightly and spoke in a friendly tone. "Joseph of Nazareth, what brings you to Alexandria? Surely this is a far distance from your home. Did you travel here to consult with us?"

Swallowing, with difficulty, the lump of fear in my throat, I took a deep breath. "Learned Rabbis, I fled before the wrath of Herod and came to this city. I thought to seek your wisdom concerning Messiah. All have heard, even in Nazareth, of the Rabbis of Alexandria."

I ended the brief statement with a salaam of homage. My eyes had not missed the stir at my mention of Herod. I could not tell if it was interest, fear, or rejection.

The eldest of the teachers fixed me with a steady gaze. "What have you done, Carpenter, to rouse the wrath of the King of the Jews?"

My heart was pounding so loudly I feared the sound would echo in the room. I took another deep breath and stared above the heads of the assembled men. I saw again the three Magi and heard their warning. I remembered my dream in the night, the hasty packing and hurried journey away from Bethlehem. I recalled Ishi's report of the slaughter of the children.

"You know of the census of Israel by order of Caesar," I explained carefully. "Each man traveled to his family's hometown to be counted for the levee. My father came from Bethlehem. That is where I journeyed to with my wife. She was near her time and delivered a son soon after we arrived." Scenes of the stable and shepherds flitted across my memory. I looked at the rabbis. "Wise Magi came from the east and on their heels came death for all baby boys under two years old. Herod feared the child the Magi sought who would be King of the Jews."

The black-robed men put their heads together for a vigorous consultation. I waited.

"Continue," the rabbi ordered at last. "How did you come here?"

"I took my family and left Bethlehem before Herod's soldiers arrived. We did not even hear of the massacre until days later."

"How did you know to flee?" A narrow faced rabbi with a pinched mouth fixed me with squinted eyes.

"I…I…"

My thundering heart threatened to silence me. All eyes were on me. Antonius placed a hand on my shoulder. The touch steadied me.

Boldly I looked into the eyes of my questioner. "God sent me a dream."

Several of the men challenged the statement.

"A dreamer are you?

"Another Joseph come to Egypt."

"Is a famine coming?"

"God speaks to us in dreams."

"Why Egypt? There are other places to hide from Herod."

I stood silent before the barrage, unsure if I was expected to reply.

Antonius spoke instead, "Learned Rabbis of Alexandria, a fellow Jew stands before you seeking answers. You have turned this meeting into the inquisition of an innocent man. My friend escaped the hand of a mad king only to be subjected to your petty questions. Is it because you have no answers to give?"

The Egyptian's challenge stopped the murmuring. The eldest rabbi bowed his head in acknowledgment.

"You are right, Antonius of the house of Ptolemy. We were distracted by the young man's story. That God would send a warning dream to this man and no other seemed to us extraordinary."

As if expecting an explanation, the old man peered at me. I returned the look as calmly as possible. No one present would believe me if I told the truth about Jeshua. It was his future and life I sought answers for. I needed to know how raise the son entrusted to me so that he could fulfill his destiny.

At last the rabbi shifted his gaze to my companion. "You both, then, seek us out with questions about Messiah?"

Antonius bowed his head slightly. "Yes. It is well known that the Rabbis of Alexandria are the most learned in the world." A neatly manicured hand gestured to the scroll lined walls. "At your hands are the records of the Jewish people. You alone of all the world have access to the ancient manuscripts that can tell us who Messiah will be and what he will do. Will this One you hope for be just for the Jews or for all people?"

His simple question set off another discussion.

"Messiah is the son of David and will lead the nation to greater glory than Solomon."

"Messiah will be 'despised and rejected', a man scorned by those he would serve."

"Kings will fall from their thrones at the coming of Messiah."

"The wisdom of God will be in Messiah. All will hear and be amazed."

"Messiah is the Son of Man spoken of by Daniel."

"Healing of the people will be the mission of Messiah."

"All nations will come to his rising."

Confused by the babble, Antonius and I looked at one another and at the ten men. Each was energetically defending his position. They stood up to more forcefully state opposing positions. The Egyptian hid a grin behind his hand. I feared it was at my stunned expression seeing such learned men acting like schoolboys.

"Gentlemen, learned Rabbis," Antonius cleared his throat.

Gradually the men quieted and resumed their seats.

"King!"

"Prophet!"

Two of the rabbis could not resist one last challenge.

My friend had resumed his regal demeanor. "Rabbis of Alexandria, we see that you are indecisive about this expected Savior of Israel. We will return in, um, a week to learn of your consensus. Come, Joseph bar Jacob, carpenter of Nazareth. We have no further interest in this wrangling."

With that the man turned and strode from the room. Head lowered in defeat, I followed. It appeared that there was no simple answer to my question. Antonius sensed my despair.

"I am certain the rabbis will find the answer you seek. You are under my patronage."

I nodded, unconvinced.

"It is not that easy," I thought to myself.

CHAPTER 23

Only the chief rabbi was present when we returned a week later. Looking less imposing without his formal black robes, the man welcomed us in the small chamber where we waited on the last visit.

"Antonius, son of Ptolemy and Joseph bar Jacob of Nazareth, I bid you welcome. Accept my humble refreshment."

With a salaam the old man indicated a low table spread with all manner of delicacies. Some I recognized but most were strange to me. Politely, our host waited while we sampled the sweetmeats and spiced fish. A servant offered goblets of fine wine at a nod from the rabbi. When we were finally seated, the old Jew bowed to Antonius and then to me before he sat down.

"I am Josiah bar Hazael, eldest of the Rabbis of Alexandria," he introduced himself. "My life has been devoted to the study of the ancient texts housed here. My father's grandfather was one of the seventy scholars who worked tirelessly to translate the scrolls into Greek. From the archaic and scattered papyrus written in Aramaic, Hebrew, and even Syrian they compiled a copy of the Law and Prophets in Greek so everyone can read them. It is a sad commentary that many of our sons are more fluent in the language of foreigners than our own tongue," he added with a sigh.

The old teacher took a moment to look from me to the Egyptian. Antonius sipped his wine and returned the glance.

A wry smile creased the rabbi's lined face. "You came before us a week ago. The question you asked caused some small discussion."

"You have a fine way of understatement, Josiah bar Hazael," my companion chuckled.

I too had to smile remembering the uproar that erupted on our last visit.

"It is true that there are many conflicting opinions on who Messiah will be," acknowledged the rabbi. "I am prepared to outline them for you and answer any questions you have. First, however, I would ask you a question, Joseph bar Jacob."

Piercing brown eyes pinned me in place. Slowly I nodded agreement.

"Yes, Rabbi," my voice sounded strained and I cleared my throat nervously.

The old man's face softened, "Do not fear, young man. I ask this for myself and not for my fellow teachers."

I nodded and took a gulp of the wine. It burned in my throat. I set the cup down hastily.

"You said you had a dream. Tell me of it," he requested gently.

I knew I could not refuse even if I wanted to. In my heart I breathed a brief prayer. I did not look at Antonius or Josiah.

"An angel came to me as I lay in my blankets. The Magi had gone their way and Bethlehem was quiet. Suddenly the angel stood before me, a shaft of light. 'Arise, Joseph,' the command roused me. In amazement I looked at my visitor. 'Take the child and his mother. Go to Egypt. Remain there until I send you word.' Then without waiting for a response, the heavenly vision was gone. I got up and awakened my wife, Mary. We left in the night with only what we could carry on my donkey. It was at the camp of Abram of Nabatea that we heard of Herod's actions. With the son of Abram we traveled here."

I finally dared a glance at my two companions. Antonius leaned back, eyeing me over the rim of his goblet. The man's expression was unreadable. I sensed bewilderment in his attitude that only deepened when Josiah spoke.

Awe filled his voice as the old man recited several pieces of the Holy Writings. "'Out of Egypt have I called my son.'

'Kings shall come to the dawning and Gentiles to the rising of the Son of Man.' 'A voice crying in Ramah, Rachel weeping for her children.' Blessed is this generation to see the fulfillment of the promises made through Isaiah."

I could only stare in silence at the old rabbi.

He leaned forward, wrinkled hands clutched together as if in supplication. "Joseph bar Jacob of Nazareth, tell me the truth. It is your son the Magi visited and your child Herod fears?"

There was no way to deny the statement. I looked into the honest brown eyes. The hope burning there was the desire of every Jew since David's empire disintegrated. Perhaps it was the dream of every person. The desire to believe God cared enough to come close as in the days of the patriarchs and that the Creator would have pity on creation and redeem a holy people.

"Yes." My soft answer was like a stone dropped into a still lake.

The ripples began immediately. Antonius slammed his goblet to the table. Red wine splashed onto the polished surface. For a moment it looked like blood.

"By the gods, what claim of nonsense is this? Joseph, are you mad? How dare you claim that your son is the Messiah prayed for by your people for generations? Do you not know what danger that will place him in?"

"Antonius, my friend," I pleaded, but he raged on.

"You, Rabbi, only a fool would fill a man's head with the dreams of a fool! No one can stand against Rome. My family is proof enough of that! Why do you Jews everlastingly prate about a Messiah that will free you from whatever government controls your destiny? It is the hope of a hopeless people—this talk of a Messiah to lead you to victory!"

The Egyptian stood up and began to pace. The rabbi and I watched him silently.

After a minute he turned to me and continued in an urgent tone. "There is no person that can accomplish freedom for any of Rome's vassals. Mark Anthony died trying, as has every other revolutionary dreamer. Joseph, do not place Jeshua into such danger! Do not fill his mind with the prattle of hopeless ambition unless you want him to die on a Roman cross."

I shuddered at the truth of the image the man presented. He stood, head bowed, clutching the doorframe. Quickly I crossed the room to put my hand on the shoulder of my friend.

"Antonius, my friend, I understand your concern for Jeshua. Too well I know that a military uprising against the might of Rome is futile. That is why I sought the Rabbis. I have to know and understand the path Jeshua must take."

"You cannot protect the child from his destiny. If he is Messiah, God will show him the road," Josiah interrupted.

We both turned to face the old rabbi.

"Antonius, you are afraid that Joseph will place his son in danger for no reason or from misguided national pride. Joseph, you fear that the child will fail God if you do not direct his way or that he will die in the attempt to do the will of God."

I was amazed at the man's perception.

Antonius turned from the door and nodded slowly, "Jeshua has become the son I lost. Because of his trust, I have learned to love again. The thought of…of…danger appalls me."

I was surprised to hear the emotion in the Egyptian's voice. That he so deeply cared for my son amazed me.

Josiah motioned to the cushions. "Friends, sit down. I will tell you what I read in the scripture regarding Messiah. Remember," he cautioned, "prophecy is incomplete until it is fulfilled. Interpretation is, of necessity, limited by our human circumstances."

Then he expounded from the books of Daniel and Isaiah. I sat enthralled hearing the familiar passages linked together to form a picture of a Redeemer. This was not the warrior king I had often heard of on the streets of Nazareth, but one set apart by God to teach relationship with the Living God. The one Rabbi Josiah spoke of was for all people not just the Jews. My heart clenched when I heard the words 'despised and rejected of men'.

Antonius interrupted abruptly, "Rabbi, you share a vision where all nations might come to worship your god, the Yahweh you claim is the only god. Yet you say that all will hate the One who comes. How can this be?"

Josiah's response was sympathetic and came from long hours of meditation. "It does seem odd, does it not? The One who can bring life is cast out. Not everyone will reject the Son of Man. Those who fear the change He will bring will fight to retain their power. The humble and meek will rejoice to hear the words He will speak. As I said both prophecy and interpretation are shadows of the reality."

I shifted my position, uncomfortable with the thought of anyone hating the innocent child in my care.

As if sensing my discomfort, the rabbi turned to me. "Already you have seen how the rich and powerful react to the hint of a threat. Herod was willing to destroy an entire town in order to preserve his throne."

"What can I do?"

"God has protected you so far. Can you trust him to continue to guide you?"

It was a difficult question. I wanted to say 'yes' but I also needed assurance that all would be well.

The old man bent forward to address me when I did not reply. "I cannot guarantee that there will not be danger or that you will not stumble. I can only tell you that in my life, God has walked with me most closely in the worst of times. Even if we cannot recognize the hand of God, it is there. When I was about your age, my wife and children were dragged from our home in Heliopolis by a mob. Helplessly I watched as our house was set afire and then my family was..." His face contorted with remembered agony. With a deep breath he concluded, "They were bound and thrown into the inferno. Sometimes I still think I can hear their screams. I was driven from the city and not allowed to seek or bury my dead. When I came here I was a broken, bitter man. Gradually I found God again and learned that the Living One had never left me."

"I am sorry," I blurted, appalled at the inhumanity the rabbi experienced.

The horror of his account left me fearful for my own family.

Josiah smiled sympathetically. "My son, God has a plan, not only for your son, but for you also. Listen for the still small voice and you will not fail."

Antonius left me without a word when we exited the Rabbi's compound. Watching the man stride up the street I wondered if I was wrong to have spoken so plainly. Many times over the next few days I pondered our conversation. I knew I could not have lied to the rabbi.

Each morning and night I bowed my head toward Jerusalem wrapped in my prayer shawl and pleaded with God. "Blessed are you, Adonai Elohim, remember your servant, I pray. God help me to trust you. Keep my son Jeshua and Mary safe. Do not abandon us. You know I am afraid."

Mary sensed my lonely pursuit for answers. "My husband, it is hard to wait for God," she said one evening.

I raised my head and stared into her eyes. They were gentle with understanding.

"I too miss Nazareth and wonder if we will ever return. It seems Messiah should be raised in Israel, yet it is not to be. Tell me what you learned from the Rabbis. What do the teachers say?"

"Mary, my love, I had no idea…forgive me…of course you seek answers too."

I leaned across the small table to grip her small hand. We talked late into the night. Her astute questions delighted me. Long after my wife slept by my side I thought about her final statement.

"My husband, Josiah is right. God has chosen you for an important purpose in the life of Jeshua. You are his father. At the right time, I believe we will return to our home. Until then, I am satisfied to wait. Surely God has not forgotten us."

I wished I had her confidence in God for I felt very alone. The discussions with Antonius and the rabbi had not eased my fears and insecurities.

Barely a week later, Mary's urgent call brought me to her side from the shop. Even before she spoke, I knew what she needed.

"Send for the midwife. You will not have to assist this time."

My feet pounded along the hard packed street as I hurried to the home of Elisheva, the midwife.

"Please come," I panted. "Mary…it is time."

Calmly the woman picked up her basket, tossed a shawl over her head and followed me back up the street.

At the door she held up her hand. "Everything will be fine. Take Jeshua. I will send for you when the child is born."

The boy stood wide-eyed in the corner of the room watching the bustle of feminine activity.

I gathered the child into my arms. "Come, my son, we are not needed."

He removed his finger from his mouth to ask, "Mama?"

"Mama will be fine. You will soon have a baby brother or sister."

"Belly," he remarked.

"Yes, Mama has been growing a baby and now it is to be born."

We passed two neighbor women at the doorway. They barely nodded at me as they hurried to assist Elisheva. I sat on the portico of the shop playing with Jeshua and waiting. Listening to the murmur of the women's voices and the occasional cry from Mary took me back to a stable in Bethlehem when God had seemed very close. Looking at the boy who was stacking blocks of wood and then knocking them over, I marveled at the memory.

Jeshua glanced up when I asked, "Could it really be that over two years have passed since that night of wonder? Lord, God of the Universe, forgive my doubts. Your hand has been on me from the start. Here I am, use me as you will."

"Abba, you pray?" He inquired with his head tilted to one side.

"Yes my son, I was praying. Do you know God is very near? The One who created all things is still working. God wants each of us to love him because…" I paused, trying to put into words my dawning understanding of a God not bound by rigid laws but rather compassionately seeking a lost people. "Because the Holy One loves us."

Bright brown eyes looked up at me. Jeshua sat on my knee with his head cocked to one side.

"You know I love you, my son?"

Solemnly the boy nodded.

"God loves you even more than that."

The trusting eyes opened very wide.

"Never forget that. God called you by name even before you were born."

"Yes, Abba, me love you and God."

Then my son looked past me and wriggled loose. I turned to see where he was headed. Antonius stood at the gate.

"Jeshua, you have grown taller." The Egyptian tossed the child into the air and made him laugh.

Then he handed the boy a treat. The ritual complete, the child was happy to take his friend's hand and lead him to me.

"My friend, it has been long since you visited." I rose to bow a welcome. "I am glad to see you."

"My pride kept me away too long," he admitted. With a tilt of his head, the man indicated the bustle in the nearby home. "Do I come at a bad time?"

I shook my head and motioned toward the bench. “I welcome the company. Mary’s time has come and I am exiled from my own house.”

A grin of understanding crossed the smoothly shaved face. “It is the way of women. Men are not needed at such a time.”

“Do you believe what I heard you tell Jeshua?” The man looked at the boy playing in the sand of the yard. When I raised my eyebrows in question, my friend elaborated. “The idea of your god loving you, like a father. That seems foreign to what I know of your laws.”

“Yes, Antonius, I do. No matter how I look at my life I have to say that Adonai has been with me like a father to guide and comfort. He has given me courage and consolation.”

“Does not that go against your own priest’s teaching? Are there not laws you Jews must follow?”

“There are Laws designed to draw us closer to God and remind us of the sovereignty of the Almighty, but God is not contained within those Laws. If God is God, he is both within and beyond any man-made Laws. Messiah will reveal all truth and reconcile us to the Holy One.”

Slowly my companion nodded, his black eyebrows tilted in consideration. “Almost you convince me.”

We had no chance for further discussion. An infant’s cry pierced the afternoon. One of the women bustled through the door.

“You have a fine son,” she announced. “No,” she held up a hand when I started toward the house, “we will come for you when Mary is ready.”

Antonius brought his hand down on my shoulder in salute. “Congratulations! Another fine boy for the house of Joseph of Nazareth.”

Jeshua toddled from his game to stand between us. The small face tilted up with a wondering expression.

I crouched to the child’s level. “You have a baby brother. We will go and see him soon. Right now he is very little and will sleep a lot. Before too long you will be able to play together."

It seemed hours later when the midwife came to escort me to Mary. "You have a healthy son," she stated before leaving me with my family.

Mary cradled the tiny bundle at her breast. With Jeshua's hand in mine I stepped toward the bed. My wife drew back the soft blanket and held out the infant for my inspection.

"See your son."

Jeshua inched forward, amazement on his face. With one tentative finger he touched the tiny cheek. He drew back, startled, and tears welled when the baby started to cry. I cradled the boy in my arms as Mary offered the infant her breast again.

"It is all right, my son. See, he is just hungry," she said softly.

Mary held out her hand to Jeshua. He hesitated only a second before cuddling against his mother.

I could not stop myself from reciting the prayer spoken through the generations. "Blessed are you Adonai Elohim, King of the Universe, you have given me the joy of a son. May he be a strong branch in your household. We will name him James to honor his grandfather. My father's name, Jacob, is James in the Greek."

Mary smiled. I saw her stifle a yawn.

"My love, you must rest. Jeshua, come away, Mama needs to sleep now. It is hard work birthing a child."

A little pout appeared and the boy clung to his mother. "I stay," he insisted.

"Mama must rest, come with me to tell Uncle Antonius."

The child was torn between the desire to stay with his mother and the hope of another treat from his Egyptian friend. I was relieved when he scrambled off the blankets and took my hand. Mary's eyes were already closing. I bent and kissed my wife on her forehead. Jeshua took my hand and we walked back to the yard. Antonius waited for us, staring into the distance. The man turned with a smile.

"Baby Ja-ames," the child announced and followed it with his request. "Sweet?"

My friend was not able to withstand the hopeful look in my son's eyes. He handed over a sugared date from the packet in his robe.

"Here you are. A big brother deserves a treat."

Content, the child sat down to savor his prize.

Antonius grinned at me. "I can see all is well. You are the very image of a proud father."

"He will be called James. I will ask Josiah to perform the circumcision."

The Egyptian frowned in disgust and shook his head. "I cannot understand your desire to mutilate your sons. Why any sane person could believe that removing a piece so skin could make you more holy... That alone would be enough to keep me from turning Jew."

"Antonius, knowing your feelings and understanding that what I am going to say is very unusual, I have a favor to ask of you."

With slightly raised eyebrows the son of the Pharaohs waited.

"My friend, I would ask you to stand as witness when Josiah performs the ceremony."

We looked into each other's eyes. His held astonishment slowly changing to recognition of the honor I asked of him.

The man rested his hands on my shoulders. "Joseph, should not the sponsor be a believing Jew not a pagan Egyptian?"

"You are the closest thing I have to a friend here in Alexandria. Certainly I have done work for my fellow expatriates but with none of them have I shared the discussions I have with you. If God is God then there can be no distinction between Jew and Egyptian in God's eyes. If God has spoken directly to the Jews then ours is the greater responsibility. We must share that insight with all our neighbors."

Antonius stared at me in silence for so long I thought he was offended. "Joseph of Nazareth, you are unlike any man I have ever met. I will be proud to stand with you when the baby is circumcised, if Josiah agrees."

"Thank you."

Jeshua's sticky hands tugged my robe as he interrupted, "Abba, hung'y."

Almost in relief we laughed together. I tossed my son into the air. "Yes, we will find something to eat."

"Peace on this house and blessings on you and your family, my friend." The Egyptian smoothed Jeshua's curls in a fond farewell.

Antonius favored us with a regal salaam before striding away up the street. Jeshua waved until the man was out of sight. I entered the house with my son in my arms. As quietly as possible, I set about making something to eat. Flatbread spread with bean curd and cheese seemed to satisfy the boy. Absently I munched some myself. Later, I carried food to Mary when she awoke. Jeshua dozed on his own mat. I sat for a long time by the small window gazing at the heavens.

"God of the Universe, blessed are you. I seek to understand your will for me and for Jeshua. You seem far off and silent, but still you bless me greatly."

Sitting in the silence of the house, I felt a presence. In my heart I knew I was not alone even so far away from land and home.

"God is greater than we have been taught," I decided. "I will talk to Josiah about my thoughts."

I broached the subject after Josiah performed the circumcision. Mary took my wailing son to comfort him.

"Josiah, have we Jews been selfish with our revelation of God?" I poured wine for the old rabbi and my Egyptian friend.

Both my companions looked confused.

Hesitantly, I explained, “If God is one, then God is for all people not just the Children of Israel. Yet we have always kept others from knowledge of God.”

Josiah stroked his gray beard before he replied, “If God wants other nations to know God, a way will be provided.”

“Perhaps through Messiah?”

“Joseph, it is not for man to plot the ways of God. Your son may be the Promised One. If so, God will show him the path.”

The old rabbi looked at Jeshua. The boy stood quietly studying the flint knife used for the ceremony and fingering the long tassels on Josiah’s prayer shawl lying beside it. I wondered what the boy was thinking. Josiah turned to Antonius.

“What do you think of the news of the Emperor’s latest appointment?”

“Which do you speak of, Rabbi?”

“Archelaus has been crowned ethnarch of Samaria, Judea and Idumea now that Herod is dead.”

My hand stopped in mid air as I reached for the wine jar to refill my guests’ cups.

“Herod is dead?” I asked, hearing my question from a distance.

Antonius and Josiah looked at me in surprise.

“You had not heard?” The rabbi asked.

When I shook my head, Antonius explained, “Just yesterday a vessel from Rome brought confirmation of Herod’s death and the news that Archelaus has set sail for Rome to be crowned by Augustus himself. It is less than Herod had hoped for. In his will he named Archelaus as king. Antipas and Philip will each be allowed a small tetrarchy to govern at the pleasure of Caesar. The real power will rest in Rome.”

“What will happen to my people now? God, are we forever to be trampled beneath foreign powers?” The anguish in the rabbi’s voice caused Jeshua to look at the old man.

He trotted over and slipped a small hand into the wrinkled one that lay limply on one knee. Josiah was startled at the gentle touch. He looked down at my son.

"You are sad," the child stated wrapping chubby arms around the old man's neck.

After a second's hesitation, the teacher wrapped his arms around the boy and buried his head against the child. We all remained frozen until Josiah lifted his head.

"Child, you remind me that there is hope for Israel." The rabbi stood up with the boy in his arms and walked to the table. He picked up his costly prayer shawl and wrapped it around my son. "This is yours, Jeshua bar Joseph. Remember me in your prayers."

It seemed an odd thing to say to a child barely past his second birthday. Josiah kissed the boy and handed him to me. Then he rolled the ceremonial knife in its sheath and with a salaam moved toward the door.

"Peace on your house Joseph bar Jacob. May the Living God bless you and yours now and ever more."

Antonius and I were left speechless watching the rabbi plod up the street with lowered head. The Egyptian broke the silence as the old man stumbled and almost fell when a dog darted into the street.

"I will walk with him."

"Peace to you, my friend."

I watched my friend hurry after the old Jew.

Jeshua squirmed to the floor. He held up the trailing prayer shawl.

"Mama, look!"

"My husband?" Mary frowned at the expensive garment in her son's hand.

"It is a gift from Josiah," I explained, bending to untangle my son from the fringe and starting to fold the material. "We will put it here for use on the Sabbath."

Very seriously the boy watched me place the garment fit for the high priest on a shelf before turning his attention to the baby cradled on Mary's arm. He stretched to reach the infant. Mary crouched to his level. My older son kissed the new addition before trotting off to play.

CHAPTER 24

I lay awake long into the night thinking about the news from Judea and a conversation Mary and I shared not long before James was born.

"Are you content, my husband?"

Looking around the neat house and through the door to the carpenter shop cluttered with half finished jobs, I nodded. "Yes, we have made a good life here. Adonai is gracious."

My wife smiled up at me and cuddled close. I kissed her soft curls.

She tangled her fingers in my beard. "We have found friends. Anna and Helen often bring Nathaniel and Rebekkah to play with Jeshua. You have become friends with Antonius. This is a good place to raise our sons."

I wondered if it would be wrong to uproot my family and return to Judea. Down the street a dog barked. Eventually I slept only to wake when the moon was high. I was tangled in my blankets and sweating. Rising I walked to the small window and stared at the orb floating in the sky. The light shone like a path toward the east. Then I remembered my dream. An angel of the Lord had come to me again.

"Return to Judea. Those who sought the child are dead."

"Why must we leave here?" I argued. "There is safety in Egypt. My business prospers and we have found friends."

"Out of Egypt I call my son." The reply was a quote from the prophet Hosea.

"Where can we go? There would be no welcome in Bethlehem. Surely it is better to wait until the boy is older."

Ignoring my arguments, the angel repeated the instructions. "The Living God will guide your way. Return to your homeland. *I AM* will go with you."

Staring at the moon and the path that pointed east, I sighed and leaned against the edge of the window. "God, you ask too much. We are happy here. Why can't we stay?"

"Joseph, what is wrong?" Mary gently took my arm.

I turned and gathered my wife into a close embrace. "God has said that we are to return to Judea."

The woman gasped and looked around the neatly ordered room. All the pretty little items in the wall niches, the tables and benches I made recently, the pottery jars in the corner, even the newly woven blankets on the bed spoke of a loved home. My arms tightened.

"When?" I heard Mary catch her breath somewhere between a sigh and a sob.

"I…I…do not know. I will have to find a caravan and make preparations," I stammered.

She looked up and pleaded, "Joseph, can we wait until Jeshua celebrates his birthday?"

Glad for any excuse, I nodded. It was easy to rationalize the delay. "It will be better to wait until after the festivals. Purim will soon be here and then Passover and the Feast of First Fruits in Sivan. By then it will be getting too hot to travel and we should wait until cooler weather. Surely we can find a caravan for Jerusalem then."

Breaking the news to Antonius was even more difficult. I waited until Jeshua's birthday celebration. It was a small gathering with Antonius and Josiah joining my family for a meal and blessing.

Afterward the Egyptian prince gestured for me to follow him. "What is this rumor that you are no longer taking on work?"

"I…we must return to Judea. A messenger from God came to me in my dreams. Just as when we were told to flee to Egypt, we are now commanded to return."

As I expected the announcement of our departure angered the man. "How can you risk returning to Judea? Any hint of the coming of Messiah will bring death from Rome. Even Herod's sons will not look kindly on such a claim."

I had to agree with a sigh, "My friend, your concerns are mine. However, I cannot disobey God."

"Here, in Egypt, I can offer you the protection of my name and patronage. I have no such power in Jerusalem."

"I must obey the Living One who has provided for the Children of Israel."

Antonius threw up his hands in contempt and anger. "Joseph bar Jacob, you are a fanatic, a religious fool of a Jew. You claim a vision from this unseen and unknowable God as an excuse to take an innocent child into danger."

"My friend, I must trust that the God of my people will protect Jeshua. The One who called the Children of Israel from Egypt generations ago, now calls his son."

Dark black brows drew together at my claim. "His son! For the sake of the child do not lay such a mantle on the boy. Even if he is the Messiah of God, he is too young now for such a burden."

Breathing heavily the heir of the Pharaohs towered over me. We faced each other and I heard in his words my own concerns. Oddly, in the face of the man's rage, I felt my own doubts dissolve.

"God will make known the path for Jeshua at the appointed time. It is not my desire to force my son's feet."

Antonius frowned silently but I sensed his rage easing. His tone was less strident when he sighed, "I fear for you. Even if I do not understand you, I must honor your belief in your God. I will pray to the gods and perhaps even to your God to keep you safe."

"Thank you my friend." Sincerely touched by his concern, we parted with an embrace.

While waiting for a sign that the time was right to leave Egypt, I often went to the synagogue to pray. I felt comfort amid a sea of prayer shawl covered heads swaying in the current of holiness.

Sometimes Josiah himself led the congregation. He called my name one Sabbath, early in Tishri, to read the Torah. The cantor unrolled the holy scroll for me. One of the younger priests pointed to the beginning line. It was the familiar prophecy from Jeremiah.

"A voice is heard in Ramah..." My voice cracked slightly as I read, vividly remembering the colorful nomad tents of Abram's camp and Ishi's words telling of the disaster in Bethlehem.

"Have you any words to say to us, Joseph of Nazareth?" Josiah asked when the reading was complete.

I looked at the old rabbi. He smiled encouragement. Looking at the sea of expectant faces, I inhaled and nodded. "Men of Alexandria, friends, I have been among you for a short time. You have made me welcome. Now I ask for your prayers, for I return to our homeland. We live in times that are changing. The Living God is acting, even now, to fulfill all that has been spoken concerning Messiah."

The gasp that greeted my statement swelled to a murmur when I continued, "You have heard of Herod's massacre in Bethlehem. Every boy child two years and younger is dead. Truly Rachel weeps for her children. The King acted from fear for indeed 'Kings have come to his rising'. Prepare yourselves for God will act."

"Rabbi, what is this?"

"Who is this man?"

"False prophet, stone him."

"Rabbi, take the Torah from the heretic."

Voices were raised in accusation and clamor throughout the room. Men debated with one another. The young rabbi rapidly rolled the holy scroll away from me and stood holding it close to his chest.

Josiah stood up and raised his hands. “Men of Alexandria.” He had to repeat himself, “My friends, Jews of the Empire.”

Gradually the tumult died down. The old man stood beside me. “This, our brother, Joseph the carpenter of Nazareth in Galilee does not claim to be Messiah. He only warns us that Messiah is coming. The prophets themselves say this. Beware lest we are so blind as to miss the Coming One by our small expectations. The True and Living God of Abraham, Isaac, and Jacob never acts as we expect. Remember Gideon, Deborah, and Samson. From human understanding they were insignificant yet through them God wrought victories. Even great David was not born to royalty but as a shepherd.”

The congregation stood silent. There were a few nods and many pondering looks.

Josiah turned to me. “Go, Joseph bar Jacob. Return to Israel and may Adonai Elohim prosper your journey and protect your family.” The old man lowered his voice as he embraced me. “The way of a prophet is not easy nor is your path as father. Listen to God’s guiding.”

My eyes were moist and I gripped his arm in farewell. Curious, but no longer hostile, looks followed me as I walked through the crowd. Just outside the door, Mary joined me from behind the women’s screen. She slipped her small hand into mine. Jeshua grabbed my other hand tightly. As a family we walked through the dusty streets of the Jewish quarter.

“It is time,” I sighed. “I will seek a caravan.”

Mary’s nodded in agreement. “Yes, my husband. I will pack. Jeshua can help me.”

Walking past the homes of men I had come to know by name, I felt a sense of loss sweep over me. Again I was leaving behind the comfortable for the unfamiliar. The streets outside the Jewish area were busy with the usual traffic. The market was filled with local merchants and traders from far away. I hoped that Tomas would be among them but did not see his grinning face or hear his booming voice. I walked on toward the Trader's camp.

"Most of the merchants are in the city," a helpful guard at the gate informed me.

I nodded, but continued toward the camp. At first it seemed deserted. On the far side of the tent city I saw movement. As I drew near, I thought I recognized the seal on one of the crates. A murmur of voices reached me. Rounding the side of a tent I came face to face with Abner, son of Abram.

I greeted my friend with a salaam. "Blessings on you and yours."

The big man enveloped me in a hug. "Can it be? Joseph of Nazareth, I had hoped to see you but did not expect it on the Sabbath. Yet, here you are in my camp! Surely God is great! Come, sit with me and tell me of your son and your wife. Surely the boy is growing tall."

Urging me forward with his arm over my shoulder we walked toward the central tent.

"Hosea, bring food for our guest. Omri, see who has come to our camp."

Quickly platters of bread and cheese were placed in front of us. Omri hurried forward to welcome me with a bow and handclasp. When we were settled on the cushions, Abner tore off a piece of the fresh bread and handed it to me in the generations old nomadic way of sharing the staff of life. When we finished eating, my young host looked at me.

"Tell me, why does a Jew seek the trader's camp on the Sabbath?"

I looked at my friend. Memories of our first meeting brought a smile to my lips. This was no longer the unsure young horseman. The young man had become the competent trader his father hoped for.

"Truly, God is great. It is time for me to return to the land of Israel," I explained. "I long for my home and my kin. My son should learn of his heritage. Herod is dead and I have been told to return. "

Abner pondered my words. Then he nodded. "The Holy One's ways are strange. The reason I travel to Alexandria so late in the season is because one of my wives was delivered of twins at the beginning of summer. We feared for their lives but God is gracious. Both boys are now strong and healthy."

"Congratulations, my friend, may the Living God continue to bless you with many sons."

Abner bowed his head briefly in acknowledgment.

"You seek a caravan returning to Judea," he guessed.

"It is true. I hoped to find Tomas but now I have found you. God willing, you can offer us a place."

The young man grinned, "The God of Abraham, Isaac, and Jacob is more than gracious. Normally, I would not be ready to leave for days. This time my horses were all sold to the house of Ptolemy as soon as we arrived. It will be a blessing to have Joseph of Nazareth and his family with us. We only go as far as Beersheba where my father, the sheik, is camped."

"There we can find another caravan. I am honored that you will include us in your company, Abner bar Abram. We will gather our things."

A polite salaam sealed the agreement. I rose from the cushions.

"I will come with you to help," Abner insisted.

"Thank you, my friend."

Abner led a camel for our household items as we walked back into the city.

"This has become my home. Everything that seemed so strange is now familiar." My vague gesture encompassed buildings and people. "Even the smells of the city, which once seemed exotic and cloying, are comforting. The constant clamor of people, chariots and animals no longer keeps me awake at night."

"The King's Highway will seem very quiet after this." Abner motioned to a particularly loud group of Romans bursting from a tavern.

"Some things will not be missed," I admitted with a grin.

We turned up the side street toward the place that had been home and shop for not even two years. A lump tightened my throat as we drew closer. At Abner's command, the camel knelt inside the small courtyard. Mary stood in the doorway.

"My wife, you remember Abner, son of Abram. He is returning to Beersheba in the morning. We will travel with him."

A shy smile and nod welcomed our guest. Jeshua stopped dragging a large bag to stare at the big man and then at the camel.

The nomad crouched to look the boy in the eyes. "You are Jeshua. I remember when you were just beginning to talk."

My son glanced at the stranger before his gaze returned to the beast calmly chewing cud behind us.

Correctly guessing the real interest, Abner held out a hand. "Would you like to sit on the camel?"

"Oh, yes!" Delight filled his brown eyes and a grin brightened my son's face. Eagerly he grabbed the offered hand. Jeshua glanced at me from his perch on the animal's saddle. "Abba, may I?"

For the first time since the angel's visitation, I found myself laughing. Mary and Abner joined in.

"Yes, my son, you will ride many camels before we reach home," I answered when finally I was able to speak.

"What is the joke?" A familiar voice interrupted.

"Uncle 'Tonius, I ride camel!"

Excited by his adventure, the boy bounced in the saddle. Unconcerned, the animal continued to chew with eyes half closed.

"So I see." The Egyptian entered the courtyard with a grin.

"My lord, thank you again for your generosity in the purchase of my poor horses." Abner inclined his head toward my visitor.

Antonius ignored Abner's comment. He looked from me to the bags and bundles by the door.

"Then you are leaving."

"I must obey my God."

The Egyptian's cheeks tightened as he controlled his emotions. "Then I will pray that your God, and all the gods, prosper and protect you and yours. My friend, I will miss you. Yet who is to say if our paths may not cross again?"

Drawing a deep breath the man smiled down at Jeshua who abandoned the camel to tug on his friend's arm. The heir to the Pharaohs swung my son up onto his shoulder. He offered a bag of honeyed dates. With an eye on his mother, Jeshua took one and then a second from the pouch.

"That is enough," the woman cautioned with a smile.

Jeshua popped one date into his mouth and snatched another before Antonius could pull the string tight.

We all smiled when Mary repeated, "Jeshua that is enough!"

Many hands made light work of loading the camel. I led Balaam from his stall. On his saddle I hung my carpenter's tools. The shop stood empty except for wood scraps and sawdust. I picked up the cloth bag containing a small ebony box made for Antonius.

With a lump in my throat I presented the gift. "My friend, you have become a brother to me here. Surely the Living God means for all men to live as family not strangers."

Tears filled his eyes and for a long time he stared at the box. "Joseph of Nazareth, you are a special man. I will not soon forget you."

When I would have bowed in farewell, my friend drew me into his embrace. "May your God give you peace," he choked, emotion filling his voice.

Rapidly the son of Ptolemy strode away. I watched the Egyptian until he was out of sight. Then I turned. Mary stood in the doorway staring into the house. She cradled James in her arms. I drew her close.

"My love, this is not the life I dreamed for you."

"Joseph," a gentle hand rested on my cheek. "It is enough that we are together. God will show us where to go."

I lowered my head to kiss my wife's curls. Hand in hand we walked outside and pulled the door closed. Abner stood beside his camel with Jeshua perched happily on the saddle. Mary and I led Balaam through the gate. A last look of farewell up and down the familiar street was all I dared take.

"Hang on." Abner warned Jeshua as he signaled the camel to rise.

A squeal of delight came from the boy as he tilted forward and then backward with the beast's movement.

"Look, Abba, I bigger than you!"

Our little group barely received a glance as we plodded from Alexandria. Too many strangers came and went through the streets for us to cause a stir. A few small boys ran behind us for a short distance, attracted by Jeshua's appearance on the camel.

That evening I settled beside Mary in the tent Abner provided. Jeshua, exhausted from the excitement of the day, had fallen asleep in my arms over his meal. I kissed his dark curls before covering him with a light blanket against the chill of the night. Mary slipped her hand into mine.

"God has provided. It is good that we will travel with friends," she remarked.

"Yes, my love, I continue to marvel at how Adonai provides help when we need it."

"It has always been so. Ever since Adam and Eve, God has sought to give us all we need. Too often we turn away and try to be self-sufficient."

With a sudden insight, I sat up. "We are like children," I said eagerly. "Our attempts are as feeble as Jeshua's wooden boxes next to the box I made for Antonius. The True God seeks to give us everything, but we, in foolish pride, refuse it."

Mary sat up in the bed with a gasp. "Joseph, for a long time I have thought of God as like a father, but I never told anyone because it seemed…somehow…almost…too personal."

"The day James was born, I tried to explain God's love to Jeshua by telling him that the Holy One loves him more than I do as his father. Surely you, of all women, must be aware of how much love God has!"

"Yes, that is true. We have only to look at Jeshua to remember how close the Living God is. I know in my heart that God is near and God cares more intimately than we can know."

My arms slipped around the woman. We held each other silently rejoicing in the closeness of the Holy One of Israel.

Dawn brought the sounds of harnesses and men's voices. Jeshua sat bright-eyed on his mat. Mary opened her eyes and smiled at me. I stood and stretched.

"My son, we must roll your blankets and get ready to leave."

"Yes, Abba."

The boy's bare feet crossed the dirt floor. Clumsily he started to bundle everything together.

Kneeling beside my son, I showed him how to fold the blankets neatly together. "This way. Now we will take it to the camel."

I slipped my feet into sandals and the child copied my actions. Outside we tied the roll to the saddle. Our other possessions were already loaded. A few minutes later Mary emerged from the tent with James. Omri and I dismantled the tent. In a short time every camel was loaded. We headed east out of Egypt toward Judea.

"Soon we will be home," I told Mary when she looked back one last time.

The journey was uneventful. Day after day the animals plodded along the dirt road hard packed by generations of travelers, armies and refugees. Abner was an efficient guide. His well-trained men barely needed instruction. Camp was erected each night in an amazingly swift manner. I noticed the respect that even the Roman commander offered the young man when we paused at the outpost beside the Brook of Egypt at the midpoint of our journey.

Commander Horatius greeted Abner with delight, “That stallion you sold me a year ago is the best bargain I have ever gotten. The heart of that animal is amazing. He will go for hours without a pause. Our Roman horses falter after a couple of hours in the heat and sand. Half the mares in my stable are with foal by him. I look forward to a fine profit from the colts. My officers are anxious to purchase his sons.”

Abner bowed to hide his grin. “I am glad you are pleased. Our horses know the desert. That is why he does not tire. When I come again I will bring a mare that will breed even better horses for your stable.”

The Roman practically licked his lips in anticipation. “I will await your return with eagerness.”

Later my friend confided to me, “It is true that the stocky animals owned by the officers from Rome cannot compare with our desert bred stock. Ours are the best and proudest horses in the world. I am careful who I sell to, though. I would never sell to a harsh man. Horses are like children. They must be treated with love as well as firmness.”

“I would not know what to do with a horse, Balaam serves me well.”

“Your son prefers to ride the camels,” chuckled the young nomad. “I have never seen the like.”

Every morning Jeshua could be found petting the long noses of even the most irritable of the camels. At first Mary feared that the boy would be hurt. However, it seemed the animals liked his attention. When he was near they did not snap or spit while being loaded. Abner even allowed my son to lead one of the animals sometimes. When he got tired, the big man tossed Jeshua up onto the camel’s saddle where he rode happily.

"Another day and we will reach Beersheba," announced Abner one cool evening.

"It will be good to rest from traveling."

"My father will be delighted to welcome you. When I returned from Alexandria in the spring, he asked if I had seen you."

Surprised that my small family had made a lasting impression on the busy man, I inclined my head briefly. "I am honored that the Sheik of Nabatea would remember me."

Abner grinned in the firelight. The crimson flames lit his bearded face and his teeth flashed. "I too will be glad to be home. I have missed my wife and children. Jeshua will enjoy playing with them."

By midmorning we could see the vast nomad camp spread out in the valley not far from Beersheba. Somewhere near the town was the well dug by the patriarch Abraham for his flocks. Even after all these centuries it still provided water for the roaming flocks. A servant rode ahead to inform the sheik of our arrival. The old man hurried out to meet his son, riding a handsome white stallion.

"Welcome home, Abner, my son. God has prospered your trading to bring you home so soon."

Then the old man turned to me. I offered a salaam from where I stood beside Balaam.

"Welcome to my humble camp, Joseph the Carpenter. My son has done well to bring you to us. I look forward to hearing of your time in Egypt. Where is your son?"

The inquiry was not surprising for Jeshua was nowhere in sight.

"With the camels," Abner laughed. "It's where we always find the boy."

"Thank you for your hospitality, Sheik Abram of the Nabatea. I am blessed by your friendship."

"You honor us with your presence," the man insisted, before turning his horse around. "Come then, let us go."

At his signal, everyone moved toward the camp. I heard Jeshua laughing when his camel settled to the ground near the tents.

CHAPTER 25

We were welcomed as family to the nomad camp. The women greeted Mary and my sons joyfully. Abner's young wife shyly held his twin sons for my inspection.

"How do you tell them apart?" I looked from my young friend to the seemingly identical pair.

I heard a muffled giggle from beneath his wife's veil. Gently Abner drew one small arm from the wrapping. He found the wrist of his other son. One sported a red band, the other nothing.

"They are so close to the same that we have resorted to this. Helab, my first born," he asserted touching the head of the infant with the red band. "Nelab is my second born."

I offered my congratulations to father and grandfather with a slight salaam. "May both Helab and Nelab grow to be a blessing in the tents of Abram and Abner."

The evening passed in feasting and talk. Servant girls danced in celebration of Abner's return. Over endless platters of food the sons of Abram gathered to hear their brother tell of his journey and trading.

"Commander Horatius is pleased with his purchase. We will be able to sell many horses to him," Abner declared.

Ezra the oldest of the sons of the sheik, frowned in concern. "We must be careful in dealing with the Romans. Selling them fine horses may not be in our best interest."

"Horatius is an honest man," insisted Abner heatedly.

Abram held up his hands to prevent an argument. "For a Roman, he may be. Your brother is also right. If our swift desert beauties fall into the wrong hands, we put ourselves at risk." Turning to me he announced. "Now is not the time for such discussions. I would hear from our guest of his time in Egypt. Why do you return now to Judea?"

"Herod is dead. Just as I was warned to flee ahead of the massacre in Bethlehem, so now I am urged to return."

My host rose to his feet. Pacing back and forth he assessed the dangerous political situation. "What are your plans? Will you go to Bethlehem where Herod's son Archelaus still holds sway? The Emperor has approved the mad king's division of the country between the three surviving sons. Philip has the land to the north toward Syria. Antipas holds Galilee and Perea. The south is under the rule of Archelaus. Philip spends much of his time in Rome. He is seeking favors from the Emperor to oust his brothers. He is more Roman than Jew. Antipas seeks to solidify his position by marriage. Aretas' daughter Phasaelis will be his bride. I spoke against the betrothal but so many of my fellow sheiks fear the Romans more than Herod's son that I was shouted down."

I looked around at the solemn faces. They all nodded in agreement with their father's opinion.

"Stay with us, Joseph the Carpenter," urged Abner impulsively.

His father nodded, "Yes, my servants will be a defense against the threat from any of Herod's sons. Archelaus especially must be feared. Already Jerusalem has been torn by riots over the martyrdom of Judas and Matthias when they tried to prevent the Roman standard from being shown in the Temple itself. When Archelaus returns from Rome, crowned by Augustus himself, there will be more unrest. Already at least four men have made a claim that they are the Messiah. Word along the caravan routes is that the Syrian governor Publius Quinctilius Varus has troops ready if the riots led by the various claimants are not stopped soon."

My blood chilled at his words. The might of Augustus Caesar stood arrayed against any who would seek freedom for the people of Israel. Memories of crosses outside of Alexandria bearing the weight of those considered enemies of the empire came to mind. My heart began to thud heavily and fear gripped me. For a moment it seemed as if the eagle of Rome stretched her talons toward my son.

I bowed my head into my hands as I struggled to erase the image from my mind. I felt a hand on my shoulder and slowly looked up. It was Abner.

"Stay with us, Joseph, my friend," he repeated.

It was tempting. I wanted to keep the boy safe. What better way to do so than to remain beyond the ken of Herod's son and Rome? I stood and saluted my hosts.

"Sheik Abram, Abner my companion, and sons of the sheik, you have given me much to ponder. Forgive me. I must think and pray. Surely the Living God would not have told me to return to danger."

Again I touched heart, lips and forehead with a bow.

Abram's hand rested on my shoulder briefly. "May the One True God show you the way."

Almost blindly, I stumbled from the circle of tents. The darkness beyond the fires beckoned. It matched my mood. I found myself pitching face down onto the sand when an unseen rock turned under my foot. I gripped fistfuls of the sharp sand, as I lay prone. Invisible, minute edges on the dirt dug into my face. I felt larger stones through my clothing. The discomfort was nothing compared to the tortured confusion of my soul.

I heard an angry voice that must be my own. "God, why do you taunt me? When I try to do what you desire, I find danger." I pounded my fists against the ground beside my head. "As a boy, I sought you in the synagogue by the laws and scriptures of your people. What was the reward for my faithfulness? You, God, took my bride for your own and forced me to choose between law and love!"

The pain of Mary's revelation swept over me anew. Remembered feelings of doubt, betrayal and rage spurred me to my feet. In the dark desert night I paced further from the flickering fires in the nomad camp. My hands were still clenched around the sand in my fist like the tight band around my heart. I shook both fists to the distant stars.

"God, I chose love and took Mary as my bride ignoring the scorn of my neighbors and kin. Did you give me peace?" My challenge rang out and I answered myself, "NO, not ever since that day have I had peace! The child was born in a stable, unattended even by a midwife. Just when I started to find contentment and a home, strange visitors came."

I stopped in my restless movement to remember the Magi with their gifts and their warning.

I hissed an accusation into the blackness, "With them came danger and death. How could you allow all those children to die? Answer me!"

My demand went unheard. My knees buckled and I pounded my hands against the ground in rage and frustration.

"Are you even God? Is Antonius right when he says that the gods are just capricious spirits who delight in tormenting mankind? Can you not stop the killing and bondage of your people? Are we even really a Chosen People? Chosen for pain perhaps, but never for joy. Look at me. Am I not an example of your disregard? You, great God, order me to flee to Egypt. When I am settled and content you command me to return to Judea. Now I find that danger lurks there still."

Tears ran down my face as I crouched in the silent night. Not even a wild dog barked. It was as if I was alone in the universe.

"What do you want from me, God?" I sobbed. "I am not worthy of the task of raising Messiah. All I ever wanted was the simple life of a carpenter with Mary as my wife and strong sons to grow up in my trade. Why am I forced to walk this path not of my choosing?"

Agonized words rang in the night as I railed against God. Silence was my only reply. My turban fell to the ground as I grabbed my head in misery. Emptiness filled me. I desired yet dreaded a reply but I heard nothing.

A moan came from deep within my soul, "Now you leave me alone to find the way. I only wanted to be a simple carpenter. Why God, why do you torment me and leave me to grope my way through the blowing sands where I cannot find your way?"

Exhausted and past guilt at confronting the Living God, I rocked back and forth on my knees. With nothing but agony in my soul, I was silent. Gradually serenity came from somewhere. I understood how Jacob felt at the Jabok after wrestling with his God. It was as though the Almighty One spoke to my soul. Comforting words from Isaiah filled my head.

"I will never leave you or forsake you. You are precious in my sight."

Face down in the sand, peace washed over and filled me.

"Return to Nazareth, to your father's house," I seemed to hear the answer in my heart. "My Son shall be called a Nazarene. You will have sons and daughters, an endless blessing around your door. Fear not, Joseph, you have found favor in my sight."

For a long time I remained prone. Peace and love surrounded me and fear disappeared. My faith was not in vain. God was close.

"God of Abraham, Isaac, and Jacob you still act in the lives of the chosen people." I committed myself to whatever lay ahead. "You have never abandoned your people. Surely you will not abandon your own son. I will trust you to direct my life."

The sky was turning rosy in the east when I finally rose. My rapid steps carried me back to Abram's tents. I was surprised to discover it was a long distance. A group of servants led by Abner were gathered at the edge of the camp. Someone pointed in my direction.

My young friend hurried toward me, almost bouncing in his haste. "Joseph, we were…"

The man's eyes widened as he took in my appearance. I raised a hand to my head realizing that my turban lay far behind.

Dirt caked my face and beard. Glancing down, I saw that my robe and tunic, too, were covered with the desert sands.

"Abner, all is well." His obvious skepticism made me chuckle. I laid a hand on my friend's arm. "Truly my friend, all is well. I have been with God. I appreciate your concern."

"When your wife came seeking you this morning, we feared you were lost."

"Mary! I must go to her!"

Brushing past the men, I hurried toward the camp. I saw the group of women then heard a glad cry. The young woman running toward me was oblivious to anything else. I caught her in a tight embrace. Tears soaked my tunic.

Finally she drew back, sobbing, "Joseph, you are safe. I was so afraid."

Then she buried her face against me again.

Contrition choked my voice. "My love, forgive me, I needed time to seek God's path. I had to get away."

My lips touched the top of the bent head. Mary stirred and drew back. Lashes damp with tears rimmed eyes wide with wonder. The woman really looked at my sand-covered appearance for the first time. She reached up to brush some of the dirt from my face. Futilely she dusted at my robe.

"And did you find God?"

Before I could answer, Abram interrupted. Concern made his voice gruff. "Joseph of Nazareth, it is good to see you safe."

Turning, I drew Mary to my side, keeping an arm around her shoulder. "A thousand pardons, Sheik of the Nabatea. I lost all sense of time as I prayed for guidance."

He gripped both shoulders in his strong hands. Steadily my host stared into my eyes. "You have found your answer."

"Yes." I added, "It was not an easy night."

"Seeking the Holy One is never easy." His mouth lifted in a slight smile. "Come, you must be hungry. Tell us what you want of your night, or keep your own counsel."

The old man turned and led the way to his tent. Already servants had platters of bread, cheese and fruit spread for us. One young man held a bowl of water for me. Another offered a clean robe. Gratefully, I splashed the water on my face and donned the garment.

Mary drew back. "I will wait with the women. I should not be here," she murmured.

"Nonsense my daughter," Abram overrode her shyness. "You have as much right to hear of your husband's night as we do. Indeed more right. Come, you are welcome. We are as family."

With a nod and reassuring squeeze of her small hand, I led my wife to the cushions. Shyly she accepted bread and cheese. Abram insisted that I partake of the food spread before us. I ate only a little, sensing the expectation in the tent. With a final sip of the wine I glanced around at the eager faces.

Looking at my wife I stated, "We will go to Nazareth. There we will live and raise our sons. God has shown me that the children of Israel are not forgotten. The Holy One of Israel does indeed care for all people as a father. God's ways are not what we expect."

Mary's lips parted and her eyes lighted with joy. "Our parents will see Jeshua!"

Turning to the sheik, I bowed. "Thank you for your offer of safety, my friend. If it was for me alone, I should not hesitate. However, the God of Abraham, Isaac, and Jacob whom you also know, has sent me to my kin in Nazareth. I do not know what awaits there, only that I must obey the One who has directed me so far."

"You must follow your God," the old man agreed. "Seldom is the way of the Almighty easy."

"Truly my friend, you speak truth."

"I will set you on your way with supplies for your journey and an escort along the coast. My caravans are known as far north as Sidon. No one will question their passage. It will be faster than through the mountains."

"Again you overwhelm me with kindness I can never repay." My voice grew husky with emotion as I bowed my head to the sheik.

"It is what I would do for any friend."

"Then I am doubly blessed to have your friendship, Abram, Sheik of Nabatea."

The rest of the meal was spent planning the trip.

CHAPTER 26

Abram rode with us as far as the city of Gaza two days later. Our departure was delayed because all the women on the camp had gifts for Mary. Abner's wife presented a soft scarf to her. One of Abram's five wives insisted we wait while she found a certain blanket for James.

"It is the one woven from the finest wool," she informed her husband. "The child will need it in the mountains of Galilee."

Another woman prepared a huge bundle of dried figs and dates stuffed with nuts that we had to find a place to pack. The sun was halfway up the sky when we finally turned toward the Great Sea. Calls of farewell and blessing rang after us.

"You have made many friends," I told Mary.

"Jeshua made friends with everyone in camp," she responded pointing to the children running beside us.

"My children, you must return to the camp," Abram ordered finally and sent them back to their mothers.

The camp we made in the late afternoon was small by the sheik's standards but we had no fear of bandits or wild dogs with his servants standing guard.

At Gaza, Abram turned back. "Abner will see you safely to Nazareth," he stated. "Joseph, may the God of your Fathers keep you safe and bless you with many sons."

The sheik gripped my arms when I would have bowed in response. He drew me into his embrace.

Then he turned to Mary. “May God be with you, my daughter.”

Gently he laid a hand on Jeshua’s head before crouching in front of the boy. “The hand of God is on you, my son. May the Holy One bless and keep you now and always.”

Rising, the old man turned back to me with a blessing, “My friend, may your son grow to be a blessing to the nations. God has caused our paths to intertwine, I pray the God of Abraham, Isaac, and Jacob, who we both serve, will prosper your way until we meet again.”

I felt tears prick my eyes at the man’s obvious affection.

“Abram, Sheik of the Nabatea, your hospitality is a blessing beyond words May the Living God bless you and your sons for you have shown the hand of God to a refugee and stranger.” I found myself unable to continue when the man again embraced me.

Abruptly he turned away. With surprising agility for a man of his years, the sheik mounted his horse. In a cloud of dust he vanished toward his home. Servants hurried to mount and follow. Abner watched his father depart before turning to me.

“We will leave at first light. I have found a caravan master willing to allow us to join him,” he smiled.

Under Abner’s direction a tent was erected for Mary. Jeshua felt no awe of the armed men who watched over the camp. To Mary’s horror and my amusement my son borrowed one of their daggers and used it to dig up an anthill. The owner squatted nearby watching the boy with a grin.

“You can play another time,” he promised when Mary called Jeshua to her side.

“Are armed guards necessary?” She asked, glancing somewhat nervously at the muscular men eating and laughing not far away.

“It is Abram’s way of continuing his hospitality. It would have been rude to refuse the offer of an escort. When we reach Nazareth, we will again be simply Joseph the carpenter, his lovely wife, and fine sons.”

Even as I spoke I wondered if we would ever simply be Joseph of Nazareth and his family. For the night I put away my concerns. Later, I held Mary in my arms until she slept. Snores outside told me that Abner and the sheik's servants also slept although I knew the men kept watch in shifts. There would be no danger in the company of Abram's men. Slowly I slid into a dreamless sleep.

The caravan Abner found was headed for Caesarea and then further north to Tyre to trade with the Romans. It carried exotic woods from south of Egypt as well as some heavily guarded, locked trunks, which I guessed carried gems from deep in Nubia. When Kasim, the trader, learned that I was a carpenter, he was quite eager to show me the lumber.

On our third day north of Gaza the man fell into step beside me.

"My friend, I am certain you have noticed the exquisite woods I carry. For such a fellow traveler as you, I would give a good price. Yes?" His oily familiarity made me shudder inwardly.

"I have no need of such fine and exotic pieces."

The man did not give up easily. He leaned closer so that I could smell his stale breath. "Ah, but you would love to work with the ebony and the mahogany. I can see it in your eyes. This evening I will show you some of the pieces. You will find that they are without knots. I only trade in the finest of lumber."

I was almost relieved when the man was distracted by a shout from one of his slaves. A load had shifted and threatened to crash to the ground.

"Stop! Stop! Fools and dogs!" He rushed away cursing to beat his slaves and oversee the redistribution of the wood on the cart.

I sighed at the delay. Each day I was more anxious to reach Nazareth and home. It seemed eons since we left the small hill town for the census. Our families no doubt thought us dead or lost forever to Egypt.

"Abba, why does that man beat his servants?" Jeshua's innocent question jolted me from my thoughts and made me aware of what was happening.

Mary sat on a rock rubbing her feet. Her brows were drawn together in concern. Kneeling beside my son, I looked with him at the scene. Kasim's whip snaked out. The men cringed away from his rage and lash. He did not seem to care if the blows landed or not. It was enough that the men in his control feared him. Even the oxen drawing the cart lowed and tried to pull away from the stinging strap. The slaves holding the beasts were hard pressed to keep them quiet. It was a scene I had grown used to in Alexandria. Richly garbed men and women shouting and beating their slaves was a common sight in the metropolis. I realized that Jeshua had never seen men who were slaves because he was not allowed far from our home. The inhumanity and brutality of slavery suddenly swept over me.

Propelled to my feet by my son's sob when the whip laid open a man's arm, I moved forward to catch the trader's upraised arm in my hand. "Kasim, this is wrong."

The wiry man twisted in my grasp. Eyes narrowed to slits by his anger, glared at me. "Jew, do not interfere in what is no business of yours."

"God did not make men to be treated as beasts." I stood my ground and continued to restrain the man.

He hissed derisively and looked around for support. "You are a fool. A Jew, trodden under the foot of Rome, seeks to reprimand me. I am Kasim, son of Pushar of Ethiopia, descendent of the great Queen of Sheba. These men are my property."

The crowd was silent. I could not judge who held the favor of the gathering. The self-proclaimed heir of royalty jerked free from my grip and began to coil his whip.

"The One God created men and women to work freely and serve only the Almighty," I stated calmly.

I did not flinch when the tip of the whip raised dust near my feet. "Do not prattle to me of religion. Has your God saved the Children of Israel from the hand of Rome? No," he answered himself. “And why not? Because the God you claim is all-powerful is a mirage. Power is in the hands of those who can take and hold it. The weak serve the strong. That is the way of the world. You would do well to learn that truth, Jew!”

Kasim’s dark face was very close to mine as he finished his statement.

Confidently I responded, “Kasim, heir of Ethiopia, know that the True and Living God is not mocked. Just as in the days of Moses, the One who created all things will act to free all peoples not just the Jews. The Queen of Sheba traveled to visit Solomon of Jerusalem. Behold a greater than Solomon is coming. His kingdom will be the one ordained by God from the beginning. The weak will not be made to serve the strong for all men will be as brothers.”

With a sneer the trader drew back. Contemptuously he curled his lip. “You are a fool and a dreamer. Jews would be wise to spend more time seeking might and less time remembering a grand past and praying for a glorious future.”

The man turned on his heel dismissing my presence.

He paused briefly when I answered quietly. “Kasim, to the Jew has been given the mandate to be a light to the nations. We have failed for we have become inward looking and fearful. The God of Abraham, Isaac, and Jacob has not changed. All men will do well to look at their lives and amend their ways.”

“Bah, keep your religion, Jew,” the trader snarled. “None of us care to hear of your empty promises. Let us move on.”

He checked the ropes holding the load of wood and signaled for the caravan to start again.

I took a deep breath and tried to relax.

“My husband, surely God opened your mouth,” Mary gasped. “I am glad you stopped Kasim.”

“Abba, you stopped bad man!” Jeshua shouted.

His words brought a serious smile to my lips. “Yes, my son, it is not right for any man to treat another as an animal. Those with power must use it wisely and for good.”

Abner joined us as I erected Mary's tent for the night.

"Joseph the carpenter, you have courage," he said with respect. "I stood ready with my father's men to come to your aid but you had no need for our intervention."

Kasim ignored me for the remainder of the journey. Another day brought us to Caesarea. Ships from across the empire rode at anchor in the harbor created by Herod.

"The bustle of the port reminds me of Alexandria," I mentioned to Abner.

The young man agreed, "For all his insanity and paranoia, Herod was a wise builder and crafty politician. He retained his hold on Israel even amid the changes of the Roman court. Despite backing Mark Anthony in the failed bid for the throne of the Empire, he remained in power. This city, on the Great Sea, is named for the Emperor to prove the loyalty of Israel and her king. His sons grew up in Rome as wards of Caesar himself. The arrangement has alienated his heirs from the people of their country as Archelaus is learning to his sorrow."

"What the children of Israel need is a Jewish king who follows the Law and the Prophets," Ishi remarked.

"The God of Abraham, Isaac, and Jacob will act when the time is right," Abner stated.

"Faith in the True God had no national or ethnic boundaries," I murmured to myself.

In the morning Kasim sent word that we were no longer welcome in his caravan. The slave who brought the message was apologetic. From the bandage on his arm, I recognized him as the man whose beating spurred me to action.

"I will find you another caravan." Abner immediately stood up, prepared to speak to the other traders camped nearby.

I stopped the young man. "There is no need. From here we turn northeast. We can cross the low coastal hills into the plains. Once across the Kishon River, we are home in the hills and Nazareth is less than a day away. The route will shorten our journey by perhaps two days."

Turning to the still hovering slave, I gripped his hand. "Thank your master for his hospitality," I ignored Abner's snort of contempt. "May the One God of all bless you and keep you."

I was surprised to see tears in the man's eyes. "Thank you, great lord. You have reminded me that not all men are cruel. May your God be with you."

With that the slave bowed to me and strode away. Sadly I saw his back slump as he neared Kasim's fire.

Chapter 27

I eagerly loaded my tools on Balaam as the sun rose over the hills to the east.

"Soon we will be climbing those hills and descending into the rich valley beyond," I told Mary. "I can almost smell the juniper and pines around Nazareth."

I turned to say farewell to Abner. The young nomad shook his head and motioned to his servants. "We will accompany you. My father told me to see you safely to Nazareth. Our friendship would have me do nothing less."

"It is not necessary," I argued. "We are close to home now. You and your men may return to your tents. We will be quite safe. God protected us on our journey from Nazareth nearly four years ago. Surely His arm is not shortened."

"Allow me this service that I may report to my father that you are safely in the bosom of your family." With a resolute look in the dark eyes above the thick beard the young man stared at me.

I grinned and shrugged, "Very well, I will enjoy showing you the way for a change."

Mary alternately walked and rode as we climbed the hills. Jeshua capered about exploring rocky outcroppings and chasing lizards until his short legs grew tired. Then Abner hoisted the boy onto his shoulders where he shouted with delight at the vistas he could see.

"The view is amazing," Abner observed when we reached the summit. "In one direction you can see the Great Sea in the distance. In the other there are fallow fields running across the valley. What is the river?"

"That is the Kishon," I responded. "This time of year, it is not the rolling torrent of spring. Across from us are the hills where Nazareth is nestled."

Mary prepared the meal when we made camp against the lower outcroppings. Abner and the sheik's servants were delighted to share the stew she offered. Afterward, I leaned back against the packs near the fire. Abner and his men also lounged comfortably a slight distance away.

"Soon we will be home." I savored the statement with a smile for my wife.

Mary looked up with a dreamy expression. "Yes, my husband, it will be good to see my mother and father. They will be so happy to see our sons!"

"You will meet your grandparents," I promised Jeshua.

The boy was busily polishing a small kettle with sand in imitation of his mother. He put the pan down to crawl into my lap.

"Abba, what are grandparents?" Jeshua's artless question reminded me of the unusual life he had led.

"They are my mother and father and Mamma's mother and father. Like Antonius and Abram they will love you very much."

"Then I will love them," the child nodded happily.

"Come, Jeshua, you must go to sleep." Mary held out a hand.

Briefly the boy considered refusing.

When his lower lip jutted in a pout I gave a slight nudge. "Go, my son, tomorrow will be another long day of travel. You must be rested. There will be much to see."

Abner chuckled when the boy ran to the tent. After the flap slipped into place we heard Mary's sweet voice begin a lullaby.

After a moment the nomad sighed, “You are blessed. It is different in the camp of my father. The women care for the children away from us men. You have a relationship to your wife and sons that I envy. That song brings back memories of my childhood, but I do not even know if my wife sings it to my children.”

“Circumstances have made my family close,” I admitted.

“Do not lose that relationship when you are settled,” the nomad urged.

I mused, “It is true that Jeshua spends more time with me than most boys his age. I remember my own father and I shared time the wood shop when he was not away on trips to other towns. Until I was ten he was gone most of the time. Even when he was home, we had little in common except the love of the wood.”

“You are blessed,” Abner repeated.

Later when I lay in my blankets, I wondered briefly if God himself seemed distant because we spent so little time seeking him. My thoughts became jumbled as I drifted off to sleep.

Morning brought cloudy skies and a chill in the air that warned of the lateness of the season.

Glancing at the hovering clouds I warned, “There is a chance of snow at least on the mountains before dark. We must get across the valley to the shelter of the far hills today.”

I set a rapid pace. Jeshua had little time for exploring. He perched on the camel, or rode someone’s shoulders as the mood suited him. Our small caravan attracted some attention from the farmers readying their fields for crops. Men waved hesitantly at our odd parade. Jeshua cheerfully waved to the workers.

“A man leading a laden donkey on which a woman and baby rode followed by a half dozen armed nomads striding down the road is not a common sight,” I chuckled to Abner. “Your camel is a curiosity rarely, if ever, glimpsed along the Kishon.”

I stopped in the lee of a cave when we met a cold wind whistling down from the heights late in the afternoon. “We must make camp. It would be foolish to press forward into the teeth of this storm since we do not have to."

"Wise decision," Abner agreed.

I admitted with a sigh, "I had hoped to go further today."

"The safety of your family must come first. We will reach Nazareth soon enough. For myself, I am not sorry to spend another night in the company of Jeshua. Your son never ceases to amaze me with his curiosity."

We all laughed when the boy emptied his pouch of the treasures collected during the day. A shiny stone, a lizard which gratefully escaped when released, wool caught on a thorn that the child spent several minutes trying to disentangle before giving up. He had exciting explanations for each object.

"Lizard was on the rock. He was pretty!"

"See the colors in the rock, Abba? Like a rainbow."

"Lamb almost got stuck but a shepherd saved it from the thorns."

I marveled at his quick mind, even as Abner remarked, "You'll be quite the storyteller when you're grown, my boy."

The clouds and storm were gone by morning. A dusting of snow lay across the valley and became ankle deep by the time we reached the top of the path.

The sun was starting its descent behind us casting long shadows on the road when I joyfully announced, "Nazareth is just ahead!"

Mary leaned forward eagerly and urged Balaam on. An hour later the village was in sight. I drew Balaam to a stop, suddenly almost afraid to continue.

Mary looked questioningly at me. "Joseph?"

The camel's harness jangled as Abner pulled the animal to a stop beside us.

I pointed out the low slung houses along the hill. "There is Nazareth. My father's home is on the far side of the village."

"Abba, why did you stop?" Impatiently Jeshua tugged my hand. "I see dogs and boys!"

"Let us go." Taking a deep breath, I took one step and then another toward the place I had called home for so many years. From my heart rose an unspoken prayer, "God of Abraham, Isaac, and Jacob, your will be done."

The boys in the street saw us first. Their excited cries to friends brought mothers to the doors of houses all along the road.

"A camel!"

"Hurry, Lisbeth, come see the camel!"

"Hester, it is a camel!!"

"Who could it be?"

Soon men began to appear. I saw Joachim coming down the hill and turned toward him. Mary slipped from Balaam's back. She thrust James into my arms and began running toward her father.

"Father, I am home," she called like a little girl.

Her announcement caused quite a buzz. All eyes focused on me.

"Could it be Mary?"

"Then is that Joseph?"

"We thought them dead."

Old Elkanah stepped forward to peer nearsightedly into my face.

"It is. Joseph bar Jacob has come home."

A clamor broke out at his statement. I lost sight of Mary as the townsfolk converged on me. My last glimpse was Joachim holding his daughter tightly in his arms. With streaming eyes he looked at the sky in praise and thanksgiving.

"Welcome home."

"Where have you been?"

"Your mother and father will be so glad."

I felt an insistent tugging on my hand and looked down. “Abba, where are grandparents?”

Jeshua’s question was greeted with laughter.

I picked up the boy so he could see Mary approaching beside Joachim. “Here comes Mamma with your grandfather.”

My father-in-law had an arm around his daughter. The crowd parted for the pair. I embraced the man.

“Joseph bar Jacob, you have returned!”

Jeshua interrupted our reunion. “Are you my grandfather?”

“If you are Jeshua, I must be.”

The child squirmed to the ground, walked to the old man and held up his arms to be picked up. The simple action delighted many. I heard sighs and sniffs from the gathering. A commotion from the back of the crowd rippled forward as my mother was ushered into my arms. Her relief and joy smote my heart. I gathered the woman close. I felt frail bones beneath her garments as I held her.

“My son! And this is your son.” Gently one hand touched James on the cheek.

I called to my first born. “Jeshua, this is your grandmother.”

Obediently the boy left Joachim. The old man lifted his hands and I saw his lips move in prayer.

“Mother, this is Jeshua.”

“Jeshua,” with awe the woman breathed the name.

The child stared at my mother before stating, “You are my grandmother. I like you.”

Tears slid down the woman’s cheeks and I saw Mary’s eyes were bright with brimming tears. I suddenly realized that my mother-in-law was not present.

“Where is Anna?”

“She has not been well,” Joachim said soberly. “Your return will be just what she needs.”

“We must go to her,” I responded to the unspoken urgency from the old man.

Joachim gestured to Abner and the sheik’s servants waiting patiently. “Your…uh…servants?”

“These men are my friends, an escort provided by Abram, Sheik of the Nabatea,” I explained.

A gasp of awe followed by whispers of speculation rippled from nearly every throat.

“I will see to their comfort and then come to your home, father of my wife. Mary should go with you now.”

My response brought almost a sigh of relief from the man. Mary took James from my arms. Jeshua proudly held his grandfather’s hand. They walked together up the road.

I slid an arm around my mother’s waist. “Come, meet a man who has become as a brother to me.”

The crowd parted and closed behind us. Everyone turned to watch the meeting.

“Abner, son of Abram, sheik of Nabatea, this is my mother Sarah. In friendship he wanted to see that I returned in safety to Nazareth.”

With an elaborate salaam, my friend exclaimed, “Surely your heart must rejoice to see your son returned.”

Shyly the woman glanced at the stranger. Then her gaze traveled to the guards and returned to my face.

“My mother is there room beyond the courtyard of Jacob’s shop for the tent of my friends?”

At my question Sarah slowly nodded, “My son, your friends are welcome at the home of your father. Jacob will be sorry to have missed meeting these men.”

Abner fell into step with me. His servants led the camel and Balaam behind us.

“Mary and I will make our home with you,” I told my mother. “Pray God there is a need for a carpenter in Nazareth.”

For the first time since my return, my mother laughed. “More than enough work, my son. You will be overwhelmed with jobs. Everyone in the area will want to have something done by the widely traveled son of Jacob.”

I had no chance to answer for we had reached the home of my childhood and youth. It looked as it always had. A squat mud-brick dwelling, whitewashed many times and even now needing a fresh coat nestled not far from the highway. Across the road was the home and shop of Elam the smith. The acrid smoke from his bellows sometimes stung the nose. Just over the rise was the residence of Simon the tanner. His walls were always hung with the drying skins of a variety of animals. The wind today blew the odor of his occupation away from Nazareth. I opened my gate and with a bow ushered my guests into the long narrow courtyard. One cart with a broken axle sat tilted near the shop door. Inside I pictured the tools and worktables.

Mother hurried into the house while I began to unload Balaam. Abner ordered the camel to her knees. The supplies and saddle were removed swiftly and efficiently. My friend joined me when I paused in the doorway of the carpenter shop. Emotion flooded over me.

“It has been more than three years since I stood here, preparing to travel to Bethlehem,” I remarked. “So much has happened.”

“This is your home. The One God is gracious.” A firm hand gripped my shoulder in friendship and support.

“Yes, through all things Adonai has been with me. It is good to be home.”

I looked around the familiar and yet strange surroundings.

“My friend, you are blessed indeed,” repeated my friend.

“I am most fortunate to have found friendship with you and Abram.” My voice sounded almost gruff as I struggled with my feelings. I could have added Antonius and Josiah, rabbi of Alexandria to my list of newfound friends.

"My son," Sarah interrupted our conversation from the door of the house.

Dropping the leather bag of tools I hurried across the short distance.

"Naomi brings word from Joachim that we should come to his home for a festive meal. Your friends are welcome at his table." A wave of her work worn hands encompassed the men nearby.

The plump serving woman who I did not recognize repeated her invitation, "Master Joachim bids all at the house of Jacob to a feast prepared in celebration of Mary's return and the birth of his grandson."

"I will bring fruit and wine. Jacob brought a rich vintage from Damascus as payment from the customer there. Perhaps your friends would help carry it?"

Sarah indicated two skins of wine in the corner. I smiled at the way my mother organized our expedition even while piling apples in a basket.

"Let us wash the dust of the road from our faces and change our robes," I replied.

Suiting action to words, I poured water into a large basin. We rapidly washed arms and faces. Clean outer garments were shaken from the packs. In a short time we were ready to accompany my mother and Naomi to the home of my father-in-law. Curious neighbors lingered in the street to watch and several children with a yapping dog ran behind.

"Anna has been very ill," Mother cautioned when we neared the house. "Do not be surprised if she cannot join us."

Jeshua's giggles could be heard before we reached the house. Joachim's hearty chuckle and a woman's laugh followed. Naomi ushered us past her through the doorway. My mother stopped in amazement.

"Anna!"

Her astonished gasp caused Joachim to turn from his wife's side. She sat comfortably on cushions laughing with my son on her lap. I noticed the thinness of her face but the pallor I expected to find was missing. A healthy blush painted the cheeks of my mother-in-law. Mary looked up from braiding her mother's hair to give me a smile. Joachim rose to his feet. He bowed a welcome to Abner. In two strides he crossed the room to take my hand.

"Joseph, my Anna is well. From the moment Jeshua climbed onto her pallet and called her 'Grandmother', she began to revive!"

I felt my heart begin to thud. My eyes sought Mary's. She nodded in affirmation.

Anna called me to her side. "Joseph, my son, come and give me a kiss."

"Anna, it is good to see you," I stammered, trying to assimilate the news.

Kneeling beside the woman I kissed one wrinkled cheek.

"You expected a dying woman," her chuckle bubbled out. "Indeed everyone in Nazareth has known of my illness."

My mother slowly came forward to settle on the cushions beside her friend. "What happened?"

"You know I felt sadder and sadder since word came that our children went to Egypt," the old woman began. "It seemed that life was not worth living. Nothing you or Joachim or the rabbi could say made any difference."

"Yes," my mother nodded with a slight frown puckering her forehead.

"Today when I heard the commotion in the street, I turned my face to the wall and asked God to let me die."

"No!" Sarah exclaimed in a shocked tone.

A slight, understanding smile curved Anna's lips. "What good is a life when you do not even care about shouts in the street announcing camels and strangers? Then I heard Joachim's voice. He said, 'She is ill, I do not know if the child should go in.' The next thing I knew, a pair of small arms came around my neck and a voice called me 'Grandmother'. I felt…" The woman paused and looked past us all. Then she focused on Jeshua and resumed her recital. "I felt…I am not sure what I felt but my sorrow was gone. I heard birds singing and the breeze blowing. I opened my eyes to find Mary beside me and this boy hugging me."

Tears ran down Sarah's cheeks. The boy scrambled from one grandmother to the other.

"Do not cry, I love you too," he assured each one.

My mother embraced the boy, sobbing with joy.

Joachim turned to Abner, still standing just inside the door. "Forgive us. My wife has been ill for a long time. We are so glad she is well that I have neglected hospitality."

"May the True God continue to bless your family," the nomad responded with a low salaam. "I too rejoice that your family is together and your wife restored. It is my honor to serve Joseph bar Jacob and bring him home to his family."

"Let us feast in celebration, not only of the return of Joseph but of my wife's recovery and your friendship!"

The man waved his arms and directed us toward the central courtyard. A table groaned under the foods prepared by Naomi and those brought by my mother. I was sure other neighbors had also contributed.

Mary hovered beside her mother ready to offer support if it was needed. The meal was truly a celebration full of laughter. Abner shared stories of Jeshua and the camel. The boy scampered from adult to adult when not exploring the courtyard for pretty stones and even a lizard that I insisted he release beyond the gate.

"Truly Adonai has been with you. I rejoice that you have returned safely by God's blessing," Joachim nodded after I explained briefly why Abram offered us an escort from his hospitality and friendship.

Jeshua finally dozed off with a pastry in his hand. I saw Sarah smother a yawn behind her hand as night settled over the town. I rose to leave.

"Joachim, your hospitality is most gracious, but it appears that my family is weary."

"Yes, we will talk more tomorrow," the man agreed.

He embraced his daughter then with a salaam to Abner and the men he escorted us to the street. Mary bent to kiss her mother's cheek before following. James was already asleep in her arms. Jeshua mumbled sleepily when I picked him up but was soundly snoring by the time we reached home. A pallet in one corner awaited my son. I stood with my arm around Mary after he was tucked in.

"Adonai has richly blessed me," I whispered into my wife's hair. "You are proof of that."

I held the woman for a long moment, before I left her to see that Abner and his men were comfortable.

In the morning the nomads prepared to set out for home. Abner surprised Jeshua with a beautifully carved camel.

The child held up his gift, face alight with joy. "Abba, look!"

I turned the little figure over in my hands. The wood was delicately incised so that each hoof and ear was perfect.

"You have great talent!" I stated in amazement.

"I found the wood last night." My friend gestured to the pile of wood scraps in the corner and turned to tighten a strap on his camel's saddle to hide his embarrassment.

"Go show your mother," I instructed handing the toy back to Jeshua.

The boy surprised us all with a quick hug for Abner before he ran toward the house.

"Mama, see what Abner gave me."

"Your son is special." The young man looked after the child "Pray God will continue to direct his footsteps for he blesses everyone he meets."

All I could do was nod. We embraced as brothers and I sadly watched the men stride down the street. Their packs were filled with fresh bread, dried fruit and other foods pressed on the travelers by Mary and my mother.

"God be with you," I whispered after the departing men. "Bring you safe to Abram and keep you and yours from harm."

When the dust settled, I turned to the shop. Each tool and bench was an old friend. I ran my hands over the sawhorses and carefully hung my own tools back on the wall. Briefly I wondered what my father would say. Sarah's comment from the evening before lingered with me.

"Jacob spends more time every year in the Gentile areas. Maybe now that you are home, he will stay here."

Joachim, on the other hand, visited every day. He never grew tired of telling me how Anna revived when Jeshua spoke to her. The neighbors smiled tolerantly at his enthusiasm. Their comments did not indicate that anyone else saw the healing as a miracle. I breathed easier even if some of the women directed barbs at me.

"About time Joseph brought the family home."

"A grandson is perfect medicine."

"She was just missing Mary."

"No wonder Anna was sick, it was fear for her daughter."

Privately, my father-in-law asked about our journeys. I told him what happened since our departure.

"Then Mary was not deluded," he sighed in relief after hearing of the shepherds and Magi.

"Joachim, God did indeed act through your daughter. We hope that here in Nazareth, Jeshua may grow as a normal boy away from any threat."

"You are wise. Adonai must determine his path."

Then one day rattling harnesses announced the arrival of someone. From the door of the workshop, I squinted into the bright winter sun. My father was leading a donkey into the yard. He stopped at sight of Balaam nibbling a pile of hay. Then the man turned toward the doorway.

"Father," I inclined my head and greeted him calmly.

"Joseph? My son, have you returned?" Dropping the harness, my father stumbled toward me.

I took a step toward the man and then another. We met in the center of the courtyard in an embrace that was welcome, forgiveness, and understanding.

"Abba, where are you?"

Jeshua's voice sounded from the house and then his feet pattered toward us. I grinned at Jacob's astonishment when he turned toward the boy. My son stared at the newcomer.

"This is your grandfather," I explained. "He is my father."

Jacob appeared at a loss for words, opening and closing his mouth while staring at the boy. Without hesitation, Jeshua left my side. Trustingly the small hand slipped into my father's big, rough, callused one. He inhaled the scent of sawdust.

"You smell like wood, like Abba."

"What is your name?" Finding his voice the man dropped to one knee to hold his grandson by the shoulders.

Confidently the child smiled at my father. "Jeshua."

The man looked searchingly into the young face. I realized he was seeking some resemblance to me.

"This is my son, Jeshua." My statement ended Jacob's inspection of his grandson.

I noticed Sarah and Mary side by side waiting for our reunion to end.

Jacob nodded to my mother. "Wife."

"Welcome, Husband, our son has returned."

"So I see," the man responded with another nod.

Later as we unloaded the donkey, I addressed my father's doubt. "Jeshua is my son and he is the Promised One of God. I have no doubts now. Mary did not lie. My wife was not unfaithful but chosen by the Living One. Any doubts you may harbor should not be directed at my son but at me."

Brows drew together as the man faced me. He growled, "You have claimed the boy as your son. I can do no less. To believe that Messiah is in that child is more than I can do. You know that I have no faith in the God of Israel whose law is arbitrary. If there is a god, obviously he cares nothing for the Children of Israel since we remain trampled by priests and soldiers."

The man turned away to hang the harness in its place. I knew he did not want to continue the conversation but I pressed on. "What if the God of Abraham, Isaac, and Jacob has been waiting for the right time to act? Were we not slaves in Egypt four hundred years?"

"Your God is a fool to think one man can raise an army against Rome. Learn from Mark Anthony and do not be so foolish."

I felt scorched by the sneer directed at me, but tried to convince my father. "What if Messiah is not a military leader but a prophet of reconciliation for all nations?"

"My son, you are a greater fool than your God if you think people will change. 'Can a leopard change his spots?' Even the Holy Writings, you are so fond of, will tell you such a thing is impossible." My father tossed the empty pack onto a shelf and turned away. "I am hungry. Let us see what your mother has prepared."

I slowly followed my father from the shop. He glanced over his shoulder. "Jeshua is a fine boy. I will never question his lineage. You would be advised to not fill his head with dreams of being Messiah unless you want to see your son on a Roman cross."

It was not the first warning I had received. I caught Jacob's arm. "We returned to Nazareth so my son could both grow up in a normal way. All I desire is the simple life of a carpenter."

"Then you are welcome my son."

I was surprised at the hand that clapped me on the shoulder in an almost fatherly way.

Time drifted into a pattern. My father and I worked together in the mornings. He was interested to hear of the styles of inlay work done in Egypt. Afternoons were spent showing Jeshua the ways of working with wood.

"Measuring carefully before sawing is as important as learning to pray and wait for God's reply. An expert carpenter does both."

"Yes, Abba. I think you are a good carpenter, but my grandfather makes prettier things. He must pray especially hard."

I lifted my head to see Jacob staring at the boy. An odd mixture of embarrassment and pride made him squint his eyes. Jeshua did not look up. He carefully marked the wood we measured. When I looked up again, my father had left the shop. Later he returned to pace the floor.

"Your son has a way of piercing to the heart of a man. I wonder if perhaps you are right and the child is more than human. However, if I believe that…"

When his voice trailed off I crossed the small room. "My father, I have asked God why Mary was chosen and why my life was turned upside down. All I can say is that God has not abandoned me, has not abandoned us, through anything that has happened."

I would have continued, but Jacob held up his hand. "No, my son, do not try to convince me."

Watching the man leave the shop, I breathed a prayer that he would find the answers he sought.

CHAPTER 28

Over the next few years, Joachim and Anna grew frailer. I built another room so they could be near us. When Jeshua was five, Mary bore twins. We named them Joses and Joanna. Just over a year later Judah was born. My family was complete when Simon and Anna came into the world a year after each other. Six years after our return from Egypt, I looked at my family gathered at the Passover table. From eight-year-old Jeshua to the infant Simon, I had the family I prayed that God would allow me. I began the familiar words of the celebration in a voice filled with emotion.

"Blessed are you Lord God, Ruler of the Universe…"

After the final cup of wine had been shared, I exclaimed, "Surely the Living One has blessed me beyond what I deserve! The Lord, Holy be His Name, has given me a rich life and blessed me with my family around me. I see not only my mother but also my father Jacob here. Joachim and Anna, you are a blessing in this house. My children, you are a sign of the favor of Adonai. Blessed are you, Lord God, like a father you give your people riches of family and love."

It was the last Passover we shared together. Sarah fell asleep one night soon after and never awoke. Jacob was heart-broken and began to spend more and more time traveling.

"I cannot bear the emptiness of the bed," he told Joachim on one of his infrequent visits. "I did not treasure my Sarah enough and now she is gone. God has taken her away."

None of us had words of comfort to offer the old man. It was Jeshua who eased his sorrow.

"My son, it is time Jeshua began to learn how to deal with the Gentiles. Let him go with me to Damascus this trip," he suggested when my son was nearly nine.

Speechless, I could only stare at my father. The relationship between the man and my oldest son had never been close.

"The boy will be company for me. You can spare him. We will only be gone a moon turning," he insisted.

I could not refuse the need in my father's eyes. "Very well."

Only then did I see Jeshua watching me from near the woodbin. His smile told me that my son had no fears about such a trip.

Ecstatically he shouted the news as he ran toward the house. "Mother, I am going with Grandfather Jacob to Damascus!"

"Joseph?" Mary stood in the doorway beside her son, one hand on his shoulder.

Fondly I looked from boy to mother. "My love, it will be good for Jeshua. Jacob himself asked for our son to accompany him."

Mary looked past me to her father-in-law. The old man was oiling the leather on the donkey's harness. I saw the struggle within her. Protective love for her son warred with compassion for the grieving man in the courtyard.

"Are you sure?"

"The Living God will be with them. Jeshua, go ask your grandfather what you should pack."

When the boy ran to Jacob, I wrapped Mary in my arms. "We cannot hold the boy so tightly. He is not ours. If my father's grief can be eased, let Jeshua go with him. Perhaps this is the hand of God to Jacob."

With a sigh, the woman nodded against my shoulder. In the morning she sent the boy and man off with smiles. The tears that soaked my tunic in the night were hidden. I walked with the travelers to the crossroads.

After hugging both my son and my father, I raised my hand in blessing.

"May the God of Abraham, Isaac, and Jacob be with you." I repeated the prayer while watching the boy and man walk away from me.

Jeshua's delighted questions wafted to me on the slight breeze. "Grandfather, how far is Damascus? Where will we stay tonight? Grandfather, what is that bird?"

If nothing else, my father would have no chance to brood with the curious child beside him. Nothing escaped the boy's quick eye and everything evoked delight and interest. I was smiling when I returned to the workshop that now seemed too quiet. My work went more swiftly, but I missed my young assistant.

One afternoon the boy burst into the workshop. "Abba, we are back!" He grabbed me in a hug. Excitedly, he tried to tell me everything at once. "Abba, I saw the temples in Damascus and the statues. It was very strange."

My son looked almost guiltily at his grandfather.

The man placed a wrinkled hand on the boy's shoulder. "You son is a good Jew. He would not look directly at the carvings, but he did find us a synagogue for the Sabbath."

My mind stumbled at the idea of my father willingly attending Sabbath prayers. I was glad that the sudden entrance of the twins kept me from replying.

"What did you see? What did you do?" Their questions ran together.

Before Jeshua could answer, Joses and Joanna turned to their grandfather. "G'anpa," they pleaded in unison.

From the depths of his leather pouch the old man produced the expected treat.

"Kiss first," he demanded with a grin.

It was an expression I had not seen for months. Hand in hand the pair ran off after a hug for their grandfather. My father stood, dusted his hands and turned to business while I unsaddled the donkey. We carried the packs to the shop and to the house.

"How was business?"

Carefully I watched my father for the normal cynical scowl.

Instead he surprised me with a smile. "The trip went well. I have several new commissions. The Egyptian style is becoming popular among the fashionable Gentiles. I am fortunate to have a son who has seen the work firsthand."

Mary rose from beside the fire when we entered.

Jacob gave her a gentle kiss on the forehead. "Mary, may the God of my fathers bless you."

My mouth dropped open in astonishment at his softly spoken prayer. Mary recovered more swiftly. Gracefully she ladled stew into a wood bowl for the man.

"My father, you must be hungry," was all she said.

Although I was anxious to learn why my father was so changed, I hesitated to ask. I was almost fearful that bringing up the subject would reawaken the antagonism and grief that were so long a part of the man's life. In astonished silence I listened to my father's brief blessing before he ate. Mary moved to stand beside me. She rested her head against my shoulder.

"He looks at peace," she murmured softly, watching the stranger who had replaced my stern father.

The man was laughing with the children about an adventure Jeshua had on the trip. He looked at Mary.

"You are fortunate, my daughter that we did not return with half the stray creatures between here and Damascus. I have never seen such a boy for attracting lost animals. I think we found homes for nearly all." He chuckled softly just as barking erupted outside. With a guilty look the man looked sheepish and shrugged. "We did obtain one pup."

Looking into the courtyard, I observed Jeshua introducing a wiggling bundle of black and brown fur to Canus, the brindle hound given to my mother when we left Nazareth. He was a large, sturdy beast who took his duties seriously even though his age prevented him from running after intruders now. The older dog ceased barking as the boy brought his squirming burden close to the watchdog. I heard Mary gasp and started forward, certain that the hound would snap.

Jeshua's lips moved as he talked to the two animals. Canus tilted his head. Then a long wet tongue licked both boy and puppy. My son deposited the small dog on the ground. Immediately the puppy began to lick his new friend's face.

"Jeshua!" Mary called sharply. "You could have been bitten!"

Shining eyes looked up from watching the cavorting pup to the group of adults staring at him.

The boy stared at us before shaking his head. "No, Mama," he asserted, "they are friends."

My father interrupted before Mary could reply. "All is well."

The woman frowned. Slowly a smile eased its way onto her lips. She shook her head in resignation and urged, "Come inside and eat."

Leaving the happy playmates, the boy followed his mother. I stood silently watching the animals. Never had I seen Canus so relaxed around another dog. We had never been able to introduce a new pet into the household.

"Jeshua has a gift," Jacob commented.

Still watching the guard dog playing stiffly with the rotund pup, I tilted my head in agreement. The man stepped into the yard. I followed silently.

My father continued his thought with something like a sigh. "A gift that is not just with animals."

We stood side by side. Jacob stared at the sky. I did not know what to say.

"Whether the boy is the Promised One, I do not know," he murmured softly. "However, if God does bring a new world, it will be with the characteristics of that child. He brings healing of body and soul. There is an aura that comforts without smothering. Jeshua is…he is special."

After that my father turned away and walked into the house. He said nothing further about the journey to Damascus. It was obvious that something had happened. The man accepted Jeshua fully as his grandson and I was grateful.

Later I lay beside Mary in our bed. I twisted my fingers gently in her hair, enjoying the sensation.

"Your father is different," she stated.

"Yes, something happened between him and Jeshua. He is not angry with God any longer. It is as you have always said, my love, the Living Lord is gracious and loving. You are proof that the God of Abraham, Isaac, and Jacob lives and acts in our lives."

"My husband, nothing we do is ever beyond the control of the Holy One."

"Mary, you have always been my love. Once I thought God stole you from me. Instead I was the most blessed of men for I have your love, a family, and my father is reconciled to God."

She nestled close and was soon asleep. I, too, drifted off at peace with my life.

Chapter 29

After the trip to Damascus, Jacob allowed my brothers to take over all the trading journeys.

"I will stay here with my grandson, Jeshua," he informed them.

To my delight he attended synagogue regularly and listened to Jeshua and his brothers recite their lessons. He even agreed to accompany us to Jerusalem when Jeshua was twelve.

We received a scroll from Mary's cousin, Zechariah, at Yom Kippur.

"The family of Zechariah invites Joseph bar Jacob and his family to John bar Zechariah's Bar Mitzvah. He will read Torah for the first time on the Sabbath before Passover. Stay with us in Jerusalem while I serve in the priestly ranks during the Feast."

Mary seemed more excited than her son. "We will go, won't we Joseph? I have not seen Elizabeth since John was born. The boys should meet each other. It will be so comfortable to stay in a house in Jerusalem for the Passover."

We had traveled to the capital for the yearly celebration several times. The pilgrim encampment, outside the city, was busy year round, but never more so than at the season of Passover. A teeming mass of humanity from around the empire filled the camp. Both Mary and I were constantly on edge watching that the children did not stray far or run out in front of a camel.

"Of course, my dearest love, we may go to be with your cousin."

She rewarded me with a radiant smile and a delighted embrace.

Immediately she began making plans. "I will start deciding what to take. We will have to have a gift for John at this special time."

"Passover is several moon turnings away." I smiled at her eagerness.

Slowly the cold, dark winter months passed. The entire family picked up Mary's impatience. She wove a soft prayer shawl for John and made a matching one for Jeshua. She draped the handsome garment over his shoulders and brushed the back of her hand across the still smooth cheek of our firstborn son.

"You will soon also be reading Torah in the synagogue," she acknowledged with a soft sigh. "You are almost a man."

The boy nodded proudly.

When the days grew warmer and longer final preparations were made for the journey to Zechariah's home. Mary arranged food and clothing in the packs. Joachim and Anna were too frail to go with us. My sister, Deborah bustled into the turmoil of packing and loading to bundle Mary's parents off to her home.

Finally we set out. Jeshua walked beside his grandfather.

"Have you noticed? Our son is only a head shorter then my father," I asked Mary.

"His muscles are beginning to fill out with the woodwork," she agreed. "Jeshua will be a strong, but gentle man. He looks at the world with confidence and empathy. I have seen adults seek him when they are distressed. Mostly he just listens or reminds us that the God of Israel is loving, gracious, and steadfast."

"Soon the girls will be trying to entice our son. Maybe not until he is no longer embarrassed about his changing voice," I added, a little sadly.

"I do not think you need to worry about the girls any time soon," Mary smiled. "He still enjoys playing with his siblings too much to consider girls attractive."

She was right. After we left Nazareth behind, James teased his brother into a game of chase. The twins spent the first couple of miles running from one side of the road to the other in search of exciting treasures. Eventually they settled down to walk beside Mary. The donkey plodded behind us, unaffected by the air of excitement we all felt. At the crossroads, I saw Mary look back.

"We will return," I promised taking her hand and adding under my breath. "God of Abraham, Isaac, and Jacob be with us and keep us from harm. Bring us back safely to Nazareth."

A small caravan bound for Jerusalem arrived as I ended my prayer.

"You must join us. It is better to journey together than alone," urged the jovial leader of the traders. He added, "Neither brigands nor Romans bother the mules of Lucius of Ephesus. I pay my taxes and keep my sword sharp."

It seemed he was right for we had no trouble on the trek through the hill country.

When we turned aside to Zechariah's home in Bethel I bid the caravan leader farewell with a prayer. "The God of Israel, be with you and bless you my friend."

"I appreciate your blessing, Joseph of Nazareth, even though our gods are not the same."

A light spring rain began to fall as the family climbed the last incline to the ancient city. The spot was holy long before Jacob, the patriarch, rested on a stone and dreamed of a ladder to heaven.

"My husband, the altar of Israel bar Isaac still stands." Mary pointed to the altar erected centuries earlier.

"Father, surely this is a holy place." Jeshua paused to stare at the stone structure.

"Indeed it is," Jacob answered. "God can transform the most unlikely of men into faithful believers. The ancient Jacob was a liar and cheat, but God made of him a mighty nation."

I turned to stare at my father. The rain began to patter more heavily and we hurried on. Elizabeth bustled out to greet us. Her white hair peeking from beneath the veil was a reminder that like Sarah and Rebekkah of old, Mary's cousin was an old woman.

"Come in, come in!"

In minutes the woman had everyone inside the warm house. A fire in the brazier standing in the center of the hall sent out waves of warmth to welcome us. A stairway led to an upper story. Beyond a door, other rooms were visible. The tantalizing smell of roasting goat drifted in from spit just beyond the kitchen.

"Mary, you have come!" Another hug buried the younger woman in the substantial form of our hostess. "And these are your children." The woman turned to smile at James, Joses and Joanna but it was Jeshua she moved toward. "Jeshua! How we have longed to have you in our home. It is such a blessing."

Elizabeth started to embrace the boy, then drew back as if unsure. She covered her quivering lips with one hand and looked toward Mary. My wife nodded encouragement, but still the woman hesitated. Jeshua himself broke the silence.

Stepping forward he took the old woman in his arms. "Cousin Elizabeth, I am honored to be here."

The plump figure only came to the young man's shoulder. His action eased the confused tension building in the room. There was no time for questions or answers. A gust of wind blew through the door signaling new arrivals. Zechariah was stooped with his age and leaned heavily on the stocky young man beside him who could only be John. Piercing black eyes scanned the visitors to pause first on Mary then on the youth still standing with one hand around Elizabeth's shoulder.

"Jeshua! Blessed are you..." He began but stopped when his father laid a hand on his arm.

"Do not embarrass the boy," Zechariah wheezed before I could speak.

With an abrupt movement, John faced his father, prepared to argue. His expressive eyes flashed.

He was silenced when the old man spoke again. "You must learn to wait for God's timing, my son."

"Yes, my father." The thirteen-year old sounded like a grown man with a deep timber already in his voice.

John bowed in obedience and helped the old man into a chair.

"Welcome to my home, Jacob bar Mattan and Joseph, son of Jacob. The husband and father-in-law of my wife's cousin are welcome in this humble home."

"Blessings on your house, Zechariah of the house of Levi," my father replied formally.

"May the God of Israel bless you," I added.

"Elizabeth, our guests will want to rest before we dine," Zechariah stated.

Servants escorted us up the stairs to a spacious room with a window facing across the valley. In the distance I could see the shrine around the patriarch's altar. A curtain drawn across the room formed a partition. Mats for the children were laid on one side and a pallet of soft blankets awaited Mary. My father was shown to a small adjoining chamber. Mary's gentle smile dismissed the hovering servant girl.

Barely had she left before James asked the question perched on his lips. "Why did both Cousin Elizabeth and John single out Jeshua?"

I looked at my wife. Mary gazed back.

"He is the oldest son." My answer did not appear to satisfy anyone. James shrugged. With a deep sigh I tried to explain. "John is six months older than Jeshua. He is a special child, a gift from God. Cousin Elizabeth was too old to have children but then God opened her womb."

"Like Sarah and Abraham?" Joses piped up, proud to show off his knowledge.

"Yes," I nodded, "just like when God gave Sarah and Abraham a son. So Elizabeth became pregnant…"

"And John was born," James interrupted impatiently. "What does that have to do with Jeshua?"

Swallowing a lump of what I recognized as fear, I looked at Mary then at my oldest son. He was standing still and silent nearby.

"All children are a gift from God. Some, like John and Jeshua are singled out before their birth. Your mother visited Elizabeth before John was born. They shared their experiences."

Jeshua stared at me. The crease deepened between the young man's brows.

"God has done many amazing things," I hedged, hoping the subject would be dropped. "There is not time now to tell of them all. When we return home I will explain everything. For now know that you, too, are a special gift from God." Lowering my voice, I added half to myself, "Perhaps more of a miracle than John."

I knew Jeshua heard my comment for he tilted his head and narrowed his eyes in confusion. There was no time for further talk for servants came to escort us to dinner. The evening passed in pleasant conversation. When the children began to fall asleep, Mary and Elizabeth disappeared to the upper regions. The men remained to discuss the political situation in Rome and Jerusalem before retiring to our pallets soon afterward.

"I am not as young as I once was," Zechariah apologized.

"Tomorrow is such a special Sabbath we will all need to be rested," my father agreed.

John proudly read the Torah standing in front of the congregation in the morning. The reading was from Isaiah, "Behold the voice of one crying in the wilderness…"

I glanced at Zechariah wondering if anyone else remembered that the reading referred to the one who would proclaim Messiah. During his short exhortation the young man kept his eyes fixed on Jeshua.

"Many have come claiming to be Messiah. Isaiah tells of a time when the true Messiah will come. There will be a messenger who will announce his arrival. May the God of our fathers grant that we hear the word of the one crying in the wilderness."

Stepping down from the platform, John accepted hearty congratulations from members of the congregation at Bethany. The feasting lasted for three days. I was sure every person in Bethany and the surrounding area came to offer blessings on the house of Zechariah for his son. A week later we set out for Jerusalem for the Passover. It was not a simple matter to move the large household, but finally we were on the road.

We reached the capital late in the afternoon after two days traveling. John and Jeshua reached a tentative friendship during the trek. The two personalities were so different that I was surprised that they found anything in common.

"We talk about God," my son explained. "John believes Messiah will come soon. He wants to live with the Essenes for they have studied much about the Promised One."

"What do you think about Messiah?"

The maturity of his answer surprised me. "God's ways are not so easily discerned. Messiah will come, but he may not be what is expected."

"Yes, my son."

"Abba, look, the walls are gold!" Joses interrupted us to drag me to the top of the small hill beside the road and show me the capital.

I had to smile at the awe in the child's voice.

"They look gilded," I agreed.

"We must hurry before the gates close at sundown," Zechariah called.

He was already heading down toward the city. We passed the familiar, sprawling pilgrim camp to join the line waiting to enter the capital.

Roman soldiers stood at attention on each side of the gate. A harassed centurion asked each traveler for their city of origin and business in Jerusalem. Beside him an obsequious man translated when necessary. Tiny eyes darted from face to face in a suspicious manner. Mary's cousin spoke for us all.

"I am Zechariah, priest of the line of Abijiah with my servants and family."

"Ah, yes, it is you Zechariah." The Roman nodded in vague recognition and waved us past.

We followed the old priest through the maze of streets to his second home.

"The house in Jerusalem is smaller than my home in Bethany," Zechariah told us before we set out so I was amazed at the grandeur that greeted us.

A splashing fountain surrounded by flowers stood in the center of a tiled courtyard. Glimpses of latticed windows on an upper level garden reminded me of the sophistication of Alexandria.

"Not even Ezra, the rich wine merchant in Nazareth, could have built such a home," I gasped.

The steward bowed to me and presented a basin of beaten copper with water for my washing. Mary gazed around in awe and even the children were quiet.

"Come, my dear, you are no doubt tired," Elizabeth ushered Mary toward a side stairway.

John, Jeshua, and I followed Zechariah up another set of stairs. The priest flung open a pair of lattices. The Temple looked close enough to touch.

"This is why I love this house. Each morning I come here to pray. During the day the smoke rising from the grounds reminds me of the Holy Presence."

Jeshua stared open mouthed at the edifice. From the street the Temple looked imposing. Looking across the rooftops to the holy place you could sense even more fully the sanctity of the entire complex. Hoarse shouts drew my eyes to the Roman fortress looming on the east side. A contingent of soldiers marched from the Antonia to begin the nightly patrol of the street.

"When Messiah comes, Rome will be swept from our city," John announced fiercely.

Zechariah frowned at his son and stated, "Come, we will join the women."

The old man led us to the rooftop where we found the women and children in a cool room, screened with lattice and vines. Silent servants placed food on the low table, then left us to our meal. Zechariah offered a blessing.

Mary turned to her cousin. "Elizabeth, this is lovely! Who would have thought that such a quiet and beautiful place could exist within the city?"

Proudly the old priest patted my wife's hand. "I am glad you like it. The house has been in the family for generations. There have been a few improvements made over the years."

"My husband, you are too modest." His wife smiled and added, "The fountain and this room are just two of the many things Zechariah has done to modernize this house."

The food smelled delicious and the two young men wasted no time dipping into the platter. We adults were not slow in following. For a time conversation lagged.

Zechariah left early in the morning for his duties at the Temple. The old man returned home exhausted, but somehow exhilarated from his duties.

On the day before the Passover itself, I took John and Jeshua with me to the Temple. The crush and noise of the crowds was overwhelming. The odor of so many bodies competed with the incense drifting throughout the Temple and across the city. Extra Roman soldiers stood alert and tense on every corner and even at the very foot of the stairs leading to the massive doors of the Temple itself. I heard taunts and curses directed at the soldiers. Obviously under orders to ignore provocation, the might of Rome remained stolidly silent.

I was not entirely surprised when John snarled, "Messiah will sweep the filth of Rome from the streets of Jerusalem."

Jeshua turned from his survey of the crowds to look at his cousin. "Would not the God who created all people care for them all, even the Romans?"

The expression on the face of the priest's son was comical, but I did not feel like laughing.

Open-mouthed in shock, the young man narrowed his eyes and curled his lip. "Israel must turn again to God, as in the days of Elijah. You, of all people, should know that!"

"I will gather my people from north and south," Jeshua quoted softly.

He looked past his cousin to the milling, intense mass of men shoving and sometimes cursing in their eagerness to reach the Temple and perform the ritual sacrifices.

"This is not the time or place for theological discussions," I pointed out. "Let us go into the Holy Place."

We joined the stream of worshipers pouring up the stairs. Inside the doors, the market atmosphere caused me to flinch and hurry the young men along. We passed the Court of Gentiles and Court of the Women. A steady buzz of prayer hung in the air, suspended by the smoke from incense and burning flesh. At last we entered the main courtyard. The massive crowd prevented us from seeing anything until John tugged my arm and led us down a back hallway to another door. From here we could see the High Altar. Several priests accepted the lambs and performed the ritual sacrifice before giving the body back to the worshipper. I had never been this close to the actual sacrifices. The sight of blood on the priests, the altar, and even the steps made me ill.

The sound of Jeshua quoting Psalm 50 pierced my nauseated fascination. "Do I eat the flesh of bulls or drink the blood of goats? Offer to God a sacrifice of thanksgiving."

The boy was pale but his eyes were fixed not on the carnage but on the heavy curtain that hid the Holy of Holies. Before long, I led my companions out of the Temple, my mind spinning not only from the sights and sounds but from my son's words.

Zechariah brought home a lamb for the feast that evening. We were joined by more cousins living in Jerusalem for the Feast. Elizabeth and Zechariah delighted in making introductions that overwhelmed me. Mary, too, seemed dismayed by the crowd of relatives. At sunset, we prepared to remember the mighty saving acts of God.

Jonah, as youngest child asked the question that started the celebration. "Why is this night different from all others?"

Zechariah responded with the ageless litany. Hours later, it seemed, we finally ate. Jeshua was silent throughout the meal and did not even join in the rambunctious search for the hidden piece of unleavened bread until his little sister tugged his arm

"Come on, Jeshua. Help me!"

Only then did my son smile and follow the girl in her search. Soon, she claimed the prize, giggling happily as she presented the bread to Zechariah. Later the twins had to be carried to bed when they fell asleep at the table. As gently as a mother, Jeshua laid his sister on her pallet, drew the blanket over her and softly brushed the dusky waves of hair off the young face.

Joses mumbled a complaint as I put him down. "Not tired." Then he was soundly sleeping.

"Abba," Jeshua spoke hesitantly.

Turning at the door, I saw my son standing in the center of the room. I crossed the floor to stand by the tall figure.

"At the Temple today…"

In the darkness, I sensed he looked at me.

He paused and I prompted softly, "Yes?"

"The blood and smell and noise cannot be what God desires. It is not possible for the God of Israel to be contained only in the Holy of Holies, is it? Surely the Holy One lives in the hearts of all who seek God. How can the people worship and serve a God that they do not really know?"

His whispered words were filled with an intense passion that I had never heard from my son.

I swallowed and tried to answer the boy. "Jeshua, I am a carpenter, not a rabbi, but I know that the Living God does speak to the hearts of men. I have felt the hand of the God of Abraham, Isaac, and Jacob in my own life."

Jeshua gripped my arm. "Abba, will I hear the voice of Adonai directing me?"

I nodded although he could not see me. "All who listen will hear. All who seek will find and be found by the Holy One."

"How will I know?"

When I did not immediately respond, Jeshua sighed.

I forced myself to answer the young man I claimed as my son. "Jeshua, you will recognize the voice of the One who created all things, in the same way you know my voice in a crowd of people."

I felt a shuddering breath run through his body.

My hands tightened briefly on his shoulders. "When God speaks, there will be no doubt, my son."

"Thank you, Abba." The boy gave me a brief embrace before leaving me alone.

I remained standing in the center of the room even after my son let the curtain fall behind him. I understood that the young man must find the One who was his Father, but it tore at my heart.

"God, your son is seeking you. He was mine for a short time, but from eternity, Jeshua is yours."

Eventually I returned to the merriment of the feast. The oil in the lamps ran low when we all sought our beds. Mary's hand slipped into mine, offering sympathy and comfort, although she did not know what troubled me. Soon her even breathing told me that the woman was sleeping.

In the silent house, I challenged God, "Why did you give me care of the boy, only to take him away? What will you give me in his place? Like Abraham, you ask me to offer up the one I love. I accepted Jeshua as my son! I cannot give him up, now! You ask the impossible."

"I love him too." The words in my heart were soft. I tried to ignore them and argued with the deity on behalf of the woman sleeping beside me. "What of Mary? You will break her heart."

Even as I raged, I remembered the worlds of old Simeon in the Temple warning 'a sword shall pierce your soul.'

Too restless to sleep, I slipped from the bed and prowled softly to the window. All around was silence. Not a leaf stirred. My children and wife slept contentedly. Loneliness swept over me. I sank down on the bench beneath the window.

"No," I barely breathed the word. "It is not time. He is too young to begin whatever is to be his mission. He does not need to know of his heritage yet. You cannot ask his mother and me to give up the boy. He is only a child."

"What of Isaac, and Samuel and David?" From somewhere came the question. I was not sure if it was inside me or beyond me.

"No, no, no!" My refusal was all the more vehement for its whispered softness.

I lowered my head into my hands. For a long time I sat slumped on the bench, raging at the unreasonable demands of God.

"How can you ask this of me, of him? I am just a simple carpenter, trying to do the right thing. God, your demands have taken me far from the life I planned. I have tried to be faithful. Now you are silent when I need your guidance. Where are the dreams and assurances now? How can I give my son back to you?"

Silence settled around me when I finally sat quiet. In my anguish my head hung down and my hands locked together behind my neck as if protecting it from blows. Eventually the rising sun and awakening household drew me from my stupor. Blearily I looked up. Morning light rested on Mary. Behind the screen I heard a whisper and then a smothered giggle. The soft patter of small feet was followed by Joses' voice.

"Now!"

From the ensuing sounds, I gathered that the twins had awakened Jeshua by leaping onto his back. The laughter resulting from his mock fury made Mary open her eyes. Her smile dimmed into a worried frown when she saw me. There was no time for any questions. A small boy and girl raced from behind the screen, shrieking with laughter.

"Save us!"

The pair scrambled into my lap as their brother followed his tormentors. James, somewhat grumpily followed, rubbing his eyes with the back of his hand.

"I have you now!" With sparkling eyes, Mary's firstborn advanced on his siblings.

I had to smile when the children pretended terror at his stalking approach. Jeshua paused, an arm's length away from his prey. He eyed the boy and girl from the corner of his eyes before leaping forward to tickle each child. Joyfully the pair jumped from my arms to attempt to wrestle their brother to the floor.

"James, help us," Johanna called.

The ten-year old leapt into the fray. Under the triple onslaught, Jeshua went down. A mass of waving legs and arms ensued. Somehow the oldest boy struggled free from his giggling siblings. He stood laughing with boyish abandon, as James became the recipient of the twins rambunctious tickling.

Mary finally restored order and sent the children to dress. Elizabeth turned with a smile when we joined her not long afterward.

"I heard the merriment in your room this morning," the old woman grinned. "How fortunate you are to have such a family. There is much to do before we start back to Bethel. Please excuse me if I seem distracted. Zechariah and John have gone to the Temple this morning. My husband hopes to interest our son in being a priest and training under the Temple rabbis."

Soon we were all at work, packing and cleaning each room until the house was spotless.

"I always leave the house ready for a stranger. It is a blessing to offer hospitality to those in need. Even though the servants are here, I feel better to have done this myself," Elizabeth confessed to my wife as she stood fanning herself with a rag late in the afternoon. "One never knows if you will return, especially now that Zechariah and I are so old."

It was dusk when father and son returned. Although nothing was said, it was obvious to us all that the meeting with the priests had not gone as planned.

CHAPTER 30

Our family group left Jerusalem amid a joyful crowd moving northward. I smiled as I looked around. Mary walked beside her cousin's litter. I guessed they talked of their sons. James and the twins made short excursions along the roadside with an ever-changing group of new friends among the pilgrims.

Our late morning start meant that we had to make camp at Gibeah, not even halfway to Bethel. A few tents were erected for the elderly, women, and children. The men planned to sleep under the stars. Evening shadows grew longer as each family gathered for a brief prayer.

"Joseph!" Mary screamed.

The panic in her voice brought me to her side in an instant. She gripped my arm so tightly I was sure her fingernails pierced the skin even through my garment.

"Where is Jeshua?"

"Isn't he with Elizabeth and Zechariah?"

Turning slightly I scanned the area. John crouched near the fire, stirring a pot of something savory. The smell drifted across the camp.

"No! He is not in the camp!" She was almost in tears.

"Have you seen Jeshua?" I asked James and the twins.

"No, Father," James responded while two dark heads shook in unison.

My heart began to thud fearfully. With an effort, I held my voice calm.

"When did you last see Jeshua?" I asked Mary.

Her eyes continued to dart around the camp as if hoping the boy would materialize at someone's campfire.

"He was at breakfast. Where could he be? It is not like my son to wander off."

"I am sure he is fine. Perhaps someone else saw him. We must ask."

"I'll help look," James volunteered.

"Stay with your mother. I will speak to our friends."

I patted Mary's hand and gently disengaged it from my clothing. A brief circuit of the camp brought the unwelcome news that no one had seen the boy since early in the day when the small caravan gathered together.

"Mary and I must return to Jerusalem," I told Zechariah who joined the search of the camp. "The boy has obviously been left behind. No doubt he hurried back to the city for something left at the house and we moved off without him."

Although my words were rational, they hid the desperate fear thundering in my mind. The capital was full of dangers for a young boy alone. Night along the road was full of peril. Bandits and wild animals lurked in the shadows awaiting anyone unwary or foolish enough to seek passage in the darkness, especially a lone boy. I dared not start back until morning myself.

I spent the night in prayer, "God of Israel, forgive me for losing the boy. Keep him safe. You alone know where Jeshua is. There are so many dangers. God of Abraham, Isaac, and Jacob, keep your chosen one safe. Have mercy. Have mercy."

Mary sat with her cousin alternately sobbing and praying. At the first hint of light, I strapped the saddle onto the donkey.

"You must eat," Elizabeth urged.

Mary shook her head. I saw tears in her eyes. "I cannot."

James stood watching his mother. Joses and Joanna hung on my father's hands. I gave each child a quick hug.

"Go with your grandfather. He will get you home to Nazareth and Aunt Deborah. Mama and I will come as soon as we find Jeshua."

"Is 'Esha in trouble?" lisped little Johanna.

Her pet name for the big brother that gave her endless rides on his back brought a slight smile to my lips. "Perhaps, but you are not to worry. You are my precious princess."

"We will meet you in Nazareth. The God of Abraham, Isaac, and Jacob will be with the boy." Jacob took me by the shoulders. His calm words and steady eyes above the gray beard comforted my heart. "Jeshua is in Adonai's hand."

"Yes, my father," I agreed and turned to reassure my family. "We will find him. Before you know it, we will all be together in Nazareth."

My hearty words helped the children relax. I lifted Mary onto the saddle. Elizabeth pressed a sack of provisions into my wife's hands. I led the donkey at a brisk trot back down the road toward the city. The sun just topping the hills sent golden shafts of light across the highway.

My mind was occupied partly with desperate prayer and partly with trying to decide where to look first for my son. Traffic increased as we drew closer to the capital. Pilgrims leaving the metropolis pushed against traders with camels and donkeys moving toward the market inside the gates. Impatiently, I threaded my way through the teaming crowd.

The Roman guard at the gate gave us only a cursory glance. A dusty man with a lathered donkey and veiled woman were of little interest to the representative of the Empire.

"Your business?" He yawned the standard question, barely caring about the answer.

"Personal," I stated.

My eyes were already roaming around the street inside the city in a vain hope that Jeshua was nearby.

"We seek our son," Mary said, surprising both the soldier and me. "Have you seen a twelve-year old boy?"

A grunt of amused derision burst from the broad shouldered man. "Hey, Paulus, have we seen any twelve-year old Jewish brats?"

"Thousands!" His companion responded with a coarse guffaw.

"Go on, you are blocking traffic. You Jews cannot even keep track of your spawn."

Mary sobbed quietly into her veil. I drew the donkey into an alley.

"He did not understand." Futilely I tried to comfort the woman.

Mary drew herself up and straightened her shoulders decisively. "We must go to Zechariah's house first."

No one at the priest's home remembered seeing Jeshua return after the family left.

"Leave the donkey here. I will have a room prepared for you," the steward offered. "You must stay here until you find the boy. It is what my master would desire."

Gratefully I nodded. We gulped down a jar of water and hurried into the busy streets.

"Perhaps the market?" Mary suggested. "Jeshua was fascinated by the sights of all the people and goods from around the empire."

Day ended as we came to the final booths. Inquiries about a lost boy were met with indifference from most of the merchants. A few agreed to watch for an unknown boy matching my description.

I drew Mary close as we slowly made our way back to Zechariah's door. Exhaustion claimed us after a silent meal. Although I meant to spend the night in prayer again, I fell into a troubled sleep when my head touched the pillow.

The gates were barely open when we left the house.

"Try the Street of the Craftsmen," suggested the steward.

Again the response was disappointing. No one had seen Jeshua.

"I have a son of my own," volunteered the tanner. "To lose him would be terrifying."

All day we plodded up and down the streets of Jerusalem. Each step took me deeper into despair.

For Mary's sake I tried to sound encouraging. "Tomorrow we will go to the Temple and offer a sacrifice. Perhaps Adonai will heed our prayers."

"He has been gone for three days," she sobbed.

I drew the woman into my arms. "My love, God spared Isaac. Surely he will return Jeshua to your arms."

The ancient story was of no comfort. Mary wept while I helpless stroked her luxuriant hair. The night passed slowly. Dawn found us standing side by side on the roof gazing at the Temple gleaming white and gold in the rising sun. Trumpets sounded from the city walls. A shofar responded from the Temple battlement. The city awakened to the familiar tramp of the troop of Roman soldiers marching from the Antonia to their positions at the gates. The daily clatter filled the streets as dust began to rise from the multitude.

Mary and I joined the crowds on their way to the Temple, ignoring the calls of merchant and beggar alike. We hurried up the endless, gleaming limestone steps to the outer court. I waited in line to exchange my provincial coinage for Temple currency. At another time I might have argued with the moneychanger over the fee but today I did not care. The dove seller accepted the shekel and handed over a perfect bird. We moved forward in the crowds. A young bored looking priest held out his hand without a glance at us.

"What is your petition?"

I could not keep a frown from my face at his demeanor, but tried to keep my irritation from my voice. "We seek our son who was lost three days ago."

Mary stifled a sob in her veil and I drew her close to my side.

"How old is your son?"

Surprised by the question and the look of interest on the young priest's face, I hesitated.

Mary burst out, "He is twelve."

"I wonder..." The young man almost dismissed us as he looked at the dusty clothing we wore. Then, as if deciding something, he shrugged, "Follow me."

Instead of leading the way toward the small altar, we moved through columns into a long hallway. Mary looked around in apprehension. Our guide stopped at a curtained doorway. He signaled silence and drew aside the drapery slightly.

I saw a group of priests, deep in discussion. A few heads were shaking. Some were nodding. Everyone was focused on the speaker.

A young voice posed a question. "Why would the God of Abraham, Isaac, and Jacob continue to send prophets if not because Adonai desires a relationship with each of us? Does not the Living God love his people?"

Mary's gasped "Jeshua!" was barely audible.

Our guide frowned at the sound. The boy seated near the doorway turned and smiled at us. A richly dressed Pharisee rose to his feet in outrage.

"What is this?"

Bowing low the young priest saluted the group. "My lords, this couple came to me for prayers in finding their son. I thought perhaps..."

The young Levite's words trailed off in the face of many frowns.

Oblivious to the undercurrent of antagonism, Mary took her son's hands. Needing to reassure herself she caressed his cheeks, hair and shoulders.

Tears rolled unheeded down her cheeks. "My son, my son!"

"Your mother and I have been looking for you for three days!" I accused, my voice was rough with emotion.

I laid a hand on the slender shoulder of the young man.

"Didn't you realize I would be doing my Father's will?" His clear eyes looked from Mary to me.

I heard my sharp intake of breath against the pain of this long-anticipated rejection.

"Not yet," his mother pleaded.

Her voice was barely audible and she tightened her grip on the boy.

"What is your business?"

The assembled men turned to me when a Levite addressed me. I wished for a moment that Antonius was beside me.

"I am a carpenter in Nazareth and I seek my son," I stammered.

"How is it your son has such learning?"

"Learning, my lord priest?"

"The boy has presented some theological arguments that I for one, would like to explore further," a tall man with a hawk-like nose and thin voice explained.

"I know nothing of that, my lords."

All I could do was shake my head. A third priest spoke.

His voice rumbled from deep within his broad chest. "Would you apprentice the boy to us? We can give him the education a mind such as his deserves."

I felt rather than heard Mary gasp, "No!"

From the corner of my eye I saw my wife tighten her embrace. I stared at the assembled priests. I was almost swayed by the eager looks on the assembled faces. The world seemed to lurch under my feet. I remembered my agonizing night of despair less than a week earlier. Was God forcing my hand? Could this be the answer I asked for?

"Adonai, I am not ready to let the boy go. He is too young. How can I break Mary's heart and leave the child here? It cannot be that You want him brought up in the Temple"

My mind flew over the history of the Chosen People. Again and again the priests were condemned by the prophets for ostentation and forgetting the people. I had only to look at the men muttering and nodding together to see wealth and power. The gilded beauty of the Temple itself suddenly seemed oppressive. The walls loomed over me threateningly. Smoke from the sacrifices and the sounds of endless prayers closed around me in a suffocating way. The priests alternately stared at me haughtily and whispered together. I sensed their disdain for my dusty, work-worn clothing and rough hands. I gasped for air and prayed for guidance. My mind whirled over the years since the girl came to me with a story of angels. There was no answer from God.

The priests were still nodding and conferring. Distantly I heard the men speaking to each other.

"Yes, the boy should learn with us."

"The wisest among us will be his teachers."

"Definitely this boy should be brought up here in the Temple."

"We will teach him the proper way to express his thoughts."

It was the last comment that stopped my indecision.

"God forgive and help me." I breathed a prayer and took a deep breath. With a low salaam I responded, "My lord priests, you honor the son of a humble carpenter too much. I thank you for your consideration."

Mary gasped, but I continued, "Surely, my lord priests, there are more worthy candidates among your own sons. You know of young men who will fill your hearts with pride at their accomplishments."

I dared to look directly at the three spokesmen. The richly dressed man looked affronted at my words while his thin companion frowned. Only the large man who first suggested the idea was smiling slightly.

I placed a hand to my heart and bowed low. "My lord priests, I beg you, allow the boy to return and learn the honest trade of a carpenter. You can see he is the joy of his mother and my strong right hand."

Despite my brave words, my heart pounded with fear. Few would dare to reject such an offer from the nobility of the land.

"You are a fool."

For a moment I thought it was my own doubts accusing me. Then I saw the speaker. At the back of the room, an old man was being helped to his feet. Leaning on his son's arm, the High Priest moved forward.

"To deny this boy a chance at learning and promotion such as we can offer is to be a shortsighted fool," Annas sneered in my face. "So be it. You want your son. Take him and pray that he will make you proud. Remember this as day you refused to give the boy a life of privilege."

In a swirl of elegant robes the old man exited followed by the remaining priests. Only the large man remained. Even our young guide disappeared.

"Bravely stated," the deep voice rumbled with approval. "I am Nicodemus."

"I am Joseph, carpenter of Nazareth, son of Jacob."

White teeth showed in the black beard when the priest grinned. I realized that our companion was not as old has his fellow Levites. My heartbeat was returning to normal and I found myself returning the smile.

"Come, I will show you the way out. Young Levi has abandoned you, it seems."

We walked through the columns toward the outer court.

"It was partly selfishness on my part to suggest that your son remain," the man confessed. "What your son said about God passionately seeking relationship with the people is something I will think long on."

I could find no reply. Nicodemus bowed in benediction to Jeshua. "Go my son, serve your father and you will be a blessing to many."

Jeshua accepted a brief embrace before starting down the steps beside Mary.

The man turned to me. "Your son will be great."

"Yes, my lord priest." Something about the man demanded honesty. "But he is not to be a priest."

"Not here in the Temple," slowly nodding Nicodemus agreed. "Perhaps we will meet again."

His eyes followed the tall boy.

I heard myself blessing the representative of Adonai, "May God be with you."

"May the God of Abraham, Isaac, and Jacob bless you and yours." His reply was formal yet I heard a longing for something more in the tone.

The priest watched me descend the stairs. When I reached Jeshua and Mary I glanced back. Still Nicodemus watched us. At the corner I looked back to see him standing between the pillars. I thought I saw the man raise a hand to me in salute but could not be sure.

My heart was at peace. I knew that Jeshua was not called to the priesthood, but to something different.

"God will show you the way, my son," I whispered, watching the young man laughing with his mother. "God will be with you. When the time is right, you will hear the call of your Father and know what to do."

I felt surrounded by love and assurance that could only be from God. I no longer had any doubts that the Holy One of Israel was in control of my life and of my son's destiny. He would grow up as the son of a simple carpenter until God made known to him the path of his life.

"God you did not steal my wife nor will you take my son. Your actions are hidden from men, but I believe you seek relationship with all people. Into your hands I commend my life."

The boy and his mother walked ahead of me. I was overwhelmed with love for them. I hurried to join them.

"In the morning we will head for Nazareth," I stated.

Mary smiled and hugged her son around the waist. "It will be nice to be home."

Jeshua looked at his mother and then at me. "I will be glad to see my brothers and sisters. There will be work for us to do in the shop, won't there Abba?"

I nodded and we walked together to Zechariah's home.

Reflection Questions

1. In this book, Joseph is in love with Mary. Do you think that idea is born out by the scriptural record?

2. Joachim and Anna are considered to be parents of Mary, although they are never mentioned in scripture. How do you think they felt about her angelic visit?

3. There was 'no room at the inn' for Mary to have her child. However, Joseph likely would have had kin in Bethlehem. How do you think you would have reacted to having an unknown nephew show up on your doorstep during a busy time like the census?

4. The years the Holy Family spent in Egypt are shrouded in mystery. If you were Joseph, would you have sought out the Alexandrian rabbis?

5. Returning to Israel, where Herod's sons still had power was a dangerous move. Would you have had the faith to trust God's messenger and travel back home?

6. The Bible gives us a very brief account of Jesus and the priests in the Temple. What do you think would have changed if the priests and Levites had trained Jesus?

LaVergne, TN USA
28 April 2010
180727LV00001B/1/P

9 780984 472307